圖書在版編目（CIP）數據

中國內地一瞥：在絲茶產區的一次旅行期間所見：
英文／（英）麥都思編著． -- 北京：文物出版社，
2020.8
（海上絲綢之路稀見文獻叢刊）
ISBN 978-7-5010-6520-2

Ⅰ．①中… Ⅱ．①麥… Ⅲ．①遊記－作品集－英國－
近代－英文 Ⅳ．① I561.64

中國版本圖書館 CIP 數據核字（2020）第 012997 號

海上絲綢之路稀見文獻叢刊：中國內地一瞥：在絲茶產區的一次旅行期間所見

編　　著：〔英〕麥都思

策　　劃：北京博悦閣貿易有限公司
責任編輯：劉永海
封面設計：書心瞬意
責任印製：梁秋卉

出版發行：文物出版社
社　　址：北京市東直門內北小街 2 號樓
郵　　編：100007
網　　址：http://www.wenwu.com
郵　　箱：web@wenwu.com
經　　銷：新華書店
印　　刷：北京雍藝和文印刷有限公司
開　　本：787mm×1092mm　1/16
印　　張：14
版　　次：2020 年 8 月第 1 版
印　　次：2020 年 8 月第 1 次印刷
書　　號：ISBN 978-7-5010-6520-2
定　　價：680.00 圓

出版説明

十九世紀初，以英國爲首的西方資本主義殖民擴張持續高漲，大英帝國希冀將勢力擴張到遙遠東方的中國。然而，當時清政府實行的閉關鎖國政策對中外貿易限制嚴格。爲了打破這種閉關自守的局面，搶佔廣闊的中國市場，英國決定先從思想上滲透中國。傳播基督教、興辦報刊、興建西式醫院等就成爲大英帝國進行意識形態滲透的重要途徑。

起初，清政府嚴禁外國人在中國境內從事傳教和出版活動。於是，傳教士們將東南亞的馬六甲、巴達維亞（今雅加達）、新加坡等地變成了出版中文書刊的重要陣地。一八四二年鴉片戰爭後，中國的大門被迫打開，原本在東南亞地區活動的傳教士紛紛踏上中國領土，進行傳教與出版活動。這批傳教士中不乏對中國近代報刊編譯事業作出突出貢獻者，麥都思就是其中卓有建樹之人。

麥都思（一七九六—一八五七）筆名尚德者，自號墨海老人。他生於倫敦的一個商人之家，成爲基督教徒後，逐漸燃起異邦傳教的熱望。麥都思自幼學習印刷技術，一八一六年受倫敦會差遣，前往馬六甲傳教站從事印刷出版工作。一八四三年，上海開埠後他移居滬上，成爲最早來到上海的外國傳教士和倫敦會上海區的開拓者。麥都思在報刊編輯事業上很有成就，其主編的中文期刊有《特選撮要每月紀傳》與《遐邇貫珍》兩種。在巴達維亞創刊並主編的《特選撮要每月紀傳》，是傳教士創辦的第二份中文月刊。一八五三年創刊於香港的《遐邇貫珍》，則是香港第一份中文近代刊物。此外，麥都思最令人稱道的貢獻在於創立了近代中國第一個機械印刷所——墨海書館。書館經營墨海書館翻譯出版了許多介紹新教信仰、西方科技與文化的書籍。前期以印刷出版中文宣教作品爲主，中後期則順應『西學東漸』的歷史浪潮，通過中國先進知識份子的翻譯，加大對西方科技著作的譯印力度，學科涉及數學、物理、化學、天文、地理、歷史等。

但與同期陸續抵滬的傳教士注重把西方科學著作引入中國輔助傳教的行爲相比，麥都思更加在意的是把中國的風俗、歷史、文化等情況介紹到歐洲社會。在墨海書館出版的書籍中，最能代表他此項意志的是《中國雜記》系列叢書。據劉立壹的博士論文《麥都思的翻譯、學術與宣教研究》可知，此書全名爲《中國雜記：旨在說明中國的政府、哲學、宗教、藝術、生產、貿易、禮儀、風俗、歷史及統計》。由書名可知作者真意，麥都思欲把中國的各項情況記錄下來展示到西方社會。可惜，整套叢書只出版了四部作品，第一部爲《中國內地一瞥：在絲茶產區的一次旅行期間所見》，其餘三部是譯作，分別是《海島逸志》的英譯本、《農政全書·蠶桑篇》英譯本和《上海縣誌》英譯本。因麥都思疾病纏身並爲各項事務所累，未能繼續完成這套極具中國特色的文化叢書。

其中，《中國內地一瞥：在絲茶產區的一次旅行期間所見》因是麥都思本人的遊記性作品，更加具有特殊的研究價值。一八四五年春，四十九歲的麥都思赴江蘇、浙江、安徽等地遊覽，幾十天後回到上海，將自己的旅途見聞寫成本書。這部作品涉及到特定歷史時期下傳教士眼中的中國南方部分地區的風土人情，在一定程度上可以説爲中西文化交流有所貢獻。目前，國内針對麥都思本人的神學思想、翻譯著述、出版活動等方面都有研究成果問世。可惜，這其中幾乎未見對本書文本内容的具體分析。所以，整理并出版這部作品，無論是出於保存珍稀資料的目的，還是完善麥都思系統研究方面都有着極高的文獻價值。

本書據清道光二十九年（一八四九）上海墨海書館鉛印本影印而成，基本保留原版圖書風貌，供各界人士學習參考。

目 録

中國內地一瞥：在絲茶產區的一次旅行期間所見

中國內地一瞥：在絲茶產區的一次旅行期間所見

〔英〕麥都思 編著

據清道光二十九年（一八四九）上海墨海書館鉛印本影印

三

THE
CHINESE MISCELLANY

DESIGNED TO ILLUSTRATE

The Government, Philosophy, Religion, Arts,

Manufactures, Trade, Manners, Customs,

HISTORY AND STATISTICS OF

CHINA.

NO. I.

A GLANCE AT THE INTERIOR OF
CHINA,

OBTAINED DURING A JOURNEY

Through the Silk and Green Tea Districts.

SHANGHAE:

PRINTED AT THE MISSION PRESS.

1849.

A GLANCE

AT

THE INTERIOR OF CHINA

OBTAINED

DURING A JOURNEY THROUGH

THE SILK AND GREEN TEA

DISTRICTS.

TAKEN IN 1845.

A GLANCE

AT

THE INTERIOR OF CHINA,

OBTAINED

DURING A JOURNEY THROUGH

THE SILK AND GREEN TEA DISTRICTS.

———◆———

DRESS REQUISITE FOR THE JOURNEY.

In order to accomplish a journey into the interior of China, it is necessary, if the individual undertaking it be a foreigner, to assume the Chinese dress, to shave the front part of

Note.   The Editor has to apologize for the inferiority of the paper, on which some part of the first number of the Miscellany is printed, owing to the non-arrival of supplies from Canton ; in future he expects to be better provided.

He also regrets, that he has not been able to furnish a better map of the journey.   A more complete one has been prepared, but it was found difficult to get it engraved properly in Shanghae at present.

Chinese dress is tolerably comfortable, and in many respects more agreeable to the wearer than our own.

A

A GLANCE

AT

THE INTERIOR OF CHINA,

OBTAINED

DURING A JOURNEY THROUGH

THE SILK AND GREEN TEA DISTRICTS.

——— ◆ ———

DRESS REQUISITE FOR THE JOURNEY.

In order to accomplish a journey into the interior of China, it is necessary, if the individual undertaking it be a foreigner, to assume the Chinese dress, to shave the front part of the head and temples, and to wear what is commonly called a tail. The traveller should also be able to converse readily in the Chinese language; and conform himself, as much as possible, to the habits and manners of the natives. The Chinese dress varies much according to the season of the year, and the circumstances of the wearer. In the summer months, of course, the dress is light and airy; but during the winter season, it is doubled and wadded, to the extent required to keep out the cold. The rich wear finer and more elegant garments, while the poor are obliged to content themselves with coarser apparel. It is perhaps well known, that the Chinese articles of dress are all roomy, and impose little restraint upon the limbs; though the large sleeves are sometimes in the way; and the long robes, wrapping about the feet, occasionally impede rapid motion; otherwise the Chinese dress is tolerably comfortable, and in many respects more agreeable to the wearer than our own.

A

The first thing put on by a Chinese gentleman is the 汗衫 hán san, and 汗褲 hán k'hoó, or perspiration jacket and trowsers; corresponding to our shirt and drawers. The upper garment is fastened close round the neck by a button, which fits into a loop hole; from this, the right flap hangs loosely dependent in a straigt line, while the left folds considerably over, so as to admit of its being buttoned under the right arm, and so downwards along the right side. The trowsers are very loose, extending from the waist to the ankles, and shaped with such a wide stride, as to allow of the legs being separated far asunder, without the least strain upon the cloth. This part of a Chinaman's dress is not provided with buttons, but is fastened round the waist by a girdle, made of a strip of cloth, doubled and hemmed along its whole length. These under garments are generally made of native cloth, mostly of a white or nankeen colour; but, in the case of very poor people, of a dark blue or black colour. Some have lately substituted European calicoes for cloth of native manufacture, as being whiter and softer; but the Chinese generally prefer the country-made cloths as more durable. A foreigner, assuming the Chinese dress, had better use nankeen, though it may feel rough and unpleasant to the skin, as less likely to excite remark. Immediately above the inner garments, the Chinese wear, if the weather be anywise cold, a wadded garment, called a 棉襖 mëên gaóu, made generally of coarse silk, and stuffed with cotton; having a short body but long sleeves, and fastened round the neck, and down the right side, in the same way as the perspiration jacket; this article of dress is, however omitted in warm weather. Over this wadded garment comes the 袍 p'haóu, or robe, fastened as the two preceding, but extending from the neck to the ankles. This robe is loose, and would be very much in the way of one's working or walking, but that it is bound round the waist by a gauze or silken girdle, the ends of which hang down or are tucked

in, according as the wearer is disposed to be shewy
in dress or otherwise. The writer, who placed himself
in this respect implicitly under the direction of his
guide, was advised to fold in the ends of his girdle,
and not allow them to hang loose either before or behind.
The robe is generally made of a kind of 四川
Sze-chuen silk, of coarse but strong texture, and lined
with white sarcenet; being stuffed or not with cotton,
according as the weather approaches to cold or heat. In the
extreme of summer, the double silk robe is exchanged for a
single one of light crape or gauze; and in the dead of winter,
for a robe of broad-cloth lined with fur. Of whatever material these robes are made, they are all provided with little
loops and buttons behind; so that the wearer can button up
the hind lappet of his garment, to prevent its being soiled by
the mud in walking during wet weather. The hinder part
of a robe, thus buttoned up, has a most singular appearance,
and looks like a little curtain drawn up by the wearer to
shew his heels. Over this robe comes the collar, which is
generally made of light blue satin or velvet, made to fit exactly
round the neck, and sewed on to a sort of tippet, with four tails,
two hanging down from before and two from behind; these
being fastened under the armpits, and the tippet being also
buttoned in front, together fix this article of dress in its position; but the appearance of such four-tailed tippet or shoulder piece, when the outer garment is not worn, is very peculiar, and to a foreigner ridiculous. Over the robe, tippet,
&c. comes the 馬褂 mà kwá, or outer jacket. This is
provided with wide but short sleeves, reaching halfway
down the lower arm, while the body of the jacket extends
only to the waist; this garment, unlike any of those previously described, is fastened by a row of buttons down the front,
and fits round the neck, so as to come under the collar, but
over the tippet; leaving the collar to fold over the neck part;
thus completing the upper part of a Chinaman's dress. This

outer jacket is sometimes made of broad cloth lined with fur, if the weather be cold ; or of camlet or silk, if worn in the summer season. Instead of this outer jacket, a longer one of the same shape is sometimes substituted, which is called the 外套 waé t'haóu, or outer coat. This is, however, only worn when in full dress, or by respectable persons.

Descending to the lower parts of the body, we find the Chinese feet cased in strong stockings, which are made of nankeen cloth, and sewed together according to an approved model, with double or triple folds about the soles of the feet ; these folds are stitched through and through in various directions, so as to make the lower part of the stocking hard and strong, and capable of enduring much wear and tear. The whole stocking is however lined throughout; and in cold weather stuffed with cotton, so that it can be easily made to stand upright like a boot. Chinese stockings have all this one peculiarity, that the leg is of the same size throughout ; and the hose, not being woven for the purpose, do not stretch as the foot passes through them, or contract to suit the shape of the leg; the legs of the Chinese, thus caparisoned, appear like pillars. When the stockings are drawn on, the Chinese pull them up over the trowsers, and tie them with green, blue, or yellow garters under the knee. The trowsers, which are very wide about the knee, being thus brought suddenly into a narrow compass at the top of the stockings, exhibit the appearance of a limb about four times the size above, to what it seems to be below. This ridiculous appearance is sometimes attempted to be remedied by a pair of 褲套 k'hoó t'haóu, or tight overalls, which are fastened at the instep, and drawn over the stockings and trowsers, up to the waist. These being made of silk of various colours, would somewhat remedy the awkward appearance of a Chinaman's lower extremities, were not these overalls destitute of a seat ; so that, while the wearer presents a tolerably neat appearance in front, he seems when viewed in the other direction. as if the hinder part of his pantaloons had been torn away.

The shoes are made of cloth or satin, with soles composed of many folds of cloth, cased by a single piece of leather underneath ; these are sewed together by many stitches passing through the whole mass. and appearing in rows at the bottom of the shoe ; by much walking the ends of these stitches get worn off, and there is danger of the bottom leather, with the many folds of cloth, coming away ; but after a time, the various layers get matted together, so as to retain their connection with each other, although the stitches should be undone. There is this inconvenience, however, attending such cloth shoes that, immediately the wearer begins to tread on wet ground, the dampness works its way up through the sole, by means of capillary attraction, so that the stocking and foot become speedily wet, and the wearer is in danger of taking cold. When once wet, these cloth shoes require a long time to render them perfectly dry ; and unless a man have a change in reserve, he must be content to go with wet feet during the continuance of rainy weather. The Chinese, however, provide themselves with a sort of leather shoes, full of iron spikes, about half an inch long. and an inch in circumference at the base, fitted into the sole of the shoe. These horrible hob-nailed clogs make a great clatter on a stone pavement in a rainy day, where the wearer is in danger of slipping about ; but on soft clayey ground, and particularly in ascending hills, they afford the wearer the advantage of a firm footing, which he otherwise might not enjoy. They do not. however, keep out the wet ; for, the leather being porous, if you tread in a slop but an inch deep, the water is attracted upwards to the top of the shoe, and even beyond it. Besides this inconvenience, they are necessarily very hard and unyielding to the foot, so that a day's march in such brogues is enough to make one lame ; as the writer knows by painful experience. To a person unaccustomed to them, all Chinese shoes are awkward in the extreme ; for not only are the soles made so thick, that they never give to the feet in walking ; but they are curled upwards towards the toe, so that the front part of a person's foot is much higher than the hinder part, and he is in danger of falling backwards. This is according to a Chinese rule, of almost universal application, viz. that of doing every thing the contrary way to other nations ; for while we raise the heel of a shoe, and depress the toe, they do exactly the opposite. The writer found it necessary to have a pair of shoes made on purpose for himself, with the soles level throughout, and sufficiently large, to admit of the toes moving freely, and enable the wearer to spring forward in walking. It would be advisable, also, for any one intending to adopt the native shoes, to try them on first with Chinese stockings, as these latter are considerably thicker than our's, and fill out a shoe more than a person would be aware of.

The Chinese almost always wear some kind of cap, both in and out of doors ; indeed they do not consider themselves as dressed without a covering for the head, as well as the feet. This is an advantageous circumstance for any one wishing to assume the Chinese garb temporarily, as the colour of his hair, and the joining on of his cue will thereby escape notice. The caps worn by the Chinese are of various kinds, as the circumstances of the wearer or the nature of the weather differ. For respectable persons, on common occasions, the round-crowned hat, with the brim turned up in a slanting direction all round, but projecting rather more before and behind, is the most common. This is generally made of broad-cloth, or satin, stiffened with paste-board, and lined with red cloth ; while the top is surmounted with a knob of twisted silk ; or, if the wearer be a literary graduate, or a government officer, this knob or button is made of brass, crystal, or lapis lazuli, according to the rank of the individual ; from the bottom of this knob hangs a congeries of red silk threads or dyed hairs, which fall over and around the outside of the crown, thus covering the top part of the cap from the view. For this cap is substituted, in the summer, a conical cap made of straw, having a round band inside, to suit the head of the wearer ; and fitted up with the same kind of knob and fringe as the hat just alluded to. These caps or hats, however, are not very well adapted for foreigners, as they do not conceal enough of the forehead, unless made large on purpose, when they are likely to attract notice from their singularity. A much more convenient hat for persons adopting the Chinese dress temporarily is the one made of felt, which is like a hollow bag, about one foot in diameter, and two feet long, closed at both ends ; one end of which is inverted and pushed into the hollow of the other, when it assumes the conical appearance of an English felt hat, before it be blocked and worked into the proper shape. In this form it may be worn as a night cap, to protect the head from the cold winds, which blow through the crevices of boats or houses, during sleeping hours ; or, with the edges turned up all round, it forms a tolerably good hat for everyday wear ; with this advantage, that the rim and crown may be made respectively large or small to suit the convenience of the wearer, either in screening his head from observation or his eyes from glare. The writer wore one of these during the cold weather, night and day, and found the article to answer his purpose remarkably well. When the hot weather sets in, the Chinese exchange these felt hats for the scull cap ; and, as it would excite notice to appear singular, the foreign traveller in China must do the same. These scull caps are shaped liked a basin ; and are either wadded or single, as the weather might require a warm covering or otherwise. Though smaller and lighter than the hats, they may still be made to cover a large part of the head, as far down as the tips of the ears, and nearly to the roots of the hairs in front and behind ; so that they conceal a great part of the head, and may be worn day and night, both at home and abroad.

Should the eyes of the traveller be of a light colour, it would be better to conceal them by spectacles, plain or coloured ; both of which may be obtained, made of rock crystal, affording sufficient protection to the eye from glare ; and, as they are very large, screening it when passing through large cities, from the curious gaze of spectators. The best kind to be worn are glasses made of 墨晶 mǐh tsíng, or tea stone, about two inches in diameter, with black varnished rims, and made to fit with strings passing behind the ears. When travelling through mountainous districts or secluded villages, however, spectacles made of plain crystal would answer the purpose, as the country people are not so much accustomed to see persons walking about with coloured glasses, as those are who live in towns. The foreign traveller had better be particular in this matter, as the eyes are the first things that attract notice, and may be the most likely to lead to the discovery of his origin. The Chinese think that spectacles sit better upon elderly people ; and to produce uniformity of appearance, the wearer might at the same time allow his mustaches to grow, which the natives commonly do at forty ; and then the spectators will consider his face and its appendages to be in due proportion.

The last, but by no means the least, change which the foreigner must undergo, in order to pass unobserved through China, is, the shaving of the head, all but the crown : and the appending of a long cue to the hair which is attached thereto. Any common Chinese barber, will perform both of these operations for a trifle, and will do them according to the accustomed mode ; care must, however, be taken to secure his secrecy, or to get the business accomplished in such time and place, as that if he does become garrulous on the subject, it will be impossible for him, or his neighbours, to discover the object or the destination of the traveller. Proper arrangements having been made, the barber sets to work, and removes all the hair from the lower part of the head, leaving that only which covers the hinder part of the crown ; he then takes a long cue of loose hairs, fastened in three divisions to a piece of silk cord, and gathering up the hinder locks of the foreigner's hair, he binds the cue on as tightly as possible, so that it may appear to be a continuation of the individual's own locks. After this he gradually plaits the three divisions of additional hairs into a tail ; towards the end of which he introduces a quantity of silk thread ; and the whole being properly fastened, the cue is complete.' The traveller should, however, not allow the barber to add too much supplementary hair ; as, if the cue be too weighty, it will cause too great a strain upon the slight tie by which it is fastened, and endanger the coming away of the whole ; as was the case once with the writer, the details of which will be met with on a subsequent page.

With a cue thus fastened, the wearer must be careful to keep on his cap at all times. Another thing likely to lead to the discovery of the traveller's origin, if his own hair be light, is the jutting out of a few straggling locks from underneath his cap ; so that the foreigner must every now and then, when not observed, put them up carefully, and not allow the odd hairs to hang about. The cue will be found to be very much in the way of those not accustomed to such an appendage ; particularly when stooping to do any work, it generally falls forward and hinders the performance of the operation ; or it catches in something from which he is going away, and suddenly arrests the individual in his progress ; if the violence of the pull does not actually detach the cue. At night also, a man can scarcely turn round in his bed, without being forcibly reminded that he has got an unusual appendage, and without being in danger of dislodging it from its position.

The way to avoid much of this inconvenience is, to bind the cue round the head, or twist it about the neck. This, however, cannot be done in company, or in the presence of superiors ;

海上絲綢之路稀見文獻叢刊

一八

中國內地一瞥：在絲茶產區的一次旅行期間所見

as it is considered a mark of disrespect to wear the tail otherwise than hanging down gracefully behind. After all that can be done, the additional hair is immediately discoverable when the head is shaved, and therefore it would be advisable for a foreign traveller not to place himself in a barber's hands during the course of his journey. The writer did this on one occasion, when far in the interior; but the village operator, being too stupid to make observations, and being altogether ignorant of the existence of foreigners, failed to remark upon the singular appearance of the head presented to him. Not so, however, the mistress of the house, who asked her husband, why the person's hair was so short, as to need a supplementary cue? Perhaps, said her husband, his wife has cut short his hair, which may account for its stunted appearance. In order to obviate the inconvenience arising from such enquiries, in future, the writer shaved his own head and beard. This had to be done generally in the dark, without a glass, soap, or brush, and with only a towel dipped in cold water to moisten the chin, and a common Chinese razor to remove the stunted hairs. At the first effort of this kind, the razor employed was blunt and full of notches, having been previously used for cutting a black-lead pencil; in this way a beard of ten days' growth was removed in about half an hour, but not without much torture, which forced tears from the eyes. With a good instrument, however, the affair went on smoothly afterwards, and the writer rejoiced in being able to render himself independent of Chinese barbers. Though, were his example to be followed by all the inhabitants of China, it would throw about a million of plodding operators out of employ.

The dress and cue having been assumed, it must not be supposed that the traveller has done every thing to screen himself from observation: he must sustain the character of a Chinese, and this cannot be done, without putting on and wearing the different articles enumerated, precisely in the same way as is done by the natives. Every thing is stereotyped in China ; there is a certain order in the putting on of apparel, which must not be departed from. Certain articles must be put on first, and certain ones afterwards ; they must be buttoned and tied in a certain way, and one over the other, according to established form ; or it will appear strange ; and the least departure from common usage cannot fail to attract observation and lead to discovery. The manner of sitting, standing, or walking ; the way of carrying the arms, and moving the legs, must all be strictly attended to, or some notice will be taken of the stranger. The individual must especially avoid walking fast, or taking long strides, or pushing past others in the street ; but must move along quietly and placidly, as if uninterested in passing events. There is time enough for every thing, seems to be the established maxim in China, and the man who is in a hurry shews that he is no true son of Han.

ON THE FOOD OF THE CHINESE, AND THEIR MANNER OF EATING IT.

In partaking of food, also, great care must be taken to eat as others do ; not only is it necessary to eat with chopsticks, but to handle them in such a way, that the instrument may appear to be in the hand of an adept. When not used, the chopsticks must be laid on the table, side by side, exactly pointing away from the individual, who has been employing them. When taken up, the fingers of the right hand must be laid slantwise over the chopsticks, by which means they may be drawn nearer, until they project a little over the edge of the table; when the thumb of the right hand being placed underneath, they may easily be taken up. As soon as they are thus taken up, the ends of them are rendered even by being placed perpendicularly on the table ; when at the same time, by a slight turn of the hand, one of the chopsticks is

中國內地一瞥：在絲茶產區的一次旅行期間所見

immoveably fixed, by being pressed against the root of the fore-finger and the tip of the middle finger, by the middle of the thumb pressing over it. The other chopstick is grasped by the points of the thumb and the two fore-fingers; by the bending or straightening of the joints of which, this stick can be moved to and fro, and made to approach to or recede from its fellow; thus forming a sort of nippers, opening and shutting at the will of the holder, and adapted for taking up or letting go the smallest article. But all this arrangement must be made while the chopsticks are held erect, with their points on the table, by the fingers of the right hand, without being touched by those of the left. The instrument being thus fairly grasped, the guests at table proceed to take piece by piece of the meat or vegetables, from one or more basins placed in the centre of the table. The stranger must take care to hold firmly the piece he wishes to secure for himself, and convey it safely to his mouth, without letting it slip or fall on the table, or the ground; a thing which seldom happens to the Chinese themselves, and which, occurring in his case, would not fail to stamp him as a novice in the use of the instrument. It would not be worth while for the stranger to feel fastidious about eating out of the same basin with his Chinese friends; as it is not uncommon for them (particularly when they profess to entertain the least respect or affection for their guests) to use their own chopsticks, and take out one of the nicest pieces of meat or fish they can find, and place it in the stranger's own basin; lest he should complain, however, of the chopsticks not being sufficiently clean, the host previously draws them very carefully through his own lips, and gives them a good suck before performing the operation. Of course, ideas of politeness differ in various parts of the world; and the intelligent traveller, accepting the will for the deed, will receive a compliment in the spirit in which it is intended.

At the commencement of a Chinese meal, the centre dishes,

whether of meat or vegetables, are arranged upon the table ; from which the guests help themselves in common. A small cup is placed in front of each individual, into which the host pours occasionally a little hot wine from a pewter tankard ; the guests take a sip of this beverage, and then a portion of the eatables, until they express a wish for rice, when the basins of rice are brought forward, and the wine cups are set aside. It is not considered according to etiquette to take wine after this. When the rice bowl is placed before the guests, it must be taken up in the left hand, and held by the thumb being placed over the rim of the basin, the fore-finger on one side, the little finger on the other, and the two middle ones at the bottom. The Chinese, however, frequently leave the rice basin on the table, and put down their mouths to it ; when, by the help of the chopsticks, they poke the rice into their mouths very dextrously. This is an operation not easily performed by a stranger ; in order to imitate the Chinese, he must place his mouth at the edge of the basin, not moving it about from side to side, where the rice may happen to be ; but conveying the rice to his mouth, by means of the chopsticks, and then poking it down. The more slobber and noise made during this operation, and the more rice a man can get into his mouth at one time, even at the risk of choking himself, is, in the Chinese estimation, the better ; but he must be careful not to spill any of it on the table or ground, nor to leave any in the basin when he has done ; as this would be a mark of waste, from which the Chinese ideas of economy revolt ; and would shew the individual to have been brought up in some outlandish extravagant school.

When one basin is finished, and the guest wishes another, he must ask for a whole or half a basin full, as he feels his appetite inclines him ; or if he has too much, he may shove a portion of it into his neighbour's basin, which would be taken kindly ; but he must not leave anything.

As for the dogs, they must content themselves with the bones which are thrown down, or put up with such coarse food, as may be prepared on purpose for them and the pigs.

It is known to most persons, acquainted with China, that the Chinese use no table-cloths; but when the meal is done, a dirty cloth is brought forward, with which the table is wiped; each person is then presented with a cup of tea, and pointed to a basin of hot water, on the side of which is a rag, with which he may wash his hands and face; and then, with a pipe, the meal is concluded. It is surprising to see, how dextrous the Chinese are with the chopsticks, by means of which they can eat peas, separate the flesh from the bones of fish, and take off the shell of a hard-boiled egg, without using anything but these two skewers. The material of which they are made is sometimes ebony, and amongst the rich of ivory; but the common people content themselves with bamboo chopsticks; more than a million of which may be sometimes seen at one time, in the places where they are manufactured or sold, and a plentiful supply of which is to be met with in every eating house or tavern, throughout the country. These are kept in a hollow bamboo, placed on the table, or hung up near the door, whence every customer takes his pair as he may need them, without enquiring into whose mouth they may have last been inserted, or what may be their condition, as to cleanliness or odour.

The viands to be met with on a journey into the interior of China, and particularly, in mountainous and unfrequented parts, are not of the most exquisite and delicate description; so that a person at all particular about his food had better not venture on the experiment. Of beef and beer, he must take his leave, immediately he quits the vicinity of Europeans; but of pork and samshoo, he will have abundance, if he has got money to pay for them. The staple article on a Chinese table is rice, sometimes white and sometimes red; but always in sufficient quantity to satisfy the cravings of the appetite. In order to tempt the rice down, the Chinese employ various condiments, the most common of which is pulse jelly, whitened and rendered solid by a mixture of gypsum. The writer remembers, attending in London on a geological lecture, when, hearing the lecturer descant upon the properties of gypsum, he ventured to observe, that the substance referred to was used as an article of food by the Chinese. Whereupon the learned lecturer lifted up his hands, with pity and astonishment, lamenting that the necessaries of life should be so dear and scarce in that country, that the inhabitants are reduced to the necessity of eating stones; in which sentiment all present cordially sympathized. Subsequently, however, the writer visited a gypsum quarry, in the north of England, and, on asking the owner of it, what they did with so much gypsum? received for answer, that a large quantity of it, was sent to the Durham mustard-makers, and not a little to the London pastry-cooks; so that the ladies and gentlemen, who pity the Chinese for eating stones, have probably, on more occasions than one, had to eat of the like. The pulse jelly so prepared is very heavy, and when placed in water sinks to the bottom; so that it must sit rather uncomfortably on the stomach; but, being warm and soft, it glides down without difficulty, taking some of the rice with it. The Chinese also make frequent use of bean-sprouts, which are tolerable.

The next most common thing on a Chinese table is the mustard vegetable, partly salted and dried, and partly decomposed and rotten. The taste of the mustard plant in this state is most disgusting, and the odour abominable; but with the Chinese it is a standing dish, and so fond are they of it, that they frequently take it off from the hedges and railings where it is hung out to dry, and eat it with relish, as they walk along the roads. The fresh mustard plant is sometimes boiled and served up, but this is so insipid that it can be relished by no one. In addition to these preparations of pulse and mustard plant, we meet occasionally with broad beans; and very often with the young shoots of bamboo, which, being sliced and served up with a little pork, form the only relishable dish to be met with in Chinese taverns; but even these are to be expressly ordered or purchased by the customers themselves, or else they do not appear.

Should the guests desire it, they may obtain a preparation of bean or wheaten paste, rolled up into very thin slices, and then cut into fine shreds, like vermicelli; this is boiled till it becomes soft, and is served up exceedingly hot; the natives take it with their chopsticks, and having got one end into their mouths, keep on gobbling and drawing it up, till they either choke or scald themselves; and then they stop a moment to fetch breath and make another effort. Eaten moderately, with a little bacon, it affords a tolerable relish, and tends as much as rice and vegetables to satisfy the appetite. Pork is only to be met with in towns or villiages, containing several hundred inhabitants; and those who wish to have meat at every meal must carry it with them, or purchase it when passing through the towns, so as to be ready for use when putting up for the night at small hamlets. The guide with whom the writer travelled, knowing what he had to trust to, generally bought a quantity of fresh pork or bacon beforehand, and having dressed it, wrapped it up in oil paper, to take along with him. Without this precaution the party would frequently have been at a loss.

In some of the sequestered spots, where nothing else was to be procured, we were furnished with a kind of double pan-cake, made of wheaten flour, with a quantity of scallions and other aromatic vegetables inserted between the layers of paste. These had certainly a taste, but it was far from being a pleasant one, which was felt more after, than at the time of eating. A very small portion of these, therefore, sufficed, after they had been once tried. No matter what was brought on table, however, the guide urged the impolicy of asking ques-

tions about it ; because the simple circumstance of making
enquiry would show that the traveller was not familiar with
what he saw ; and, to be unacquainted with what came upon
the table every day, would be a display of ignorance, that
would be unpardonable even in a child, and could not fail to
mark out the individual as a stranger or a foreigner.

The same care, to avoid seeming surprised at anything,
was especially enjoined on the writer on all occasions by his
companion ; as being likely, if neglected, to involve all parties
in difficulty. Those who travel in China, therefore, must
abide strictly by the advice given children at home, viz. to
hear, and see, and say nothing. In consequence of disregard-
ing this maxim, the writer had frequently to experience
the disappointment of getting no answers to his questions ;
and finally discovered, that the best way to obtain information, was to appear indifferent about it ; and gather it, as
best he could, from the desultory conversation of those by
whom he was surrounded.

The wine brought on the table, during the writer's
journey, was generally a distilled spirit, colourless, but not
very strong, nor altogether unpleasant to the taste. When
this spirituous liquor was introduced, however, it was always
served up in very small cups, holding only a few tea-spoons
full, two or three of which was the modicum usually consumed by each guest ; after which, the rice was served up,
and the wine put by. This kind is called 高粱 kaou
lëâng, or Barbadoes millet, because distilled from that grain.
Another sort, is called 紹酒 shaóu tsèw, because it comes
from the prefecture of 紹興 shaóu hing; this is a little
weaker than the former, and possesses an unpleasant taste.
A third kind, called 水酒 shwùy tsèw, or water wine, is
very common, and from its mildness, sweetness, and flavour,
forms a very good beverage ; this latter is served up in larger
cups than the two former; still the drinking of it is not continued after the rice is brought in. As a general thing, we

C

may venture to say, that there is not much drunkenness to be seen at Chinese dinners ; their wine-shops are not provided with accommodations, for customers to sit down and fuddle themselves at, but each one must take his portion standing, outside the counter, and then depart ; there is little or no urging one another to excessive drinking. In the tea-shops friends meet, and pass their evening hours together ; but the beverage they there consume exhilirates without intoxicating, so that the customers return home as steady and sober as when they came. On the whole then, the Chinese would be a sober people were it not for opium ; but the use of this is confined very much to the sea-girt provinces and large cities ; and the people in the villages and open country are tolerable free from the vice of opium smoking.

CHINESE INNS AND TEA-SHOPS.

The houses of entertainment throughout the country need to be described. On all the great roads, where there is much traffic, these houses are found at the distance of every five or ten miles. They are known by the sign, generally hung out in front of the door, 中伙便飯 chung hò pëén fán ; intimating that they afford middling accommodations and convenient meals. The reader, however, must not suppose that he will find therein anything like what is to be met with in the commonest inns in Europe. In country places, these rice-shops, or eating-houses, are generally cottages, of one story, with clay floor, and planked sides ; having a small shop in front, and accommodations for strangers behind. After passing through the shop, you cross a small yard, and enter an open room, called a hall, wherein a table and a few benches are placed ; on each side the hall you find what is denominated a sleeping-room, and sometimes behind this range there is a kitchen and two other bedrooms. Should the house be two stories high, the upper rooms or lofts are appropriated to the coolees and chair-bearers who accompany the guests. The strangers must not expect to find bed and table linen, as such things are unknown even in respectable houses in China. The tables are sometimes wiped on the entrance of a guest, and after a meal ; but this is done with a bit of rag a few inches long, which merely serves to remove a little of the extraneous dust, while an inch thick of dirt is frequently left adhering to the table. It is a very rare thing to see a broom pass over the floor, which being made of earth easily imbibes the slops, and conceals them from view. The mud brought in by passengers only adds to the material of which the floor is composed, and all bones, rice, and other eatables, are carefully cleaned away by the dogs.

The first question, on entering such a house of entertainment, is, whether they have got any rice and vegetables ; which is generally answered in the affirmative, coupled with a polite confession of the poverty of their preparations. A confession, the truth of which the writer has seldom felt himself at liberty to dispute ; the accompaniments to the rice provided on such occasions being the poorest and most insiped imaginable ; should any customer wish anything further, he is at liberty to send out for some pork, should such be procurable. The sleeping rooms are seldom provided with windows, and the only avenue for light is through the door, which, opening into another apartment, admits but a feeble ray of light. It is perhaps as well that such is the case, as were the room better illumined, its dirt and deformity would be more conspicuous, and fastidious strangers might be deterred from entering. The bed-room is sometimes provided with separate bed-places for each individual, consisting of a frame-work about six feet long, three broad, and two high, upon which is spread a layer of straw, covered with a mat ; but more frequently one end of the room is occupied by a larger frame-work, about six feet wide and ten long, upon which three or four guests may sleep together.

Should the strangers not be provided with coverlets, the establishment undertskes to furnish a cotton wadded quilt to each customer; but as the coolees and chair-bearers, with all sorts of dirty fellows, have been in the habit of using these quilts for months or years; adding to the stock of filth and vermin which they contain, every successive time; it follows, that such coverlets are anything but agreeable, and of course only the lowest class of customers avail themselves of the benefit. Each traveller must therefore take with him his own mat, quilt, and pillow; and, with every precaution, will find it difficult to escape coming in contact with the dirt and noxious insects already present in such dormitories. One of the most disgusting articles of furniture, in such bed-rooms is the pail, which sends forth an odour, that is too powerful for any but Chinese olfactories. The floor is sometimes boarded, but washing is entirely out of the question; and the cobwebs in the corners, indicate the entire absence of brooms, ever since the erection of the building. In short the whole establishment partakes of the united qualities of stable and pig-stye, falling far short of what those respectable receptacles are in most civilized countries. The only agreeable thing is the basin of hot water, which is invariably presented on entering, for the purpose of washing the face, hands, or feet of travellers; and the cup of warm tea which immediately follows.

The lowness of the charges in some measure reconciles the helpless traveller to his fate, in putting up at such hovels; being sometimes 80 cash or three pence for supper and bed, with breakfast before starting next morning; or, if the traveller chooses to pay separately for each article, he may get a bowl of rice for twelve cash, one of vegetables for the same, and a a cup of tea for half as much, which will serve him for supper; his breakfast next morning will be the same, leaving 20 cash for fire-wood, waiter, parlour, and bed-room; but the lumping system is generally considered the best; as, when the passengers trust to the honour of the host, they stand a chance of obtaining a bit of pork to their meal, should such be procurable.

The keepers of these lodging-houses are tolerably civil : a stranger on entering makes a slight bow to the people in the shop, and passes on the reception-hall in the centre of the building; whither he is followed by the host, whose first business is to wipe the table, (an operation by no means unnecessary), after which he pours out a few cups of tea. If he be polite, he will ask the surnames of the guests, and whether they desire any thing particular to be provided for them. The guests may also take this opportunity of asking about the nature and distance of the next day's march; though, if he be a foreigner, the fewer questions he puts the better, lest he should excite suspicion. The host also seldom troubles his guests with his conversation, after the first interview, which under certain circumstances is to be prefered. On leaving, the people of the house always wish the travellers a pleasant journey, while the travellers on their part use some complimentary expressions towards those who remain.

Foreigners should be careful to avoid, while putting up at taverns, the persons who may happen to be lodging there, at the same time. There is a certain inquisitiveness about the Chinese, and they have an unpleasant habit of asking a variety of questions, about the name, surname, age, circumstances, origin, birth-place, objects, and destinations of travellers, which queries it is not always convenient to answer. All this is done, not so much with a view of prying into other people's business, and obstructing their proceedings, as out of mere custom, and in consequence of a habit which they have formed ; believing, at the same time, that such queries are pleasing to the parties to whom they are proposed. There are individuals to be met with in such taverns whose object it is to annoy travellers, with the view of getting them into a difficulty, and then making a market of them.

A number of vagabonds are frequently to be met with, wandering about the country, who, under pretence of searching for smuggled opium, require travellers to open their baggage; and, having ascertained what their boxes contain, lay plans to rob them, or endeavour to extort money from unwary stangers, by the threat of bringing them before the mandarins; As a stranger is sure to lose, and never gain, by coming into contact with officials, many persons would rather pay a small sum than be brought into court, however innocent they may be. A foreigner should, of course, avoid such 匪徒 fei t'hoô, rascals, who live by making a disturbance, and whose interest it is to bring others into trouble; and, as they are not easily distinguishable from honest people, except by their debauched appearance, and villainous looks, the greater necessity is there for circumspection.

The writer will here detail a circumstance, which occurred on his march; the party with which he was travelling fell in with an individual, who was going the same way, and was even a fellow-townsman with one of our number; the man who came from the same district, however, took little notice of his neighbour, while another of the company, became very friendly with him. The other reproved him when alone, saying, "Though the man is my townsman, I do not lay myself open to him, and why should you be so free and familiar? do you not know, that road-side acquaintances should be carefully avoided?" Should a stranger, however, need information or assistance from a traveller who might fall in his way, it is easy to put him into a good humour, by asking how old he is, and then complimenting him on his looks; or oue may enquire, how many brothers he has got, whether his parents be yet alive; and, whether any of the brothers be yet at home, to wait upon the old people. The next step is, to offer a piece of tobacco; which, if the party accept, a good understanding is immediately established.

In addition to the eating-houses, there are tea-shops to be

met with, in much-frequented roads, at the distance of a mile, or even half a mile, from each other. These tea-shops are a grade lower in point of comfort and accommodation than the eating-houses, and do not pretend to furnish more than tea or cakes to the weary and hungry traveller. Each shop is provided with a number of tables and benches, arranged in rows under a shed, which projects out in front of the shop, and generally covers the road. Immediately on a stranger stopping at one of these, and taking his seat, a basin is brought out, and placed before him. The hot water is in most instances ready, and a pinch of tea being thrown into the basin, the boiling water is poured over it. This, being left to draw, in about two or three minutes, is ready for use, and the stranger sips it, of course without milk or sugar, from the original basin ; taking care neither to scald his mouth, nor choke himself with the tea-leaves. When he has swallowed about half of this beverage, the shopman stands ready with a fresh supply of hot water, to fill up the basin ; and so on, if the customer require it, for the third or fourth time. By this time, the strength of the little tea put in being entirely exhausted, he pays his six cash, or one half penny, and departs. At these tea-shops, there are generally half a dozen or more travellers, whose observation it would be advisable for a foreigner to avoid, by sitting on one side, or in the more shaded and obscure part of the shop ; not mixing in conversation with those a-round him.

ON THE MODES OF CONVEYANCE.

The modes of conveyance in the interior of China, depend very much on the region, through which one may have to travel. In the neighbourhood of the sea coast, or in the vicinity of the great rivers, the mode of procedure is by water ; and so much more convenient is water than land carriage, that the Chinese have managed to connect most of their great rivers and lakes with each other, by means of the canals, which have been dug in all directions, and which spread like veins and arteries, to almost every part of the empire. As far as the experience of the writer has gone, and a glance at the map will confirm the observation, the Chinese have no walled cities or large towns, except in places which are accessible by water. In the hilly districts there are no navigable rivers, and therefore no large towns ; but immediately you arrive at a stream, large enough to admit even of rafts, you may expect soon to meet with a mart of business. In the level country, if a river or lake is not sufficiently accommodating to extend its arms to human dwellings, busy and restless man excavates a canal to connect his abode with the grand thoroughfare of nations. Most of the canals which the writer has seen are straight, about fifty feet broad and ten deep ; sometimes they extend but a short distance across a strip of land, that divides one lake from another, and sometimes they stretch over a space of fifty or a hundred miles, in order to facilitate the communication between distant cities. They are spanned, at intervals of a few miles, by bridges of one arch, which in the route travelled by the grain junks, must be at least twenty feet high, to admit of those bulky vessels passing under them, even when the masts are lowered. Wherever a bridge is seen spanning a canal, the traveller may be sure of finding a number of houses and shops, on each side of the water ; if there be not a considerable village in the vicinity, or a road leading to one. These arches are generally well turned, but when the buttresses give way, as is not unfrequently the case, the arch then exhibits a flattened appearance on one side or the other ; and the writer has met with several instances of their having fallen in, or greatly needing repair. The Chinese generally use for their bridges long blocks of stone, five feet in length, alternating with shorter ones of one foot, all purposely chiselled into a curved form, to suit the bend of the arch, with the sides somewhat wedge-shaped, at the point of junction with the other stones ; on the top of the arch, where we should fix the key-stone, the Chinese place one of these long slabs, and arrange the smaller stones on either side, so that they have many key-stones instead of one. When they construct bridges of several arches, they make the intervening buttresses so small, that the arch is thereby considerably weakened, and not unfrequently falls in. The middle arch is generally very large, in proportion to the side ones, so that the passengers have to ascend to a great height, by steep steps on either side of the bridge, in order to cross it. This of course would render them unavailable for the passage of heavy-wheeled carriages ; which in other respects could not pass over their bridges, on account of the slight construction and narrow width of the same. Chinese bridges being destitute of a parapet wall, and the road for passengers being immediately over the stone slab which forms the tops of the bridges, they look from a distance, as if they were made of paste-board, and the passengers appear to be walking in the air. Some bridges have, however, been met with of a very substantial kind, with strong buttresses, equal arches, parapet walls, and level roads along the top, across which carriages might easily pass. These will be described in the following journal, as they occur on the route passed over by the writer. Wooden bridges are frequently met with, spanning mountain torrents, but these are invariably provided with iron chains passing from one side to the other, through the various compartments of the bridge, in order to prevent the whole being washed away when the freshets come down. One such chain was observed, precisely like the chain cables used for European vessels, large enough to hold a brig of 200 tons, and in a position several hundred miles from the sea, whither it is not likely that chain cables of European manufacture could be conveyed ; it is to be pre-

中國內地一瞥：在絲茶產區的一次旅行期間所見

三五

sumed, therefore, that the natives made it themselves, near the spot where it is found.

ON CHINESE BOATS.

In travelling along the canals and small rivers of China, covered boats are used, which are divided into several apartments, with windows and doors, suited for the convenience of passengers. The boats usually employed are about 25 feet long, by six broad; the whole of which space, (with the exception of four or five feet forward, and six or eight astern, left open for the purpose of enabling the people to work,) is inclosed and partitioned off, in the following manner. First comes the outer cabin, about six feet square, with an entrance in front, and a door behind leading into the central cabin; a window on each side admits light and air, while a few stools placed round render it a very neat vestibule for the reception of visitors. The central cabin, is higher, longer, and broader than the first, with several windows on each side, a bed-place at the further end, seats all round, and a table in the midst: here the passengers may eat, drink, sleep, and work, with ease and comfort, while the boat is under weigh. Astern of the central cabin is a small berth, athwart the vessel, a few feet wide, where the boat people sleep; and abaft this is an open space, covered in by a mat, where the men stand to scull the boat. Their sculls or stern oars are powerful instrumemts, working on a pivot, fixed into the stern of the boat; and being slightly bent, the boatmen are enabled to give the scull a curved or spiral motion in the water, by means of which the boat is propelled; a rope is fastened from the end of the scull to the deck, by working which the scull is turned half round; while one or two other men, grasping the scull in the hand, move it backwards and forwards or guide its motions. Large boats are provided with two stern oars, and those which are still larger, have a couple of additional sculls forward; these sculls appear better adapted for canal boats than oars, as these vessels have to be moved along very narrow water communications, and may be seen passing under bridges or between close walls, only just wide enough to admit the boats themselves ; the scull however sends them forward, where there would not be room to row or paddle them. The boats now alluded to are provided with a curiously-shaped mast, fitted on a cross piece of timber passing over the top of the central cabin, by means of two hinges, which admit of the mast being easily lowered abaft, whenever the boat has to pass under bridges : the mast itself is double, rising up from either end of the cross beam just alluded to, and meeting in a point at the top, in the form of a Greek Lamma ; the mast is thus prevented from going over the side, by the width of its base, and is steadied longitudinally by means of a rope, which passes from either end of the boat to the mast head. It is thus easily lowered, and as easily raised. A second and smaller mast, of the same kind, works in the larger one, and is raised occasionally for the purpose of towing the boat, Masts of such a construction are convenient in small canals. with numerous bridges, where both mast and sail have to be lowered every half hour ; but, on account of their weakness, are ill adapted for large rivers, while by their broad base they they do not admit of the sail being drawn much aft ; and hence such boats can only sail with the wind a-beam, and cannot, like single-masted and sharp-bottomed boats, beat against a head or a strong wind. Vessels navigating the Yang-tsze-këang, and other large rivers, are of a different ld, and thus better adapted for withstanding heavy and erse winds.

ON CHINESE ROADS.

but the roads of central China are better than a stranger could expect to find them ; considering that they are not made for the passage of two-wheeled carriages, and only for foot passengers, with occasionally a wheelbarrow, and a

中
國
內
地
一
瞥
：
在
絲
茶
產
區
的
一
次
旅
行
期
間
所
見

few animals, the path-ways are on the whole exceedingly good. In some places they were found fifteen feet wide, paved with flag stones in the middle, and with well-laid pebbles on each side. For hundreds of miles, the traveller may be assured of meeting with good stone roads, at least three feet wide, formed of slabs of granite, mica slate, sandstone, or lias, according to the nature of the adjacent rocks, and the supply of stone in the neighbourhood. Over mountain passes, one or two thousand feet in height, roads are to be seen, cut into steps, six or eight feet wide, and laid with great care and exactness, for the convenience of passengers. The ascending of hills, and the passage over plains, is thus much facilitated, by the sure standing which the foot meets with. At the distance of a mile from each other, sheds are to be seen, built over the road, and provided with seats, where the weary traveller may refresh himself by a little rest, and prepare for further exertions. These roads and sheds, together with the bridges and canals, are, as far as can be ascertained, all the product of voluntary and benevolent effort. Sometimes an individual makes a vow to repair a certain line of road, or mountain pass, or build a bridge ; and sometimes a subscription is put round, headed by some rich and liberal person, for the purpose of setting some such useful measure on foot ; the money seems readily collected on such occasions, and is perhaps faithfully laid out ; at any rate, a stone tablet recording the date and circumstance of the erection or repair, and the amount contributed by each individual, is usually stuck up at the head of the road or bridge ; and sometimes when successive repairs have been made, a ring of such tablets may be seen, giving everlasting publicher (as they express it) to the benevolent donors, who land earned such imperishable fame by their exertions.

Another gratifying circumstance we have to record is, that we do not remember to have met with a single turnpike gate, toll-bridge, or canal-charge throughout the country ; all is free, as the light of heaven, or the air we breathe. Ferries are to be met with, where travellers may get rowed gratuitously across rivers, the boat and its ferry-man being provided by a public subscription, so that there is not a halfpenny to pay. More than all this, there are societies in the interior of China, for providing tea and soup for weary travellers ; and the writer has frequently felt himself indebted to some unknown benefactor for a pleasant and refreshing beverage, when faint by the way. Sometimes the gratuitous tea is provided in such a shed as has been above described, where some old woman is constantly in attendance, to keep the water boiling, and to supply fresh tea leaves, all day long ; and sometimes it is made ready in a temple, where the priest does these offices of kindness, as a part of his duty. The expense of keeping up one such tea-shop, is perhaps a dollar a day, and in the green tea district there are hundreds of them.

Another benevolent provision, made by the Chinese for the use of travellers, is the lighting of lamps along frequented roads, and near to dangerous bridges ; these are made of thin layers of oyster-shells, fitted into a wooden frame-work, and either suspended from a lamp-post, or fixed in a recess in a stone pillar ; the light they afford is of course dim, but it serves to shew where the bridge or road is, and displays the good intentions of the persons setting them up. There is no charge either for paving or lighting as in England.

MODES OF LAND TRAVELLING.

The mode of travelling along the roads of central China, is on foot, or by means of sedan chairs ; while some avail themselves of wheel-barrows, or asses. Coolees are easily procurable for the conveyance of goods, and at rates not very exorbitant. The sedan chairs met with in the interior are of the simplest construction imaginable. They consist merely of four upright posts, about five feet high, made of

海上絲綢之路稀見文獻叢刊

三八

small hollow bamboos, about an inch in diameter. These together with transverse and horizontal pieces of the same kind, above, below, and on either side, are fastened together by means of fine rattans ; a bottom and seat made of boards, a top of wicker-work, and a cloth to go round the back and sides, complete the machine, which, independent of the poles, cannot weigh more than ten pounds. The poles are made of very elastic wood, about three inches in diameter in the centre, tapering off towards the ends. They are about 16 feet long, in consequence of which they possess an elasticity, very convenient and pleasant to the rider. When the se dans are not engaged, the bearers take out the poles, and turn the chair upside down ; one man placing the top on the bottom, and letting the seat rest on his shoulders, walks away with the sedan ; while the other follows with the pole. When carrying a passenger they take long steps, and in as cending a hill, keep their legs wide apart, and put one very slowly before the other, by means of which a swing is given to the chair, like the pitching of a vessel in a head sea when this operation is gently performed it is not unpleasant, but with some persons it would produce a sensation not much unlike sea-sickness. The distance which the chair bearers will travel varies from 20 to 25 miles a day, and the expense from one dollar to a dollar and a half. The agreement is generally made for the former sum, but the tea, cakes, rice, and vegetables consumed by the bearers on the way, for which they manage to indent on the kindness of the person they carry, amounts to the odd half dollar. They are a troublesome and noisy generation, making great professions on starting, and always receding from their promise before the journey is half over. Opium is the main cause of their apparent elevation at one time, and the want of it occasions their breaking down subsequently ; while gaming, drinking, and other vices to which they are addicted, both annoy their employers and impoverish themselves.

The coolees who are engaged in carrying burdens, are very similar in character to the chair-bearers ; like them they get their money with much difficulty, and spend it with the greatest ease. Every coolee is provided with a pole, about six feet long and two inches wide, made of elastic wood ; it is somewhat flattened on one side and rounded off on the other, being about an inch thick in the centre and broadest part; and half an inch at either end. The pole is sometimes a little curved, and when in a horizontal position, the bow part is kept downwards, and the two ends elevated ; near the ends are some short pegs to prevent the strings by which the goods are suspended, slipping backwards or forwards. The pole thus prepared, is placed across the shoulder of the bearer, and the goods suspended from either end, something in the way that pails hang from either end of the yoke, borne by milk-maids in England ; with this exception, that the yoke of the Chinese coolee is straight, and rests only on one shoulder at a time ; when the bearer is tired, he rests his burthen, or shifts it to the other shoulder, at his convenience. In order to facilitate this operation, the coolee is provided with a staff, tipped with iron at one end, and grooved at the other ; it is about as long as his own shoulder is high ; this staff is placed with the ferule downwards and the groove upwards, underneath the bearing pole ; the burthen at one end resting on the ground, while the coolee removes one shoulder, or applies the other to the load, as he thinks fit. Having taken up his burthen again, he uses the staff as a sort of lever, resting on the vacant shoulder as a fulcrum ; with the short end, which is a little flattened, underneath the bearing pole, to help to sustain the weight, and his own hand, applied to the long end where the iron ferule is, as the power. When they arrive at a stopping-place, they place the staff again under the pole, allowing one side of the burthen to rest on the ground, and the other to recline against a wall or tree, where it remains till the bearer wants to proceed ; the object gained by this manœuvre is, the keeping of the cords stretched, the goods in their proper places, and the burthen in such a position, that it can be taken up without much effort on the part of the labourer.

For the same reason, the chair-bearers prefer taking up the chair when empty, and leave the passenger to get into it as best he may, while it is on their shoulders ; that they may not have to put forth additional effort, in raising the weight, when their bodies and knees are in a bent position. There is an art in getting into the chair, while on the bearers' shoulders, which a novice is not acquainted with ; and the bearers can tell by the way of a man's mounting the sedan, whether he be accustomed to such a mode of travelling or not. This of course must be attended to by a foreigner, or he will soon be known to be such. While the bearers are standing with the chair, ready to start, he must insert his head between the poles, with his face in the direction in which he is going, and not towards the chair, as Europeans are apt to do ; then he must place his hands on the poles, on either side, and raising one heel to the foot-board, he must gradually elevate himself to the proper position, and seat himself gently in the chair ; taking care not to bounce into it with violence ; as it would not only make the bearers exclaim against his weight, but lead them to conclude, that he has never been in a Chinese sedan before.

Before quitting the subject of the coolees and their bearing poles ; we may allude to an invention seen amongst them which they call a third hand ; it consists of a small bamboo tube fitted into the middle of the bearing pole, for the purpose of holding an umbrella, so that in rainy weather, they can prosecute their journey without being wet, and without the trouble of holding a screen over their heads. Coolees and chair-bearers are also generally furnished with a quantity of oiled-paper, with which they cover over their goods, ar)d preserve them from being injured by damp, in a rainy day.

The weight generally borne by a coolee, is about 110 cat ties, or 146 lbs. with this they will easily travel thirteen miles a day, and cross mountain passes with their load. If it be an object to get the bearers to go quickly, one half of the above weight only must be laid upon them, and then they will go double the distance ; but what is thus gained in velocity, it is evident, will be lost in power.

ON THE BEST MODE OF TRAVELLING.

The best way to travel overland in China, if a person can afford it, is, to take a sedan chair, and, packing up one's luggage into small loads of thirty or forty pounds each, to let the coolees bear the baggage after the traveller, at the same rate at which the chair-bearers travel, viz. twenty-five miles a day. Should the loads be heavier, the coolees will certainly fall behind, and the traveller be obliged to wait for them. But for a mere traveller much luggage is not necessary ; a mattress, coverlet, and pillow, with two or three changes of under garments, will be quite enough ; what he wants more, he can buy at every town, and throw away when unnecessary. A good pedestrian would make his way with ease through the provinces of China, with only one faithful servant, to carry a light pack, and act as guide ; for, the fewer persons a stranger has about him, the fewer will he come into close contact with, and the less chance will there be of molestation or discovery. Wherever water communication is available, the most convenient mode of travelling is by boat ; as a stranger may then shut himself up from observation, when approaching densely-peopled and suspicious places ; while he can throw off restraint, and go freely abroad, where there are few likely to observe, or harrass him. In many parts of the country, indeed, the people seem never to have dreamt, that there are such things as foreigners, and would as soon think of seeing a ghost, as meeting with a barbarian.

中國內地一瞥：在絲茶產區的一次旅行期間所見

Sometimes persons are met with travelling on horseback, or making use of asses and mules ; but this plan can by no means be recommended to one from abroad ; as the elevation renders him more conspicuous and exposed, and, there being no relays of horses on the road, he would be unable to change his beast, at the end of a stage, or when tired down. Travelling by means of wheel-barrows, is one of the methods used by the Chinese, but rarely ; and, as there are many parts of the road where wheel-barrows could not pass, this mode is not to be recommended to one who has to travel far.

KNOWLEDGE OF THE LANGUAGE REQUISITE.

A traveller in China ought to be well acquainted with the language ; it is generally known, that the provincial dialects, in various parts of the empire, differ much from each other ; but strangers are not aware of the amazing extent of this difference.   The dialects vary so much in the several provinces, that the natives of one are incapable of making themselves intelligible to those of another : even in the several parts of the same province, or prefecture, the dialects differ.   This of course is a great bar to travelling, and were it not for the Mandarin dialect, would be an insuperable obstacle to convenient locomotion.   The keepers of rice and teashops, however, and all those with whom travellers are likely to come into contact, are generally acquainted with the court dialect ; so that a person, knowing this, can make his way through the eighteen provinces ; but then he ought to know it thoroughly, and be able to converse in it without mistake. It is very possible for a man to have studied Mandarin for years, and to have read in it all the books of Confucius, in addition to various ancient and modern authors ; and even be able to compose essays, and write books in the language himself ; and yet be ignorant of the commonest terms, and the most familiar phrases.   The language necessary in an

四三

eating-house, is very different from that used in a study; and yet were a person, putting up at the former, unable to express himself about eating, drinking, and sleeping; and were he puzzled, when addressed on subjects of every day occurrence, the by-standers would not fail to set him down as a very extraordinary individual, if not a barbarian. The writer, after many years of patient study, has often found himself at a loss for words, where the commonest coolee would not be deficient. Such acquirements are not to be obtained from books, but from life; and it is only by frequent intercourse with the Chinese, that a man could expect to attain such a knowledge of every-day conversation, as would carry him unobserved through the country.

COMPLEXION TO BE ATTENDED TO.

The complexion of the foreign traveller is another thing that must be attended to, in order to avoid the observation of the Chinese. The skin of the inhabitants of China varies from a dull pale white, to a copper or an olive colour, and sometimes assumes a hue approaching to black. The northerners, are much fairer than those from the south, and have frequently a ruddiness which the latter do not possess There are very few who exhibit the fair or florid complexion of Englishmen. Should such travel in summer, their faces would soon be tanned by the sun; what the sun could not do, however, would soon be effected, in the same way that the Chinese themselves get their complexions tinged; viz. by never using soap in washing. The Chinese wash their hands and face several times a day, but without soap. A basin of hot water, almost scalding, is brought in to the guests, at taverns and on board of boats, into which a dirty-looking cloth is dipped; this, when squeezed out, is rubbed over the countenance once or twice, and the moisture occasioned thereby is then left to dry on. A stranger travelling incog. through China, must of course do as the Chinese do,

and the least fastidiousness on this point, or the determina-
tion to resort to the use of soap, would lead to observation.
It is evident, however, that this process can never thoroughly
cleanse the face, and, when used repeatedly and constantly,
must obscure the natural fairness of the skin, while the
scalding hot water tends to give that sallowness and pale-
ness to the complexion, which is observable among the
Chinese. Added to which, the living in close rooms, satura-
ted with the smoke of tobacco, and lamp oil, will soon bring
countenances, originally differing much in colour, to pretty
nearly the same hue.

THE GUIDE.

In the course of the preceding pages, much allusion has
been made to a guide, a most indispensable personage in such
expeditions, as the one herein detailed. The writer was fortunate in meeting with a man, who combined the qualities of
daring and caution in an eminent degree. He was adven-
turous enough to undertake the business, and yet sagacious
enough to perceive every slight appearance of danger, and
avoid it. He would venture through crowded places, with
his charge, and yet scrutinize the countenances of individuals
at every stopping-place. He was fully alive to the danger
he ran, and yet, for the sake of the object he had in view,
willing to encounter it. The way in which he came to undertake the business was as follows. Having heard, at the
city of 杭州 Hang-chow, of the arrival of foreign teachers
at the newly-opened ports, and seen some of their publica-
tions, he determined to seek their acquaintance : and on his
arrival at 上海 Sháng haè, called upon the writer. There
was something peculiar in his manner, which could not fail
to strike, at a first interview ; a solidity, an earnestness, an
apparent sincerity, which excited an unwonted interest in
him. Subsequent opportunities of conversing with him tended to increase that impression, and a peculiar friendship

soon sprang up between the writer and his future fellow-traveller. Listening to the doctrines of Christianity, he fancied
he could trace some resemblance between them, and the
dogmas of his spiritual guide, to whom he paid great deference. On enquiry, it was found, that the instructor to whom
he referred was a very enlightened Chinese, who had extracted all that was good from the Confucian, and other systems
within his reach, with reference to a Supreme Being, and
purification of the heart. The old gentleman alluded to
had compiled a number of essays, which contained many
good things ; and, what with one system and another, a
scheme was got up, which far surpassed any that had hitherto been culled from native sources. Our new acquaintance
had conceived the idea, that if he could effect an interview
between the compiler of these essays, and the preacher of
foreign doctrines, he should get them to agree; and, while the
one brought an element, which China did not possess, of spiritual and experimental godliness, the other would assist in clothing such ideas in the best possible language ; and thus the
present and future ages be benefited. His teacher, however,
was old, and could not travel ; what then was to be done ?
The writer proposed a solution of the difficulty, and offered
to go and see the Chinese reformer. This, after some deli-
beration, was acceded to, and the parties agreed to start on a
given day, as friends, and without any self-interested object.
Having seen something of the habits and manner of life of
Christians, the Chinese guide had conceived a favourable
idea of the Gospel ; he believed that there was only one
Supreme God, that Moses was his lawgiver, and that Jesus
was a true sage, who had suffered much for the benefit of
mankind ; but, his ideas were still very confused on many
important topics, and he needed to learn which be the first
principles of the oracles of God. He belonged, however, to a
school of superior men, and had been accustomed to exercise his mind in deep reflection. It was thought, therefore,

中國內地一瞥：在絲茶產區的一次旅行期間所見

that, by a visit to his usual abode and fellow disciples, some
thing might be done towards benefiting the individual, and
paving the way for the introduction of the Gospel into central
China. On these principles, the journey was undertaken
and though in itself an infraction of existing political regulations, exposing the individuals undertaking it to much inconvenience and risk, yet, in dependence on the Divine guidance,
it was hoped, that it would be accomplished without loss.

Such a guide was far better than a hireling, who would engage in the enterprize only from a prospect of gain; but the
travelling in such company was attended with some unplea-
santness; as the writer was obliged to put himself entirely
under the control of his Mentor, to confide every thing to
his care, and to recede from his own will and way, whenever it crossed that of his director. And it was but just so
to do; for if a man from disinterested motives exposes himself to some risk on account of another; the least the other
can do, is to study his safety and convenience; sacrificing
everything of private feeling and advantage to secure his
friend from harm. It was certainly an exercise of patience,
to allow one's-self to be directed in every movement, and
checked at every turn: submitting to the judgment of another,
where the propriety of an arrangement could not be exactly
seen, in order to ensure the success of an enterprise, and the
exemption of its conductor from responsibility and blame.
But so terrible would have been the visitation, had the poor
fellow been discovered, in leading a foreigner into the country, that the writer was willing to do anything to screen
him, and would have deprecated above all things having
been the cause of involving the guide and his family in the ruin,
which, under an arbitrary government, would have followed
detection. By the good Providence of God, however, such
consequences did not ensue, and the man was not made
to suffer for his kindness to another.

COMMENCEMENT OF THE JOURNEY.

1845. March 27th. Having dropped down to Woo-sung, the preceding evening, I sent for a Chinese barber from the town, to attend me on board one of the ships lying there. I told him, that I wanted my head shaved, and a Chinese cue appended to my hair. He did not seem at all surprised at the request, and, without remonstrance or delay, proceeded to deprive me of my locks, without the least ceremony. He had brought a quantity of hair with him, but finding me already provided, he made use of what was nearest at hand, and fitted on the new tail in a very dextrous manner. He told me, however, that though the junction was tight for the time, yet after a few days, it would be necessary to splice it anew. A dollar satisfied him for his trouble, and he promised to keep the secret. The cue being wound round my head, and covered with a large cap, I proceeded, still in European clothes, on board a ship, then passing up the river, without the generality of those on board suspecting the change which my head had undergone. Arrived at 上海 Shàng-haè, I remained below until the evening; when I retired into one of the cabins, and changed my dress, having carefully provided every requisite beforehand. In a quarter of an hour, I appeared completely changed, and astonished the ship's company not a little, who could not understand how such an individual had come on board. The captain kindly volunteered to put me on shore in his own boat, and I set out on my new expedition. Just at that moment, however, a most fearful thunder-storm came on; the heavens were as black as death; not an object was to be seen at more than a foot distance, except when the lightning glared, which, dazzling the eyes, rendered the subsequent gloom still more impenetrable. The thunder roared in a terrific manner, and the rain descended in torrents. As it happened, the captain was a complete stranger to the place, and did not know, even if he could have seen, where to put me on shore ; thus, when we reached the river side, we knew not where to land, and had to poke about in the dark for a landing place, but in vain ; at length we saw a light on shore, and sent one of the sailors to borrow a bit of candle, which, by holding it in his hat, he managed to keep lighted, notwithstanding the high wind, and guided the bewildered traveller, over some sticks of timber, on to firm ground. On gaining my feet, and looking round, I soon found that the place where they had landed me, and from whence they had borrowed the light, was the native custom-house, to the officers of which I was well known. Those on duty at the time, however, were too lazy and too much frightened at the storm, to look out at the door, and I was too glad to escape their observation. Assaying to proceed on my way, I soon found the darkness so great, that not a step could be taken without danger of falling, or getting into one of the many pits, which I knew to abound on the road side, or at least getting off the pathway which was very crooked. At length, I stopped at a blacksmith's shop, to ask for a light. They enquired, whence I came, and whither I was going ; I reiterated my request for a lantern. They said, they had none. I then asked for a bit of candle ; an inch of which, after much hesitation, and many marks of suspicion, they at length gave me. With this I went on a little way, but the wind soon blew it out, and I was as badly off as before. By degrees, however, I got my eyes more accustomed to the darkness, and preferred stumbling occasionally, to exposing my face to the gaze of the passengers, who, assisted by the glare of a candle, would the more easily recognize me. Not adverting to an inequality in the road, I fell near the banks of the river, but immediately getting on my feet, I pursued my course, sometimes ankle deep in water, and perpetually drenched with the pelting shower. Now and then I availed myself of a friendly lantern, that might

carried past at that time ; but these being borne sometimes
wn side streets, or into houses, frequently left me in dark-
ss. Being well acquainted with the streets, however, I
naged to reach the neighbourhood of the spot where I had
reed with my guide to meet me, near the south side of the
wn. Here, turning the angle of a lane, I spied a glimmer-
g light at the farther end, and approaching it, found my
ithful friend, true to his promise, standing in the place of
ndezvous, dripping with rain. Not a soul else was near,
d our mutual recognition was not observed. Having
ined company we proceeded to the river side, where the
at he had provided was in readiness; we embarked forth-
ith, and creeping into the hole allotted for my residence,
divested myself of my wet garments, and covering myself
ith the bed-clothes, soon fell asleep.

March 28th. On waking this morning, I was rejoiced to
ind that the boat was already under weigh ; but, being
shut up on all sides, I could not ascertain in what direction
it was going ; when, after a quarter of an hour's rowing, it
came to an anchor. I thought this might be in order to wait
or the opening of the bridge-gate at 新閘 Sin-chă, or to
top until the tide would admit of our passing ; but what
vas my vexation to find, by listening to the conversation of
he boatmen, that they had only got to the entrance of the
岸涇浜 Yâng-king-pang, which, owing to the lowness of
he water, they could not enter till the afternoon. Thus I
aad to lie, with scarcely room enough to allow of my sitting
upright in the boat, and hardly light enough to enable me
o read ; being only just able to see, through the matting that
overed me, to about one foot distance from the boat. As we
ere here surrounded by other boats and vessels, and exactly
a front of an English merchant's counting-house, I did not
vish to make any further effort to see, for fear of being seen.
I had now time to survey the inside of the boat and to as-
ertain its dimensions. My own berth was nearly at the

F

head of the boat, forward of which was an open space, abo
two feet long by three wide, where a boatman stood occasiona
to pole the boat ; in the bulk-head, which separated my be
from this space, there was a little door, through which a pers
might just creep, but which was rarely opened.   Immedia
ly astern of my berth was the central part of the boat, eig
feet long by five wide, which was occupied by my guide a
his partner in business, who was aware of my foreign origin
this space was merely high enough to allow of the
sitting upright by day, and lying at full length, side by sic
at night, with one of the boatmen stretched across at the
feet ; a bulk-head with a door-way separated this centre cab
from the hinder part of the vessel, which was not mo
than six feet long, by five broad ; in this place the oth
boatman slept, and here they both stood up by day to pr
pel the boat. Thus her whole length was not above 22 fee
long, by six broad in the widest part, narrowing towards th
end ; while the roof of the cabins was only three feet high.
The covering of the boat was of matting, spread over a frame-
work, high in the centre, and lower towards the sides and
ends ; so that the boat on the outside assumed the appearanc
of a lengthened egg-shell.   Underneath the deck was
sort of hold, which contained the half a dozen boxes c
my fellow passengers ; and below the platform, on which
the boatmen stood astern, was the fire-place and apparatu
for cooking.   Thus cooped up and confined, in silence
and darkness, I was compelled to spend the whole of the
forenoon, surrounded by bustle and activity, and yet unable to show myself, lest, by an untimely discovery, th
whole expedition should be defeated at the outset.   Afte
mid-day the tide answered, and we entered the small cree
above-named, which, though only a few yards wide, is one
the mediums of communication with 松江 Sûng-këang, 薊
州 Soo-chow, and the rich districts to the westward.   This
narrow canal, on account of its security from danger by storms

l freedom from annoyance by Mandarins, is chosen by
ll boats, in preference to the 吳松 Woô-sûng creek,
ich runs paralled with it ; and the 黃浦 Hwâng-poo,
ch, after a few miles of southing, is navigable for vessels
a large size, proceeding to the westward. The entrance of
洋涇浜 Yâng-king-pang, is very unprepossessing ;
g lines of beggar-craft, and manure-boats skirt the sides
he creek ; these, originally very offensive to both nose
d eyes, send forth a doubly disagreeable odour after a
vy shower, which the close proximity in which we pass-
gave us the full benefit of. At length, after clearing the
allows of the creek, we came to an anchor in the broader
rt of the canal, within an hour's walk of the town. Our
ening repast finished, the boatmen were induced, as the
le was favourable, to go a little further, and by night we
ached the village of 紅橋 Hûng-keaóu, or red bridge,
out eight miles from Shang-hae. At this place there
e about a hundred houses ; but the red bridge, which for-
rly gave a name to the place, has been replaced by a
oden one.

March 29th. We proceeded early on our way, and after
wing three or four miles, reached 七寶 Tseĭh-paòu, or
e Seven Precious Ones. This is a considerable town,
ith about ten thousand inhabitants. A large stone bridge,
one arch, spans the canal, somewhere near the centre of
town ; and a smaller one crosses it, at either extremity of
settlement. The streets are occupied by shops, the
k pers of which carry on a small trade ; while there are a
number of large mercantile establishments, which do considerable business in cotton and grain. Besides a subordinate
civil officer, a sub-lieutenant, (巴總 pa tsung,) with eight
soldiers, are stationed here. There were formerly two temples, one at the north, and the other at the south side of the
town, which were dedicated to the seven precious stars of
Ursa Major, hence the name of the town ; it is fifty-four le,

or sixteen miles, from 青浦 Tsing-poo, and twelve fro
Sháng-haè. After passing Tseĭh-paòu, we left the princip ab
canal, and proceeded along a narrower channel, until wna
came to 北幹山 Pĭh-kan-shan ; this is a small roun be
topped hill, about two hundred feet high, on the summit ors
which there formerly stood a temple, dedicated to some bravia
general, who is said to have tried the metal of his sword, beig
cutting a rock in twain. The natives shew a rock, at tl a
back of the hill, which consists of two parts, with sideji
resembling each other in shape, as if it had been cut in twqhe
this they call the 試劍石 try-sword stone. They alaic
shew an indentation in another rock, which, they say, waoc
caused by the heel of the general's boot, when he stamped ob
it in his rage. The temple, however, is now destroyed, ano
only the foundations of it remain. At the foot of the hilj
is a small village, where a little trade is carried on ; an
from the top of the hill are visible, to the southward, a loce
range of hills, in the neighbourhood of 松江 Sûng-këangh
from between which the pagodas of that city appear. To t'gh.
north, is seen the pagoda of 清龍 Tsing-lûng, near whime-
the remains of the ancient city of 青浦 Tsing-poo may nd
seen ; while to the westward, is visible the modern Tsing-po c
with its high pagoda.

Quitting this interesting spot, we passed on to 青浦
Tsing-poo, which we reached in the evening. This cih
was founded in the Ming dynasty, about 250 years ago, hu:
already shews some signs of decay. The walls are abo ce
two miles in circumference, twenty-three feet high, v 2
1,725 embrasures, and seven bastions ; there are five gaee
and four water-gates ; three of the former are provided wh
half-moon bastions, and double entrances ; the ditch roue
the walls, is thirty feet wide by ten deep. The embrasu
have been some of them in ruins, as also a part oi
the wall, but have lately been repaired. A large bridge in
the northern part of the town, has been broken down

ms

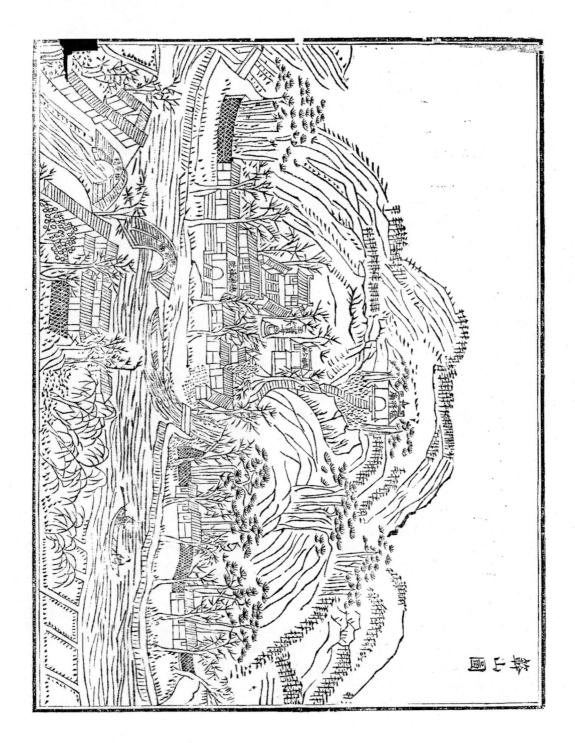

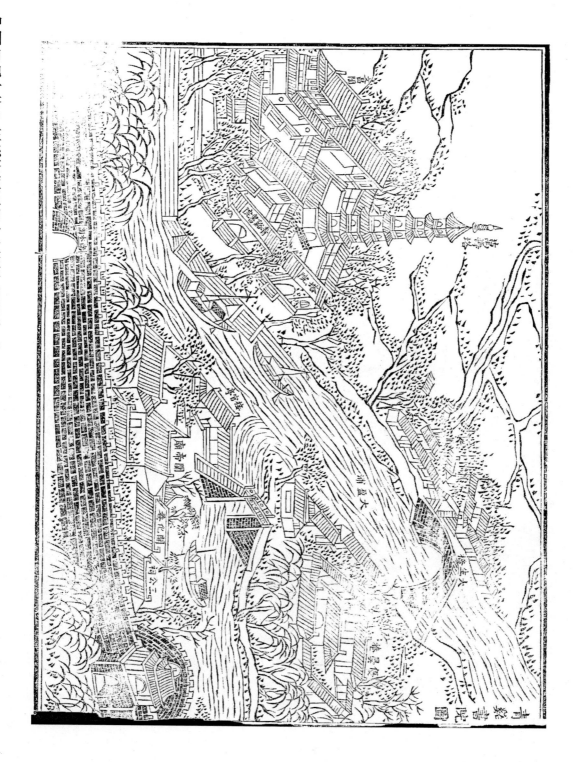

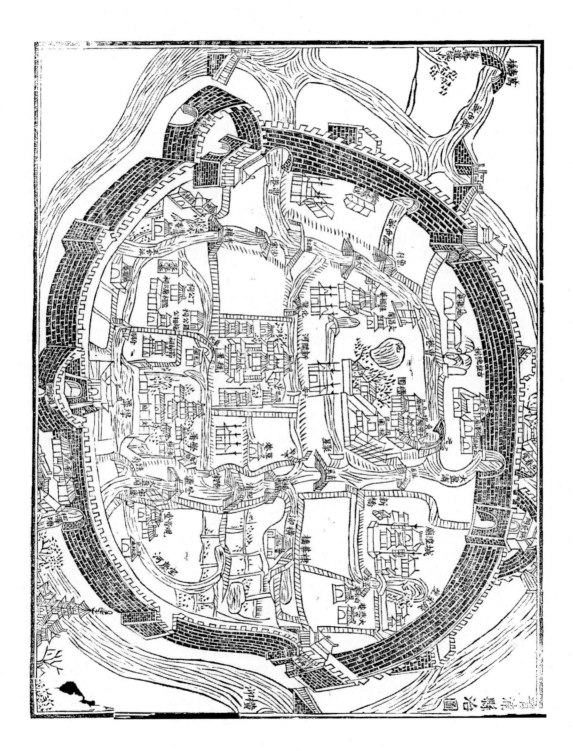

or sixteen miles, from 青浦 Tsing-poo, and twelve fro
Sháng-haè. After passing Tseïh-paòu, we left the princip
canal, and proceeded along a narrower channel, until w
came to 北幹山 Pïh-kan-shan ; this is a small roun
topped hill, about two hundred feet high, on the summit
which there formerly stood a temple, dedicated to some brav
general, who is said to have tried the metal of his sword, b
cutting a rock in twain. The natives shew a rock, at t
back of the hill, which consists of two parts, with side
resembling each other in shape, as if it had been cut in tw
this they call the 試劍石 try-sword stone. They al
shew an indentation in another rock, which, they say, wa
caused by the heel of the general's boot, when he stamped o
it in his rage. The temple, however, is now destroyed, an
only the foundations of it remain. At the foot of the hil
is a small village, where a little trade is carried on ; an
from the top of the hill are visible, to the southward, a lo
range of hills, in the neighbourhood of 松江 Sûng-këan
from between which the pagodas of that city appear. To t
north, is seen the pagoda of 清龍 Tsing-lûng, near whi
the remains of the ancient city of 青浦 Tsing-poo may
seen ; while to the westward, is visible the modern Tsing-po
with its high pagoda.

Quitting this interesting spot, we passed on to 青浦
Tsing-poo, which we reached in the evening. This c
was founded in the Ming dynasty, about 250 years ago, l'atu
already shews some signs of decay. The walls are abo
two miles in circumference, twenty-three feet high, v
1,725 embrasures, and seven bastions ; there are five ga
and four water-gates ; three of the former are provided w
half-moon bastions, and double entrances ; the ditch rou
the walls, is thirty feet wide by ten deep. The embrasu
have been some of them in ruins, as also a part o
the wall, but have lately been repaired. A large bridge i
the northern part of the town, has been broken down
storms

some time, and the people do not seem to have wealth energy enough to repair it. Much money, however, has bee , from time to time, expended on the city, which has paved, though narrow streets, numerous bridges, temples, public offices, and triumphal arches, in abundance ; most of these outlays are the result of private effort, and have been expended by the inhabitants, with the view of rendering their residence more comfortable and secure. Outside the city walls, at the south-east corner, is a pagoda seven stories high, built about a hundred years ago, from the top of which, there is a beautiful view of the adjacent hills and lakes ; but the steps being now out of repair, it is difficult for strangers to enjoy the prospect. A sketch of this pagoda, taken by the Chinese, is annexed. In the neighbourhood of this city, is a temple, and a tomb, supposed to contain so ie of the clothes and ornaments, formerly possessed by

fucius, which were said to have been dug up by a c ntryman in his field ; since which time, the natives have honoured the relics, as though they had actually belonged to the sage ; and it is reported, that one man having slept a single night on the spot, had a dream, by means of which he got a clearer insight into the true meaning of Confucius' wr tings, than he could have obtained, through the medium of all the commentaries. Confucius, however, never was in Tsing-poo, during his life-time ; and, when he died, he was buried in Shang-tung, about 1,000 le to the northward.

1 urch 30th. Sunday. Our boat proceeded onwards this mo ning, and being embarked with others, I was obliged to mo e with them. I availed myself, however, of the quiet ret ement of the boat, to read the Scriptures, and was ple ied to see my fellow-travellers do the same ; while I ea stly prayed, that the perusal of the Sacred Writings, mi be blessed to their spiritual good. We quitted Ts- poo s ditch, that winds round the sonth city n aaed-

proceeded along a canal, called the 漕巷 Tsaôu-k ...
ior about four miles, when we arrived at a place ...
朱家閣 Choo-këa-kŏ ; on approaching this town, ...
canal gradually widens, into a large sheet of water ; ...
further end of which, is a high bridge, of five a ...
with a pavilion, three stories high, on the south side ; ...
southward of this pavilion lies the town, above allud ...
't contains fom ten to twenty thousand inhabitants, ...
eing situated near the borders of the 泖湖 Maou ...
and just midway between Soo-chow and Sung-këang ...
is a place of considerable trade. It dates its rise ...
the Ming dynasty, and was founded by a man, ...
named Lŭh, since whose time it has grown to its p ...
size. The bridge is the most prominent object on appr ...
ing the town, as the central arch is very high, the tw ...
each side gradually decreasing in size, so that the b ...
has the appearance of a small hill, and those who p ...
over it have a fine view of the surrounding country.

About noon, we passed a village, the name of which ...
could not learn, and crossed at intervals several lakes, ...
ther several arms of the same lake, connected by narrow ...
nals. These sheets of water, were about two miles wide ...
the range of lakes thus formed is called the 連湖 Lë ...
or connected ponds ; northward it extends to the 薛 ...
Seïh-tëen-hoô, and southward to the 泖湖 Maou- ...
the centre of which latter is an island, with a pag ...
it, visible from a considerable distance. It appea ...
reference to Chinese historical records, that at on ...
of this lake, called 長泖 Châng-maou, in the dis ...
鼠山 Kwăn-shan, there was formerly a city, cal ...
卷 Yêw-keuén, which in the time of 秦始皇 T ...
hwâng, the Emperor who burnt the books, (B. C. 24 ...
rishing condition: but about the close of the ...
the city was swallowed up ...

when the weather is fine, and the sky clear, the streets and houses of the old city are to be seen, at the bottom of the lake ; it is also said, that in the reign of 萬歷 Wán-leĭh, of the Ming dynasty, (A. D. 1,573), when the modern city of Tsing-poo was built, the old people of the place informed the magistrate of the district, of the existence of this subaqueous domain, and that he ordered them to dive down into the water, by which means a quantity of materials were obtained, for the erection of the present city. In the middle of the lake, there is an island, with a pagoda on it, called 潮音閣 Chaôu-yin-kŏ, which is said, to have been the centre of the ancient city of 由卷 Yêw-keuén.

At about 3 p. m. this day, we passed the small village of 生塔 Săng-tă, and in the evening arrived at a lake, called 三百浪 San-pĭh-lâng, the 300 waves ; after crossing which, we anchored for the night in a small canal, opposite the cottage of the boatman. His children and nephews spied the boat from a distance, and hailed his approach with delight, crowding round him on landing, and jumping about with the greatest glee, while he received them with much fondness. The appearance of the children indicated the health and happiness of the family, but their little chubby faces were so begrimed with dirt, that it was difficult to tell of what colour they originally were. I was surprised, and, under other circumstances, should have been somewhat chagrined, to see the little notice which the women and children took of me, whenever I met them ; scarcely looking round as I passed, and if they did, not deigning a second gaze. This appeared the more strange to me, as I had been accustomed, as other foreigners are, when walking about in the garb of my country in Sháng-haè, to be stared at and followed from place to place ; but being clad in Chinese costume, the people did not seem to imagine that there was anything peculiar about me, and passed me as they would another Chinaman, a class by no means rare in these regions.

We had travelled this day about fifty le, or fifteen miles and I was glad in the evening to get out of the boat, and take a short walk in the adjacent fields.

March 31st. This morning we again got under weigh, and after crossing two or three more lakes, we came to a place called 平望 Pìng-wáng, containing several thousand inhabitants.* In this town, we observed a temple, with 十誡 Shíh-keaé, the ten commandments, written over it; this, does not refer, however, to the Ten Commandments delivered by God to Moses, but to the ten prohibitions of Budha ; which are directed against 1. The killing of animals. 2. Theft. 3. Adultery. 4. Falsehood. 5. Discord. 6. Railing. 7. Idle talk. 8. Covetousness. 9. Envy. and 10. Heresy : the town of Pìng-wáng lies about W. S. W. from Tsing-poo, at a distance of eighty le, or twenty-two miles. The water-communication, which we had hitherto sailed along, here crosses the imperial canal, the course of which is north-west and south-east ; it is defended by a strongly built causeway, leaving only a small opening about thirty feet wide, through which the water rushes to the north-eastward, with considerable velocity ; this opening is spanned by a flat bridge formed of immense blocks of granite, reaching from one buttress to the other. † We had some difficulty in

---

* Pìng-wáng is a most important place for trade, being situated near a confluence of the lakes, and on the Grand Canal, joining Soochow to Hang-chow ; it therefore attracts traders from all parts, who open their shops, and spread out their wares and provisions for sale. There is a small civil officer resident at the place, called a 巡檢司 Seun këen sze, or inspector, and a military officer of the rank of lieutenant.

† This bridge is called 通安橋 T'hung-gnan-keaóu, "extending tranquillity bridge," and 畫眉橋 hwǎ-meî-keaóu, "painted eye-brows bridge ;" it was built in the Sung dynasty, repaired during the reign of the Ming sovereigns, and under the Emperor Kang-he was rebuilt, entirely through the exertions of a priest named 果緣 Kwò-yuên, who obtained the money by begging.

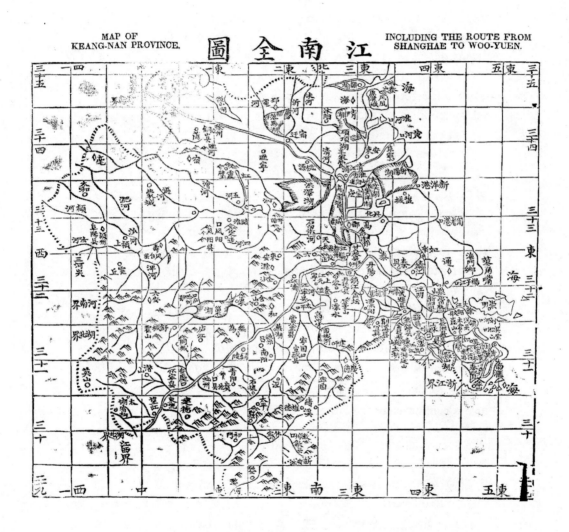

MAP OF
KEANG-NAN PROVINCE.

江南全圖

INCLUDING THE ROUTE FROM
SHANGHAE TO WOO-YUEN.

getting through this bridge; but when we effected our purpose, we were gratified with the prospect which presented itself; on the eastern side was the causeway, with the bridge in the middle, and the temple just alluded to at the northern extremity; along the north side of the lake, was a long range of wharves, with a busy population; to the south, in the centre of the lake, was an island, upon which was erected an elegant pavilion, called the 湖心亭 Hoô-sin-tìng, or temple in the heart of the lake; and on the west, an open country, across which we were about to travel. The whole of the fields, along which we had passed since leaving Tsing-poo, had been mostly occupied with the mustard-plant; this the Chinese cultivate for the sake of the seed, from which they manufacture oil, used in lamps, and for cooking. The soil generally appeared low and damp, not above two feet above the level of the water, and the mustard-plant being just then in flower, the whole country exhibited a beautifully yellow appearance, as if covered with gold. So low was the ground, and so little elevated above the water-level, that if an inundation were to occur, thousands of acres must be overwhelmed, and multitudes of people deprived of a home, and of the means of subsistence.

Along the canals, and throughout the lakes, which were not above eight feet deep, the people were employed in raising mud for the purpose of manuring their fields. We also observed several boats provided with fishing cormorants, about twenty in each boat, which, at a given signal, were made to plunge into the water, and dive after fish. The boatmen all the while beating the surface of the water with long bamboos, in order to make the birds dive the more frequently; when a single cormorant obtained a prize, he was assisted by means of the bamboo to get into the boat again; and having a ring or string round his neck, which prevented him from swallowing his prey, he was obliged to disgorge the fish, and dash into the water after more;

G

In this way the fishing was carried on, until the fishermen were satisfied ; when the cormorants, with the ring taken off, were allowed to fish for their own advantage. It is said, that a good cormorant will sometimes take fish larger and heavier than himself, which the others will assist him in bringing up into the boat; after which, they will sit quietly on the edge of the boat, without presuming to touch any more than what is given them.

In the course of conversation this day, the guide related an old story, which when told with spirit appears amusing, at least to the Chinese. Formerly, he said, Confucius, Laou-keun, and Buddha, the founders of the three sects of religion professed in China, were talking together, in fairy land, of the want of success which attended their doctrines in the world ; and proposed a descent into these sublunary regions, to see if there were any right-minded persons, who might be commissioned to awaken the age. After travelling for some days, through town and country, with little success, they came at length to a desert place, where the smoke of human habitations was not visible. The three sages, being wearied with their journey, looked about for some place where they might quench their thirst; when suddenly they espied a fountain, and an old man sitting by, to guard it. They concluded that they had better ask him for a little drink, and consulted together upon whom the task should fall of soliciting the favour. Come, said the other two to Buddha, you priests are in the habit of begging, you had better go forward and obtain permission to drink of this fountain. Buddha accordingly advanced, and put in his petition. The old man asked, who are you ? I am, replied he, Shikyamuni, who formerly appeared in the west. Oh! you are the celebrated Buddha, then, of whom I have heard so much; you have the reputation of being a good man, and I cannot refuse you a draught of water ; but you must first answer me a question, which if you can do, you may have as much water as you please ; but if not, you must go empty away. What is it ? said Buddha. Why, said the old man, you Buddhists constantly affirm, that men are equal, and admit neither of high nor low ; how is it then that in your monasteries, you have different degrees, viz. abbots, priests, and noviciates ? Buddha could not answer, and was obliged to retire. The sages then deputed Laou-keun to go and ask for water, who, on coming up to the old man, was asked his name ? I am Laou-jen, was the reply, Oh ! the founder of the Taou sect, said the old man ; I have heard a good account of you ; but you must answer me a question, or you can get no water. What is it ? Pray annnounce it. Why, you Taouists talk about the elixir of immortality, have you such a thing ? Yes, said Laou-keun, it is the partaking of this that has rendered me immortal. Well then, said the old man, why did you not give a little to your own father, and prevent his decease. Laou-keun could not reply, and was obliged to retire ; saying to Confucius, Come, brother, you must try your skill, for I can make nothing of the old man. Confucius, therefore, advanced with the same request. And who are you ? said the ancient. I am K'hùng-chúng-nê, of the Loò country, said he. Oh ! the celebrated Confucius, the sage of China ; I have heard much of your discourses on filial piety, but how is it that you do not act up to them ? you say, "when parents are alive, do not wander far ; and if you do, have some settled place of abode ;" why then have you strayed away to this uninhabited region ? Confucius was unable to reply, and retired. Upon this the three worthies consulted together about this old man, and came to the conclusion, that as he was such an intelligent man, they could not light upon a better individual to revive their doctrines, and spread them through the world. They therefore came to him with the above-named proposition. But the old man replied, with a smile, Gentlemen, you do not seem to know who or what I am. It is the upper part of me only that is flesh and blood, the lower part is stone ; I can't talk about virtue, but not follow it out. This the sages

found was the character all mankind, and in despair of reforming the world, returned to the aërial regions.

After passing Ping-wang, we sailed along a branch of the
imperial canal that flows east and west, when we saw the
first mulberry-trees on the banks of the river ; but they were
only small plants, about three feet high, just budding forth
their leaves. These were planted between the rice-fields,
and on the borders of streams, while the whole face of the
country was taken up with other kinds of cultivation.

In the afternoon, we observed two hills about ten miles off,
to the north-west, which were the eastern and western, 洞
庭 Túng-tíng hills, situated in the 太湖 T'haé-hoô, or
great lake. The westernmost of these hills appears about
700 feet high ; it is very steep, and perforated with caverns ;
hence the name, which means "cavernous hill." It is also
called 包山 paou-shan, "embraced hill ;" because it is surrounded and embraced by the waters of the lake. On account of its deep caves, which pass under the lake, and
are supposed to penetrate into the bowels of the earth, it
is further denominated 地脈 té mĭh, the earth's artery. It
is covered with wood, and surmounted with temples, from
which the tinkling bell and solemn chant are often heard.
It has several peaks, on ascending the highest of which you
have a beautiful view of the surrounding lake, and its various
islets, with the distant hills to the south-east and south-west.
Many pagodas, terraces, knolls, precipices, and dells, are
pointed out in this vicinity by the lovers of the picturesque ;
the whole land is said to be free from wild and noxious animals, while orange and citron groves cover its verdant slopes.
The easternmost hill is called 莫釐 mŏ-lé, from 'the
circumstance of a general, of that name, having once fixed
his residence there ; it is smaller than the western hill, but
in many points resembles it. A camp is formed upon it, over
which is a military commandant of the rank of Major, who
controls all the troops in the vicinity of the lake. The com-

MAP OF
CHE-KEANG PROVINCE.

浙江全圖

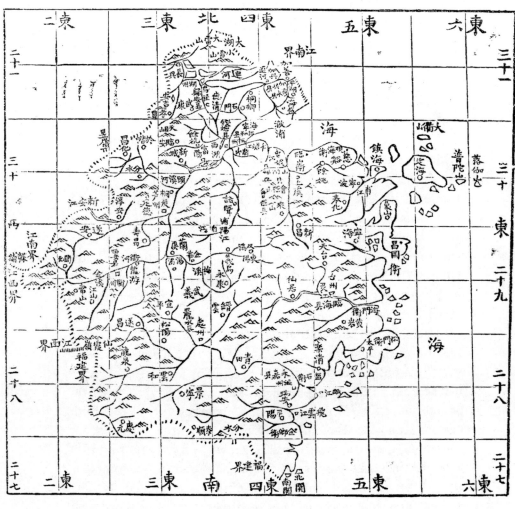

mon saying is, that he, who was not travelled to the 洞延 Túng-ting hills, knows not what mountain scenery and lake beauties mean.

We passed on the canal a great number of rafts of wood and bamboo ; one of these rafts was estimated to contain a hundred thousand bamboos, and was about a third of a mile in length ; its conductors seemed to be on their way to Soo-chow, Hang-chow, and other populous places, where there is a great demand for building materials.

During the afternoon, we passed a village, called 梅堰 mei-yen, "the plum dike ;" it has a small military guard stationed at the place.

Towards evening, we were pleasingly struck with the view which presented itself before us. A beautiful pavilion, three stories high, with a granite foundation, and a scolloped roof, met the eye, rising up from the midst of the broad canal, and throwing its lengthened shadow across the still waters. It was about fifty feet wide at the base, which was four-square ; on a terrace, formed of large blocks of stone, rose the pavilion, about 50 feet high, with its neatly-painted windows and doors, its fantastic gables and concave ridges, each of its many corners terminating in a bell, and each of its row of tiles being turned up with variegated porcelain. The name of this handsome structure, was 慈雲禪司 Tsze-yûn-shen-sze, " the hall for contemplation covered by favouring clouds;" it was built in the Súng dynasty, and, after having been re-paired under the Ming sovereigns, was rebuilt, in the 20th year of Kang-he. Beyond the pavilion appeared a pagoda, six stories high, surmounted with a crown, very elegant and in good repair. At the foot of the pagoda, was a town called 真澤鎮 Chin-tsïh-chin, containing about 10,000 inhabi-tant. The name of the place, signifying " well-watered town," was given in consequence of its vicinity to the 太湖 T'haé-hoô, or great lake, from which it is not above five miles distant; there is a civil officer stationed here, called a 巡檢司 Seûn-këen-sze, or inspector; and there are four military stations at the four quarters of the town. Several large stores were observed, at which rice and oil were sold, but the houses in general seemed in a dilapidated condition; one building was observed three stories high, but that also was out of the perpendicular, and would certainly have fallen, had it not been for the adjoining houses. We passed the night in the centre of this town, in our boat, but were much disturbed by the watchmen's rattles. We travelled this day about 80 le, or 24 miles.

April 1st. This morning we started at daylight, and after a course of fifteen or twenty le, about five miles, we crossed the borders of Këang-soo province, and entered Chĕ-këang, approaching the town of 南鄩 Nân-tsîn; this town is seventy-two le, or twenty-two miles, to the west of Hoô-chow; it is a place of considerable size, being nearly two miles in length, and containing two large stone bridges, the arches of which were about twenty-five feet high, and fifteen broad, very strongly built of red sand-stone, mixed with lias. At this place we observed, a number of boats, laden with young mulberry-trees, which were bound in bundles, roots and all, and brought thither for sale, with the view of extending the cultivation of the plant. On the sides of the canal, were numerous timber-yards, the materials contained in which were however short, and rather adapted for small Chinese houses, than large mansions. The market of this town, is supplied with all kinds of commodities, and the trade is flourishing. In the time of the Yuên dynasty, the town was surrounded by walls, which, in the following dynasty, were broken down, to repair those of Soo-chow. The remains of the ancient Nân-tsîn city, are still traceable; and a map of it, as it formerly stood, is preserved in an adjoining temple. After passing this town, about two or three miles, we observed the mulberry-trees more thickly studding the banks of the river, and covering the adjacent country;

these trees were more advanced than those which I had previously seen, being about ten feet high, and the stems a foot in circumference. Wherever the land was a little elevated, at least six feet above the water-level, the mulberry was diligently cultivated, and every preparation made to meet the wants of the forth-coming silk-worms.

This morning we observed a boat proceeding in the same direction with ourselves, bearing a flag with this inscription, "The Superintendent of the grain department of Chĕ-këang," and a little further on we fell in with two boats, having inscribed on their flag, "The chief magistrate of the district of 丏陽 Mëen-yâng, in the province of Hoô-kwàng;" on seeing these, I supposed, that of course the officers whose flags were thus borne aloft were on board, and began to puzzle myself, in order to find out, in what way the gentlemen could get to Hoô-kwàng or Chĕ-këang, according to the course which they were then steering. I afterwards discovered, however, that it is not an unusual thing for boatmen to beg the flag of any mandarin they may happen to carry, in order to hoist it afterwards. In the same way, many poor fellows may be seen in towns, carrying about lanterns, with the titles of high officers painted on them, in order to screen themselves from the annoyances of petty policemen, and make people believe, that they are respectably connected.

About noon, we passed a considerable branch of the canal, bearing to the southward, which probably leads to 杭州 Hang-chow, and forms the chief medium of communication, between that and 湖州 Hoô-chow. Going on a little further, we passed under a bridge, which was in a very ruinous condition, and almost threatened to fall on us as we went under the arch. As we advanced, we beheld four small hills in front, two on each side of the canal, as though guarding the approach to the city of Hoô-chow; their names are the 昇山 Shing-shan, 蜀山 Shŭh-shan, 昆山 Pe-shan, and 孺山 Joô-shan; the larger and smaller 雷山 Lûy-shan,

海上絲綢之路稀見文獻叢刊

in the 太湖 T'haé-hoô, or great lake, likewise appeared, at some distance to the north-west. On the south-west, also, a high hill was visible, with two tall pagodas, or stone pillars on the top of it, respecting which the boatmen observed, that when we were so far advanced, as to shut in this hill behind some of the others, we should see Hoô-chow; this saying proved true, for we had no sooner shut in the pagoda hill, than the masts of the junks lying off Hoô-chow appeared. I have been the more particular in mentioning these hills, as since our leaving Sháng-haè, with the exception of the few hillocks about Tsing-poo, and those in the Túng-tîng and T'haé-hoô lakes, we had scarcely seen a hill; but now we appeared to be getting into the midst of them, and were about soon to be surrounded by lofty mountains, which would delight and bewilder us by their beauty and magnificence. Few rocks also, had been seen, and the whole country had hitherto appeared one continuous mud-flat without a stone; but now we were approaching a region, interesting to the geologist, and replete with nature's wonders.

During our journey through the lowlands, we had frequently observed the people busily employed in getting up mud from the bottoms of the lakes and canals, for the purpose of manuring the rice-fields; and before quitting this region, it may be as well to describe the process. They used for this purpose, two slightly concave baskets, about two feet in diameter, which fitted on to each other, like the two valves of a cardium shell; these were each fastened to the ends of long bamboo poles, which poles crossed each other at a pivot, about a foot distant from the baskets, and ten or twelve from the opposite ends. The workman standing in a boat, thrust down the machine, (which was something in appearance like a pair of old-fashioned sugar-tongs,) with the baskets downward, into the water. Holding the two upper ends of the bamboos apart, he of course kept the mouth of the

tongs open, till having pushed them into the mud, he closed
the valves by bringing the top part of the poles close together, and then drew up the machine with a load of mud;
emptying his charge into the boat, he sent it down again and
again, till the boat was full, or the period of labour expired.
It was worthy of observation, how the labourers availed themselves of the known property of water, to support bodies in it
until the near the surface ; for they appeared scarcely to care
about exerting themselves, in raising the weight of mud from
the bottom, until it was near the surface, when they put
forth all their strength to lift it over the gunwale into the
boat. I have been thus particular in describing this operation, because of the many thousands of people engaged in it,
and because of its great importance in Chinese agriculture.
Having obtained a boat-load of mud, the peasant proceeds to
that part of his field which adjoins the river, and having made
a hollow pit on the bank, he with a scoop throws up the mud
into the place prepared for it. Should this be lower than
the level of his field, they use a bucket, with a rope fastened
to each side of it; two persons holding this rope, one on
each side of the mud-hole, by alternately slackening and
tightening it, giving it at the same time a jerk on one
side, manage to throw the mud up on the field. In this
labour, a man is generally assisted by his wife or daughter;
for the women in China do not scruple to engage in any,
even the most dirty, occupation, if it have but a reference
to the multiplying of the means of subsistence.

THE CITY OF HOO-CHOW.

Approaching Hoo-chow, we passed a vast number of grain-
junks, employed in receiving on board the Emperor's tribute,
and preparing to convey it to the capital. They were moored to each bank of the canal, sometimes two deep on either
side, leaving but a small space for the passage of boats between them. These junks were larger and newer than any I

H

had hitherto seen, and were some of them very gaily painted. The sailors were numerous, and appeared both haughty and indolent. On board of several junks, I saw the process of taking in rice from the boats along side. A pulley was slung to the mast, and a rope being rove through it, a dozen men were attached to it, in order to raise one bag of rice, which could not be done, even with all that power, without much singing and noise. Others were engaged in hooking on the bags, and others in stowing them away, or writing down their numbers ; so that a score of men were found necessary, to take each single bag of rice on board ; which in a private vessel would have been easily done by one man. I was pleased to see, however, that the sailors were very particular in keeping their junks clean ; and as each boatman had his own private speculation, the decks were covered with birds, dogs, and other animals, which might meet with a ready sale in Peking. The number of these grain-junks, I could not exactly ascertain, but they extended along the canal for more than a mile in length, and there could not have been less than five hundred of them. It appeared necessary to anchor them a few miles out of the city, because of the quarrelsome disposition of the sailors ; as well as on account of the narrowness of the canal, which would not admit of their approaching nearer the city without impeding business.

In the evening we arrived at Hoo-chow, but the lateness of the hour prevented my observing much of its beauty. The walls appeared in good repair, about 25 feet high, and twenty thick. The canal passed through the city, under the walls, where there was a water-gate, spanned by a finely-turned arch, at least 20 feet high. On passing through, we were detained by an old man, who demanded money of us, because it was dusk ; our people offered him five cash, but he rejected that sum with scorn, saying that nothing less than fifteen would satisfy him. He was, however, contented with ten, and lifted up the bar to let us pass. Having entered the city, we found the canal wider than on the outside, with many vessels coming and going; while the banks of the canal were lined with stores and ware-houses, giving the appearance of a very populous and commercial city. About the middle of the city, we came to a large bridge of three arches; the centre one was about fifty feet wide, and the other two nearly equal to it. The top of the bridge was almost flat, and not elevated as most of the Chinese bridges are. The name of the bridge was 把牙橋 pà-yây-kenôu, or "hold-your-tongue bridge;" every Chinese on passing under it, feeling it neccessary to hold his tongue; more out of superstition, however, than in obedience to any public order. There are several pagodas, and many temples in Hoo-chow, but as the evening was far advanced, we had not an opportunity of seeing them. Having passed the residence of the 知府 Che-foó, or prefect of the city, we thrust our boat in among a number of others, near a market place, and, after the din of voices around us had subsided, we fell asleep.

Hoo-chow is the same with the 楊州 Yâng-chow, spoken of in the days of Yù, B. C. 2,205, (see Translation of the Shoo-king, page 97.) During the 夏 Hëá dynasty, it constituted the country of the 防風 Fâng-fung; during the 周 Chow dynasty, it successively belonged to the 吳 Woo, 越 Yŏĕ, and 楚 Tsoò countries. When the Emperor 秦始皇 Tsin-chè-hwâng, who burned the books, divided China anew, this region was called 會稽 Hwúy-k'he. In the time of the Three Kingdoms, it fell to the lot of 吳 Woo. In the 唐 Tâng dynasty, it was denominated 湖州 Hoô-chow, which name, with occasional interruptions, it has retained ever since.

Hoô-chow is situated to the south of the 太湖 T'haê-hoô, Great Lake, from which it probably derives its name. This lake, together with the various rivers and canals connected with it, has rendered the region now under consideration very fertile, and afforded easy communication between it and the surrounding regions, hence its growing wealth and importance. It is classed under the 浙江 Chĕ-këang province; the prefecture of Hoô-chow is 190 le, (or about 58 miles) from east to west, and 138 le, (or about 42 miles) from north to south. In an easterly direction the city of Hoo-chow, is distant from Soo-chow 210 le. In a wester-ly direction, it is distant from 廣德州 Kwàng-tĭh-chow 130 le. On the south side, it is distant from 杭州 Hang-chow 120 le. And towards the north it is 38 le, to 小雷山 Seaòu-lûy-shan, in the 太湖 T'haé-hoô. From Hoô-chow to Peking, the distance is reckoned at 3,700 le.

The city of Hoô-chow was built on the site of 烏程 Woo-chîng, where the famous 項王 Hëáng-wâng, who flourished about the commencement of the Christian era, held his court. According to the records, one 郭璞 Kwŏ-pŏ, of the 晋 Tsín dynasty, wished to remove the seat of his government to the eastward; when his daughter, who was acquainted with geomancy, dissuaded him, on account of the supposed perpetuity of any city built on this site. In the 4th year of 武德 Woô-tĭh, 李孝恭 Lé-heaóu-kung built the city of Hoô-chow, 24 le in extent. In the 元 Yuên dynasty, the boundaries of the city, being considered too wide, were contracted to 13 le and a half. The gates, which in the Tâng dynasty were nine, have been since reduced to six. A branch of the grand canal enters the city, under a large arch near the eastern gate; which, after traversing the centre of the city, is led out under a similar arch, near the west gate. Large sheets of water are interpersed throughout the space within the walls, various parts of which are spanned by noble bridges. Islands here and there appear in these pools, on which temples and pagodas are reared. The highest pagoda, called 飛英 Fei ying, is situated on the north side of the city. The mansion of the Che-foo, or pre-fect, is in the centre, while the residence of the two district magistrates are placed in the east and west quarters.

As Hoo-chow is the principal seat of the silk cultivation in China, it may be expected that some account would be rendered of that important branch of industry ; which I cannot better do, than by giving some extracts from a work on the silk culture lately issued by the Treasurer of the Province, in order to encourage and direct the inhabitants of this district, in extending and improving it. He begins by remarking

ON THE DIFFERENT KINDS OF MULBERRY-TREES.

The mulberry being the most essential requisite for the silk-worm, to rear the latter the former must be attended to. There are two kinds of mulberry, the 魯 Loò, found in the north, and the 荆 King, in the south part of China ;* the former has large leaves, with but little fruit, and a firm root ; the latter kind has smaller leaves with much fruit, but it is comparatively a more hardy plant. Most of the mulberry saplings are derived from the southern species ; and the best plan is to plant this kind first, and graft the northern mulberry upon it, when you get a firm root, with abundance of leaves.

ON THE MODE OF 接桑 INGRAFTING THE MULBERRY.

Take a twig of the northern variety three inches or more in length, and cutting off a portion of it slantwise, in the shape of a horse-shoe, about an inch or more long, insert it quickly within the rind of the southern mulberry plant ; then bind it round, and cover it with a lump of earth. But this can only be done at a favourable season, by an expert and careful hand ; added to which the binding must be

---

* 魯 Loò is the ancient name for 山東 Shan-tung, and 荆 King is the old designation of 湖北 Hoô-pïh ; hence we infer that by the former is meant the northern, and by the latter the southern species of mulberry.

tight, and the plastering thick. Choose some time just before or after the vernal equinox, when the weather is fine ; and on the sprouting of the buds, retain only one, which in autumn will become a mulberry sapling.

ON 移裁 TRANSPLANTING AND 翦桑 CLIPPING THE MULBERRY.

In planting the saplings, a space of five feet or more must be allowed for each tree, and they must be disposed in a triangular form, like the character 品 p'hin, and not one opposite to another. In the month of February following when the weather is pure and genial cut off the top of the plant, at the height of two feet from ground. When the buds shall have sprouted forth, retain only two, which will become branches in the latter part of autumn, about five or six feet long. Then in the month of February of the next year, cut off the tops of these branches, to within a foot or more of their stem. thus giving the plant the appearance of the letter Y ; and retain as before two buds on the end of each branch, cutting off all the rest. In the ensuing year, clip off the new branches again. always leaving a foot or more, according to the former method ; and thus go on, clipping and retaining again and again, and the branches will continue to double their number. In about five or six years or more, a little after summer sets in, commence cutting and clipping, both branches and leaves, in order to feed the worms. After having clipped the plant for a number of years, the tree will assume a knobbed appearance, having upon it from sixteen to seventeen knobs or fists, when it gets the name of the 拳桑 fist-like mulberry. Upon the larger knobs, you may retain three or four branches ; and on the setting in of the ensuing summer, you may clip off from the knobbed parts, both twigs and leaves, to feed the worms. This is done, on the one hand, to save labour ; and on the other, to enable you to hang up the inverted branches in an airy place, lest the leaves should have been moistened by rain or damp; after a short time they will become dry, when you can take them to feed the worms with.

METHOD OF CUTTING OFF 科斫 THE MULBERRY TWIGS.

In cutting off these, never retain the central branch, and then the branches will spread on all sides.   There are four kinds of branches which must be pruned away; 1st, the 瀝水條 leĭh shwùy teaôu, water-dropping branches, or such as droop down; 2nd, the 刺身條 tszé shin teaôu, self-stabbing branches, or such as grow inwards; 3rd, the 駢枝條 ping che teaôu, double branches, or those which grow together, of which only one must be selected; 4th, the 冗脞條 yuen tso teaôu, thick-set branches, or such as grow thickly together, although otherwise in proper form.

After the mulberry twigs have been clipped off, loosen the earth carefully near the roots, and bury about them oil-cakes that have been dissolved in hot water, a cup-full or more to each plant.   When the sprouts re-appear, they are called 莓條 mei teaôu, fresh shoots; these by autumn will have grown eight feet in length.   In the winter you should apply some thick dung, and rich mould; when in the ensuing year, the exuberance of the foliage will be redoubled.

GENERAL REMARKS ON THE 蠶性 NATURE OF THE
SILK-WORM.

(陽)

As silk-worms belong to the 揚 yang, superior principle of nature, they love fire and hate water, thus it is that they eat without drinking.   Silk-worms are naturally fond of stillness, while they dislike noise; they likewise prefer to be warm, but abhor dampness. Whilst in the egg-state, they must be kept particularly cool, but as soon as they are hatched, they must be kept very warm; on awaking from their first sleep, they require warmth; but after their principal sleep, coldness is requisite, as they become old, the warmth must be gradually increased; and when put upon the bush to spin, they must be kept extremely warm.

Silkworms require to be 齊 tsê, equal, in three things; the eggs should all be laid together, they must all be hatched together, and begin to spin together. There are five things, 宜 ê, proper for silk-worms; when beginning to sleep, they require to be kept dark and dry; after awaking, they require light; when going to eat, they require plenty of leaves, and fast feeding; and when awaking again, they are afraid of wind, and at such times require few leaves and slow feeding.

There are seven things which they 忌 kè, abhor; from the time when they are first hatched up to maturity they abhor smoke; they also abhor wine, vinegar, and all kinds of acrid things; they abhor musk, and the smell of oil; on being fed, they abhor damp leaves; they likewise abhor hot ones; they cannot bear to be near were people pound in a mortar; neither do they like mourning, nor pregnant women. Those who are skilful in rearing silk-worms, take care that the grubs are produced about the middle of April, and that they come to maturity in twenty-seven days; in which case they are seldom ill, consume few leaves, and produce abundance of silk.

ON 浴種 WASHING THE EGGS, 生蟻 AND HATCHING THE GRUBS.

The collection of silk-worms' eggs, is called a 連 lëên, card; which are the eggs from the coocoons of the last year's worms. In the beginning of April, soak the card for a quarter of an hour in pure water, and then take them out; this is called 浴蠶 yŭh tsân, bathing the silk-worms; then spread them out in an airy place, till they are dry; after which wrap them up first in paper, then in cotton, and put them aside in a clean quiet spot. In seven days, take them out, to look at them; and when their colour shall have turned to a pea green, they must be looked at every day. Should three or four come out before the rest, let them be brushed off with a feather as useless ; these are called 行馬蟻 hing mà ê, or galloping grubs, and would, if retained, cause the worms to be unequal in age. When about one third of the grubs have come forth, still wrap them up as before ; for, should these not feed on leaves for one day, it will be no matter. On the next day, take the cards out and spread them in a warm spot, when the worms will all come out together. The grubs come forth mostly from ten to twelve, in the morning.

ON REMOVING THE GRUBS 下蟻 FROM THE CARDS.

When the 蟻 ê, grubs have all come forth together, take some mulberry-leaves, cut into threads, as fine as silk, and scatter them over the surface of the card ; wait until the grubs shall have crawled on the cut leaves, and then take them up very gently with the 蠶箸 tsán choo, silk-worm nippers, and move them away over to one place ; you must not on any account use a goose's feather, to brush them off with, as it will injure and wound the grubs. Should the grubs not have come forth all together, wrap the card up again, and on the morrow take it down as described above ; but place the grubs that came out last in a separate spot, and on no account deposit them in the same place with those previously hatched, lest you should have worms of unequal ages together. In removing the grubs, let them be equally distributed ; the keeping them too much apart, and huddling them together, are alike to be avoided. The worms must be removed only twice ; should any remain upon the card without coming out, lay them aside, for they are weakly diseased grubs, and it will be useless to rear them.

When the black grubs have all come forth, weigh them together with the cards, and put down the exact weight : after which weigh the empty cards, and you will be able to ascertain the neat weight of the worms. For every ounce weight of grubs you may obtain about 150 or 160 ounces of silk, and the worms will devour about twenty peculs, (each pecul 133 lbs. avoirdupois) of leaves. Thus you should weigh the leaves which are given to the worms, and be careful not to exceed the proper quantity.

ON FEEDING 飼蠶 THE WORMS.

The leaves first given to the worms must be picked from the outside of the trees, and cut fine with a sharp knife; every time you cut the leaves, be sure to wash your hands; let the leaves be renewed five or six times in the course of twenty-four hours, and when the leaves are done, give the worms a fresh supply; the leaves must not be too thick, but be spread about in a regular manner; as soon as you have given the worms their leaves, place them inside a curtain, to protect them from the wind and cold. Use the small silk-worm frame, upon which the trays in which you put the silk-worms must be well fitted, that the worms may get warmth; do not on any account pile the trays one over the other, lest the worms generate damp, and become sickly. In rearing silk-worms, it is necessary to keep the temperature even; if it be too cold, they will be a longer time in coming to perfection; if too hot, they will become dry and shrivelled. When the weather is cold, you must not suddenly heat them, but gradually increase the warmth; neglecting which precaution, they will get the yellow sickness, and become weak. So also, when hot, you must not suddenly introduce cold air, but gradually open the windows; neglecting which advice, the worms will become white and die. In hot weather, if the temperature be suddenly reduced, the worms will refuse to eat; in such case you must instantly warm them, by means of a gentle fire, and raise the temperature, after which the appetite of the worms will return. In rainy and cold weather, first make a little fire in the room, and then give the worms their leaves, which will prevent sickness. The mulberry-leaves should be gathered at an early hour, or after sunset ; for the worms dread both damp and heat. If they eat damp leaves, they will get the diarrhœa, become white and die ; if they feed on hot leaves, they will be troubled with constipation ; their heads will become large, and tails small ; and then should they eat ever so much, they would fail to attain maturity, or form cocoons.

ON DIMINISHING THEIR FOOD 斷飼 IN ORDER TO EXPEDITE 睡 THE TORPOR OF THE WORMS.

It is necessary to expedite the sleeping of those worms that have not yet fallen into the state of torpor ; for this purpose, observe when one third or one half of the worms have assumed a yellowish bright appearance, and diminish that proportion of leaves. The leaves also must be shred finer and thinner than usual, and the number of meals increased. If two thirds of the worms have become yellow, then reduce two thirds of the leaves ; let the leaves also be much thinner, and the meals more frequent. When they have nearly all gone off into the torpid state, and there be still a few pale and white worms, that have not yet fallen asleep, it would be better to reject them, as irregular and sickly worms. Take the torpid ones up gently, and put them in a still place, when they will cease eating ; after this, wait until they have generally revived, when you can supply them with food ; if when only eight or nine tenths of them have got up, you forthwith supply them with food, they will arrive at maturity at unequal periods. It will not hurt them, however, to let them fast a little at the time of awaking, because in the first place, their mouths are accustomed to eating, and they can the more speedily consume the leaves ; and secondly, because they easily increase in size, when arrived at that stage. When the worms begin to revive from their torpor, they must not be roughly moved, because their skins are tender, and they easily sustain an injury ; they also dread the wind, more than before dozing, when their skins were tougher. After they have begun to eat again, do not cease giving them leaves ; and if you keep on feeding them systematically, you will soon bring them into a regular state.

ON REMOVING THE 起底 EXCREMENT OF THE WORMS.

When the worms first come out, they must be removed from the tray once a day; for this purpose some finely-cut green leaves are spread over them ; upon these the worms will crawl and eat ; seeing which you must take the little nippers or chopsticks, and raise the top layer of leaves with the worms upon it ; then carefully gather the other layers that are underneath ; this done, the residue and the excrementitious matter must all be thrown away. After the second torpor, the worms daily increase in size, and every time they are removed, they must be put wider apart ; in doing this, you may use your fingers, and gently raise the upper layer with the worms upon it. In giving the leaves for food, they must not be in the least coarse. After the third torpor, should the weather be fine, they may be taken out of doors, but not if it be windy. After the great torpor, in removing the excrements, you may use the silk-worm net, and spreading it over the worms, with a few good leaves upon it, the worms will mount up ; and when they have had two or three nibs, then let a couple of people remove the net over to an empty tray; and throw away the excrements and the fibres of the mulberry-leaves, in order to prevent the sickness arising from damp or steam. When the worms are fallen into the great sleep, put them into a broad tray. For every three pounds weight of worms you must supply 100 pounds of leaves ; and they will produce five pounds weight of cocoons, which will yield eight or nine ounces of raw silk. After the worms have slept, and are just about to eat again, for every portion of leaves that are reduced, there will be a corresponding reduction in the quantity of silk obtained. After the fourth torpid stage, should the weather be warm, they will arrive at maturity in five days; but should the weather be cold, it will take them seven days to arrive at the same stage. Then take up the more advanced worms, and put them on the bush; every time you take any up you must scatter leaves, which are called 上馬桑 Sháng-mà-sang, the 'mount-horse leaves;" in half a day or a little more, they will all have arrived at maturity. Silk-worms have either three or four periods of torpor: the treatment, however, is in both cases the same. The fourth period is the great torpor.

ON PUTTING THE WORMS 上簇 ON THE BUSH.

For bushes, or receptacles for spinning, use the straw of late-growing glutinous rice; scrape off the outer rind of the straws, and bind them firmly round the middle; let the straws be about a foot and a half long, with both ends even; the place where these receptacles or bushes are put must be dry and airy; they must be elevated on bamboo or wooden frames, crossed with mats made of rushes; upon which must be placed the straw receptacles or bushes, arranged in order. Then take those worms which have arrived at perfection, and put them in a Canton-varnished tray, from which, after having washed your hands, spread them about the receptacles or bushes, neither too close nor too far apart; should the weather be cold or rainy, place a fire under the rush frame, and heat them well; the warmer they are, the more easily will they be able to form the cocoons, and the more readily will the silk be wound off; after five days you may select your cocoons, and stripping away the waste silk that surrounds them, you may wind off the threads; but do not let the worms get damp, which may impede the formation of the silk.

Then follow some directions about sacrificing to the spirit that presides over the silk-worm.

ON THE SUMMER 原蠶 SILK-WORM.

The 原蠶 Yuân-tsân are also called 夏蠶 hĕá-tsân, summer, or 二蠶 ûrh-tsân, second-crop silk-worms ; the cultivation of these is not generally encouraged; first, because the rearing of them happens at a time when people are busy with their harvest, and it interferes with the business of agriculture ; secondly, because when silk-worms are abundant they affect the horses, * the breed of which will not then be numerous ; hence the ancient classics forbad the rearing of these worms; and thirdly, because after the spring worms have been fed, the mulberry-leaves become scarce : and if you denude the trees of their leaves any further, you are likely to injure them, and spoil the next year's crop. But when the spring worms fail, and the mulberry-leaves are still plentiful, it is a good thing to fall back upon the summer worms, to supply the deficiency. In rearing the second-crop worms, you must be uncommonly diligent in changing the trays, and giving them leaves, when, after 21 or 22 days, they will arrive at maturity. You must endeavour particularly to keep them from the attacks of the large flies, and prevent their being injured by by heat : for, while spring worms must be kept warm, summer worms must be cool.

ON GETTING 收種 PROPER SEED.

The most important thing in rearing silk-worms, is the getting of proper seed. The worms that are intended to be

---

* This arises from a mistaken idea, that, because horses and silk-worms are under the influence of the same constellation, viz. that of 房 fâng, or Scorpio, therefore the increase of the one will necessary involve the decrease of the other.

reserved for seed, should be nourished with double care. From these select the best sort of worms, and give them extra feeding ; when come to maturity, set apart those that appear most healthy and strong, just when they mount the bush; five days after the cocoons are formed, pick out those that appear thickest and fullest upon the bush, and clear away the waste silk from them ; let there be an equal number of males and females ; the former are known by their being smaller, more tapering and brisk ; while the latter are to be ascertained by their being rounder, fuller, and more slow ; put the males and females on separate trays, and when their time is up, the moths will come forth of themselves; those that have stunted wings, bald eye-brows, scorched tails, as if yellow with smoke, or that have red bellies without hair, also those that come out either before or after the others, must all be rejected ; keeping only the perfect and good, this is the way to secure good seed from the very first. The moths come out generally from three to six o' clock in the morning ; the conjunction takes place between 7 A. M. and 2 P. M. when their energies are exhausted ; after that time, it is better to remove the male moths. and arouse the female ones by a gentle tapping. that they may cleanse themselves from their dirt. Having previously pasted some thick sheets of paper, stretched out on a plank, arrange the moths regularly on the card that they may lay their eggs ; those that are laid from 2 to 6 P. M. are reckoned good seed ; but those subsequently laid, are weak and useless. Having removed the female moths, hang up the card in an airy place, until the seed becomes of a proper colour and consistency, when they should be washed in clean water and dried. After sprinkling some ashes over the cards, roll them up, and suspend them in an elevated place, where they will not be affected by damp or moisture ; they must also be kept out of the way of smoke. In the beginning of autumn, you can free them from the ashes; and in the middle of January take a decoction of mulberry-leaves, that has been left to cool, and steep them in it, for a quarter of an hour, to strengthen their energies; after which, you must dry them, and having wrapped them up, suspend them in their former elevated position.

TWELVE RULES FOR 繰絲 WINDING OFF THE SILK.

1. About a fortnight previously, put some river-water into an old jar, and let it settle, till it becomes clear. River-water is better than spring-water, and running than standing water. If you have had not time to let it settle, you can throw a handful or two of shells into the water, to clear it for use; but beware of using alum.

2. When you plaster your furnaces, you can plaster at the same time the bottom and sides of your pan; at the mouth of the pan, the plastering should be about four fingers in thickness, gradually thinning towards the rim; wait until your pan is dry, and when you want to use it, fill it nearly full with water, heated to a proper degree; for this purpose, old pans are preferable. Formerly it was thought, that cold pans were better than hot ones, but now people do not use cold ones. Once also, it was recommended, that there should be a board to divide the pan into two parts, that two people might wind together; but now this practice is discontinued. Burn dry wood under your furnace; and, in order to try the heat, observe whether the chrysalis sink or swim; if they come to the surface of the water, reduce the heat; and if they sink, increase it. The degree of heat, also, must be regular.

3. According to the old plan, the winding-frame should be put by the side of the furnace, even with the pan; all the apparatus for winding should be placed on the right side of the furnace, as the most convenient for the performance of the operation; the reel should move easily, and be kept steady, by means of a stone placed on it; but let not this

interfere with the arms of the reel ; the pins for fastening which should be knocked in repeatedly to make them firm.

4. When the water is warm, put in your cocoons, and stir them about a little with your hands, so that the cocoons whirl round ; then search for the ends of the filaments, and, getting hold with the left hand of the coarse ends of the same, slightly jerk them several times on the surface of the water, and lift up the coarse ends of the threads, all below which is fine silk ; gently pluck off these coarse threads ; then with one hand taking up the fine silk, and with the other using a perforated ladle to keep the cocoons down in the water, wind the silk upon a peg, to be ready for reeling.

5. When you have got a number of these filaments, put them together in separate lines upon the reel, and pass them through the little eyes, that are fixed upon the board of the spool frame ; after this, lead them over the rattling spools, where the threads are crossed, and made to move along with the silk, to be drawn over the reel ; this done, turn the reel with your foot. In putting the threads on, you must be careful to arrange them well, and put them through the little hooks, or rampins, until the silk being wound off, the chrysalis sinks ; the cocoons in the silk-pool being now fewer, take some of the fine silk-threads from the peg. and add them on, taking care that the lines be of a regular thickness ; and when you have wound off until the chrysalis appears, and the covering over it be as thin as paper, then disengage it, and do not let it break off of itself, lest you suddenly sever the line, or soil the silk.

6. Should the thread break in the middle, and the cocoon be disengaged, you must endeavour to join it, by taking up the separated cocoon, and placing it on one side, look out for the clue, and then, getting hold of the end of the thread, draw it out, and join it to the other.

7. In drying the silk, use an old porcelain basin, and heat it over hot charcoal, until all that is within the basin

becomes perfectly dry ; for if the silk be damp, it will lose its gloss. The basin must be put at a little distance from the reel, lest the heat injure the silk thereon. It must also be held slantwise, with the mouth turned outwards ; one person should attend to this duty.

8. The oftener the hot water, in which the cocoons are placed, is changed the better ; observe when it becomes a little foul, and then throw away about one third of it, putting some clean warm water in its stead ; this operation also, should have some one to look after it.

9. The band that turns the machinery should be frequently wet, in order to keep it tight ; that the different threads may be regular in winding, and not become irremediably ravelled ; if the band be not tight, the rampin-board also will easily get out of its place, which is called the disarrangement of the board.

10. The old method of getting the silk off the reel, was as follows : the frame of the reel being loosely tied together by means of hemp threads, in order to keep in the pins, and the small ends of the wooden pins being fixed in their places, a few smart blows with a hammer would disengage them ; after which you may take the reel off the frame, with the cloth and the silk that were upon it.

11. There are various methods of managing the cocoons. In some the clues are blown about by the wind ; these after being put on the wheel break in a turn or two, in which case it will be necessary to increase the fire, and work with boiling water. There are some filaments that blend in the raw state, and are no sooner on the reel, than they get together in knobs ; in which case you should avoid cold water, and use warm. There are some again, that blend only when matured, and when they have been half wound, suddenly come off ; these should be removed. There are some filaments that both float about, and yet easily blend ; if the water be hot, then they blend into knobs ; and if cold, then they float about. Some-

times we meet with cocoons of the 野蠶 yây-tsân, wild silk-worm, which must first be well dried, and then thoroughly boiled, when you can get hold of the clues: put the cocoons of one whole bush into the boiler together, and wind them off; as soon as you have wound them half off, take the cocoons of another bush and join on to the former; you have no need to make the water in the pan very hot, it only requires to be lukewarm.

12. Refers to some superstitious observances not worth recording.

FOUR RULES INCULCATED AT THE SILK ESTABLISHMENT OF 丹徒 TAN-TOO, IN CHIN-KEANG-FOO.

1. On planting the mulberry. It is necessary to have your mulberries grafted, which grafts come to perfection in three years; it is better to use those cions which have been grafted in Hoô-chow, by which much trouble will be spared. About the beginning of January in each year, employ an experienced planter of mulberries, from 溧陽 Leïh-yâng, near Nan-king, to go to Hoô-chow, and buy your plants, making a bargain with him to pay only for such as live.

2. On feeding the worms. The year after your grafted plants have come to perfection, hire a silk-worm feedster from Leïh-yâng, who will teach girls of fifteen and under to feed the worms.

3. On hiring ground. Make your agreement for ten years, paying the rent every year. On each mow (or sixth of an acre) you may plant 40 trees; after two years every tree will produce thirty catties of leaves; the leaves of five trees, or 150 catties, given to the worms, will produce one catty of silk; thus each mow will produce eight catties of silk, which if woven will make twenty small pieces of silk-stuff, value 50 dollars; this, deducting half for the hire of the ground, and the labour and food of work-people, will yield a tolerable profit.

4. Plan for raising the money. Having a number of tickets

drawn out by some respectable man, let each one get his relations and friends to advance the money, no matter how much, and give them tickets from the establishment for the amount ; after three years, when the proceeds are realized, pay off the principal and interest, at the rate of ten per cent, per annum, with three per cent, on the interest, for the three years. When the women of the establishment, are willing to lend to the concern, such monies as may be over and above what they need for their support, give them a memorandum of the same, and pay them every month, at the rate of fifteen per cent per annum interest, beside refunding the capital at the end of three years. Should the officers subscribe anything, pay them also according to the amount, when the term is expired.

TWELVE MORE RULES REGARDING A SILK ESTABISHMENT.

1. As to the fence. According to the old books on agriculture, in the winter months, you should plant long twigs of willow and ash mixed, and set very closely together ; when they have begun to grow, bend them down on either side, and plait them together crosswise, binding them with the fibres of the coir palm ; outside of the hedge thus formed plant sour dates, small oranges, thorns, briers, &c. the more prickly the plants are, the better.

2. On setting up a sign. On the sign let there be written in large characters, " an establishment for the encouragement of silk-cultivation." Beg also of the local officers to issue out a notice, forbidding idle people to tread down the plants.

3. On opening out a sluice. If you can lead in the river water to irrigate your field, you will save the expense of digging wells ; while at the same time, you can breed fish and keep ducks in your canal, or cultivate the water-lily, water-caltrops, water-cresses, water-chestnuts, &c.

4. On manure. In the winter months you must nourish

the roots of your plants, for which purpose make use of rotten fish preserved in jars, or the juices of decomposed vegetables.

5. On planting fruit trees. In the fourth month, plant your mulberries; in the winter, loosen and water the earth round the plants; and then in the spring, they will shoot out new branches; in the following year, besides gathering your mulberry-leaves, should there be any vacant ground, you can plant it with fruit trees, such as arbutes, pomegrantes, apricots, or pears.

6. On cultivating vegetables. Beneath the mulberries you can plant onions, leeks, and melons, or potatoes and yams; select those that need most frequent irrigation, and then the mulberry-leaves will be the more plentiful: in order to prevent the locusts from eating the mulberry-leaves, you may plant the more yams.

7. On medicinal herbs. Withered mulberry-leaves, the parasites of the mulberry, together with white and diseased silk-worms, may all be used as medicine; but the snails found on the mulberry must be carefully caught, lest they injure the leaves.

8. On using the wood for timber. The mulberry-trees useful for feeding silk-worms, are generally saplings; some persons, however, allow the trees to grow large, for the sake of the timber, of which various articles may be made. Various descriptions of mulberry-wood are mentioned, all of which are useful.

9. On growing bamboos. On the establishment, there is need of ladders, tables, and sieves, all of which are made of bamboo; hence the necessity of cultivating that plant.

10. On feeding goats. The leaves of the old mulberries are good for fattening goats, and goat's-dung is good for feeding fish. Hence goats may be kept with advantage.

11. On dividing the establishment. When the resources of an establishment are abundant, others may be set up, in order to extend the cultivation.

12. On amity amongst neighbours. After the mulberries are planted, there will be an abundance of young plants, and should neighbouring farmers wish to increase their number of trees, or any cions be needed for public use, you may allow people to come to your ground, and take a few young plants gratuitously. You can also keep on hand a few copies of a work on the silk cultivation, which you can distribute to such as need them.

In all matters, sparing and economical plans should be pursued ; thus in the silk culture, it will be sufficient to have one principal planter of the mulberries, and one chief rearer of silk-worms, which will obviate the necessity of referring to pictures and representations. With regard to plans for raising the money, let all the labourers who contribute have a share in the profits, and not be necessitated to set their money out to interest elsewhere ; thus your applications for assistance will always meet with a ready response. As to hiring ground, you can make trial of any vacant land, that may happen to be uncultivated, and then you will not be blamed for hindering the production of the necessaries of life.

The above directions were published at an establishment, in Chin-këang foo, and in two years the undertaking became very prosperous.

DESCRIPTION OF THE IMPLEMENTS USED.

1. THE WINDING-MACHINE. 車狀

This winding-machine has four posts, the hinder ones are two feet four inches high, with a groove on the top of each, to receive the axle of the reel. The front post on the left must be two feet seven inches high, having on the top of it a ring, to receive the rampin-board ; the front post on the right should be two feet three inches high, having on the top a pin or tenon, on which the box or nave turned by the band revolves.

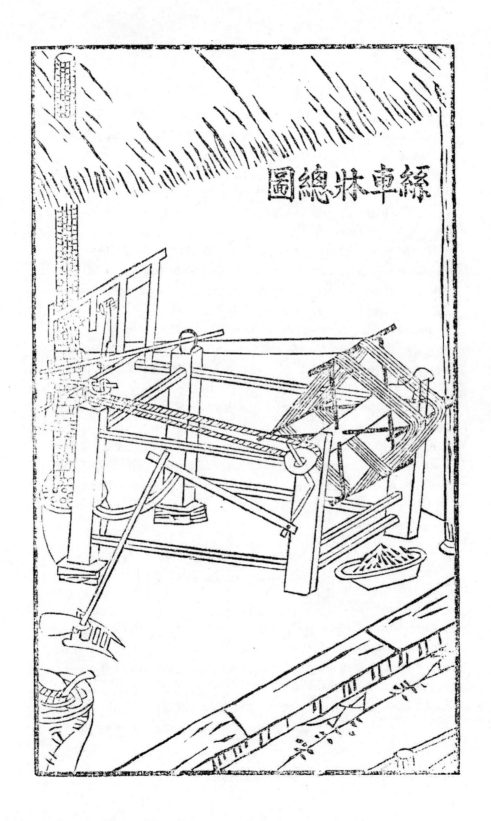

絲車牀總圖

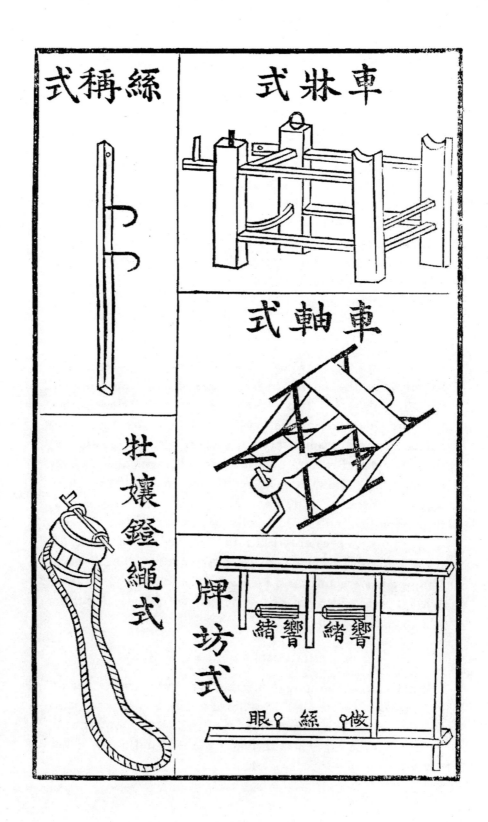

絲稱式

車牀式

車軸式

牌坊式

牡孃鐙繩式

響緒 響緒

做絲眼

2. THE REEL. 車軸

This reel is made of hard wood, two feet five inches long; near the head, which is round, the shape is octagonal, for the band to turn on; and at the end of the axle, there is fitted on a piece of wood, six inches long, with another short piece of wood transverse to the former, to act as a crank. Round the axle on the four sides are holes, and to each hole, there are arms each a foot long; horizontal battens or rails are fitted on to these arms, and round them a cloth is stretched for the silk to be wound on, which may be easily taken off the reel.

3. THE SPOOL-FRAME. 牌坊

This frame is provided with two long posts, each two feet high, on the top of which is a transverse beam; depending from this, are two short pieces of wood, three inches long, which are connected with the long posts, by a long bamboo pin, passing through a perforation in each of them; upon this pin, revolves two rattling spools, which are made of hollow bamboo, about five inches long; these bamboos are cut so as to leave a knot or joint at each end, through which holes are made that will just fit the pin. Two pins with eyes are fixed into a board underneath, for the silk to pass through; these are made of thin pieces of iron or copper, about three inches long; in one end of these is a flat hole, which must be smoothed, so as not to cut the silk-threads in two.

4. THE RAMPIN-BOARD. 絲耙

This is intended to regulate the silk, and cause it to wind slantwise on the reel; it is made of a flat piece of wood, two feet five inches long, in one end of which is round a hole, that fits on the cog-wheel turned by the band; the other

K

中國內地一瞥：在絲茶產區的一次旅行期間所見

end, is put through the ring on the top of the front left post of the winding-bench. Upon the rampin-board are two iron hooks, to guide the silk in its passage.

5. THE BOX OR NAVE AND BAND. 牡孃鐙

This box is made of mulberry-wood, it is three inches high, and six in circumference, it may either be eight-sided or ten ; in the middle, there must be a round hole, to fit it on the pivot, at the top of the post of the winding-bench ; let there be an indentation in the middle, for the band to pass round ; on the top, leave a couple of ears or handles, through which may pass a round stick, four inches long, (with a pin in one end) to receive the rampin-board. For the band, twisted cotton is the best ; it should be about four feet long, the two ends should be joined fast together ; first, let it be put over the box or nave, and then over the handle of the reel ; in the middle, let the band be crossed once, when it will cause the box to move in conformity with the reel.

6. THE WHISK. 做絲手

This is made of a slip of bamboo, about two inches broad and eight long ; about six inches from the end let there be a knot or joint, to strengthen it ; and from this part, divide the bamboo into seven or eight strips, like the fingers of a hand ; this is used to get hold of the ends of the filaments in winding.

7. THE FOOT-BOARD. 踏腳板

For this purpose, use a piece of wood, about a foot and a half long, and six inches wide ; upon it fix a couple of grooves, on which the shoe-board is to rest ; again, take a thick board eight inches long, in the shape of a shoe, on each side put a pin, to fit on to the grooves of the bottom board. Upon this fix a piece of upright wood, two feet

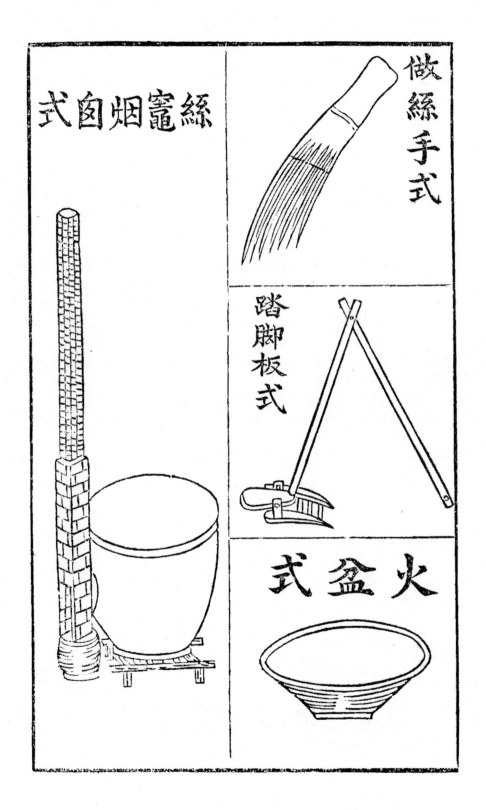

絲竈烟囱式

做絲手式

踏脚板式

火盆式

long, on the top of which, let there be a mortise ; besides this take another piece of equal length, and join it at one end to the upright piece, by means of a bamboo peg passing through both ; at the other end, make a round hole, which will fit upon the handle of the reel ; so that, when a person treads upon the foot-board, these pieces of wood will come into play, and the reel thereby be turned.

8.   THE FIRE-PANS. 火盆

These must be of two kinds, large and small ; the one is a yellow clay pan, to contain charcoal ; for, wherever the ground is shaded by hills, you should warm the silk-worms ; also when winding, make use of fire-pans, to prevent dampness.

9.   THE FURNACE AND CHIMNEY. 絲竈烟囱

The modes of making the furnaces are various : some use an earthenware furnace, made out of a small yellow jar ; on one side a hole is left for a fire-door, which must be well plastered, within and without.   Some make use of a stuccoed furnace, built of bricks, piled one over another, two feet five inches high, broad enough to hold a large iron pan ; this furnace must also be well plastered, within and without. There are both open and close furnaces : those constructed under a high shed, are called open, in which there is a good vent for the fire, and a saving of wood ; the close furnaces, on the other hand, have no flue, and occasion great inconvenience from the smoke.

Silk is very apt to be discoloured by the smoke of the furnace, hence the necessity of constructing a chimney, to lead off the smoke ; for this purpose, use thin slips of bamboo, intertwined in a circular form ; the bottom may be about six or seven inches in diameter, and tapering towards the top ; it should be ten feet high, passing through the roof of the shed. On the two sid ? of the fire door, and all along the chimney, within and without, let the whole be well plastered with mortar.

10. THE SILK-BOW. 絲箶

This instrument consists of a board, about two feet long, three inches thick, and four broad; at each end a hole is chiseled out, and a thick slip of bamboo, three feet four inches long, and four or five inches broad, is bent at both ends, and fixed in the above-named holes, thus taking the form of a bow; this 'is used for stretching the hanks of raw silk on.

11. THE SILK-REGULATOR AND THE BOBBIN.

托繡父墜梗

The silk-regulator is for regulating the silk in spinning it; it is made of brass, and has a wooden handle, fitted underneath, about three feet long. The hanging bobbin is made of bamboo about a foot long; it must be shaved round and smooth like a skewer; at one end let a knob be left, and at the other end let a spiral groove be cut, into which the silk may be inserted, and kept from falling down; if you want to make the bobbin heavy, string a score of copper cash upon it; on the outside of this bamboo pivot, put a hollow cylinder made of reed, about six inches long; varnish it at both ends, and use it for winding the thread on.

12. THE BLOCK ON WHICH TO CHOP THE LEAVES. 切桑礎

This block is made of rice-straw, stripped clean of its dry leaves, and bound firmly together by three bamboo hoops, the ends being cut off even on both sides; the block thus formed is four inches high, and upwards of a foot in diameter.

13. THE SIEVE FOR SIFTING THE LEAVES. 葉篩

This sieve is made of fine basket-work, it is about eight inches in diameter, and three inches high ; the finer the holes are the better, while the bamboo should be shaved very smooth. In feeding the young worms the leaves are put into this seive and sifted, by which means the pieces are obtained of an equal size.

14. THE SILK-WORM BASKETS. 蠶筐

The natives of Hoo-chow, in feeding silk-worms, use this basket as a measure ; for the little black worms, one dram of leaves go to a basket ; for those of middling growth, 20 or 24 ounces go to a basket ; and after the period of long torpor, five or six catties of leaves are reckoned a basket-full. The names of these are various ; they are called either sieves, trays, or flat baskets ; when the worms are first born, the receptacles for them are called sieves ; when middle-aged, they are denominated trays ; and when the worms have gone through the second torpor, flat baskets. If winter bamboos be used for these baskets, the grubs will not attack them ; the larger trays should be about three feet seven or eight inches in diameter, with sides an inch and a half high ; the smaller ones, two feet or two and a half in diameter, with the sides one inch high ; the larger sieves should be about two feet and a half, and the smaller two feet in diameter, with sides an inch high. When the holes of the sieves and trays are too large they may be pasted over with paper.

15. THE SILK-WORM NET. 縻蠶網

This net is made of string, like a fishing-net ; the length and breadth being according to the size of the basket. The meshes of the net should be close or open, according to the size of the worms, the small worms requiring a close, and the larger ones a wide-meshed net.

16. THE LARGER FRAME FOR SILK-WORMS. 大蠶植

This frame must be three-cornered, with three posts each eight high, between which there must be nine tiers of cross-bars, each eight inches apart so as to admit of the silk-worm baskets being taken in an out. The front cross-bars must be six feet long, and the hinder cross bars three feet long. In each of the front cross-bars, there must be a tenon about four inches long; and in the end of the hinder cross-bars should be corresponding mortises, which are to be fitted on to the short tenons in the centre of the front cross-bars; a hole is made through both, into which is fitted a bamboo peg, by means of which one may turn the back part of the frame to the right or left, and fold it up at pleasure.

17. THE SMALLER FRAME FOR WORMS. 小蠶植

For the smaller silk-worms use smaller frames, four feet high and as many wide, with five or six tiers of cross-bars; the frame is made thus small to admit of its being put inside a set of bed-curtains.

18. THE FEATHER FOR REMOVING THE WORMS. 担蠶毛

This is generally a goose's feather, the lighter and softer the better, lest the worms should be injured in the removal; when the little black worms are just born, they are as fine as hairs, so that they cannot be gathered up by the hand, but may be moved along by means of this feather.

19. THE SILK-WORM NIPPERS. 蠶箸

These are made of bamboo, about five inches long, and of the size of common skewers, only tapering towards the end; they must be rubbed fine and smooth, and then they may used for the purpose of taking up the silk-worms.

中國內地一瞥：在絲茶產區的一次旅行期間所見

20. THE BENCH FOR FEEDING WORMS ON. 飼蠶橙

The thicker this bench is the better ; the face of it may be about a foot wide, and the legs two feet high ; on the top of the bench make a round hole, midway between the two legs to the right and left ; there insert another piece of wood, at right angles with the bench ; on the top of this cross-bar make a hole, similar to the one on the top of the bench ; use another round piece of wood for a back leg, about two feet high, perpendicular to the cross bar, and place a second cross-bar even with the one on the top of the bench ; then fit the two cross-bars, into the upper and lower part of the bench, on the top in the former of a letter T ; in order to fix these, insert wooden pins through the hole on the top of the bench, and through the hole in the cross-bar likewise, by means of which it can be turned to the right hand, or to the left, and serve as a stand for the baskets, in which the the silk-worms are fed.

22. THE LOW BENCH FOR FEEDING THE WORMS. 地蠶橙

This bench should be a foot high, seven or eight feet long, and eight inches broad ; the stronger the better ; when the worms are spread about over the ground, so that people have no place to stand on, then they can be put on this bench, for the purpose of feeding them.

23. THE FRAMES, MATS, AND ARBOURS. 山棚蘆草帚

The mats should be made of reeds, which are to be spread over the frames, without which, there would be no place for the worms to spin on ; the length and breadth of these mats, should be according to the size of the house ; each house may contain four or five of such mats, so as to fill it. The bushes or arbours, should be made of rice-straw. There are two modes of binding these. Some take a handfull of straw, about two feet long, tied fast round the middle, and both ends spread out in a slanting form, these are called 墩頭帚 the single-headed arbours. Others take a bundle of straw, about three feet long, and having tied it fast in the middle, double it into two; then, taking hold of a few straws in each division, and crossing the straws of the original ligature, bind them round again several times, so that the ends open out, like an umbrella; these are called 折頭帚 the double-headed arbours.

24. THE BASKET FOR COCOONS. 繭籃

This is made of fine wicker-work, either large or small, according to fancy, but smooth and well-woven.

25. THE MULBERRY-SHEARS. 桑剪

The branches of the mulberry must not be broken off, but cut by means of shears, which are to be made of steel, with the head about an inch and a half long, and the body five; the shoulders should not be too wide, the handle convenient to take hold of, and the edge hard and sharp.

26. THE MULBERRY-LADDERS. 桑梯

These are either high or low, the medium being about nine feet; there should be a ladder on each side, one opposite the other; on one side of the top-board, let two iron rings be fixed, through which a thin piece of wood may be passed, so that when you move them out, the two legs may be opened wide, and when you fold them up, the props may be joined.

27. THE MULBERRY-HOOK. 桑鉤

When the mulberry-branches are long, and you cannot reach them with the shears, you must use a hook, to draw them towards you; the iron head of the hook should be five or six inches long, and shaped like a parrot's bill; at the near end of it, make a round hole longitudinally, to receive the handle, which should be two feet eight inches long.

28. THE LEAF-BASKET. 葉籚

This basket should be made of split bamboos, about a foot and a half in diameter, and two feet or more in height;

across the top there should be a cross piece of wood, for the convenience of carrying it on one's shoulder ; a piece of rope tied across will do. The openness or closeness of the meshes are immaterial.

29. THE MULBERRY-SAW. 桑鋸

When the branches of the mulberry-tree are tough and hard, and cannot be clipped by the shears, they should be cut off by means of a saw ; this instrument may be a foot and a half long, half an inch wide, and the twentieth of an inch thick, provided with a row of small teeth ; the bow should be of iron, at each end of which the saw should be fixed, with a short piece of wood for a handle.

30. THE KNIFE FOR GRAFTING MULBERRY-TWIGS. 接桑刀

This knife should be about five inches long, and half an inch broad, as sharp as possible ; for the grafting depends mainly on the splitting of the branch, so that the construct tion of the knife, is not a matter of indifference.

31. THE MULBERRY-SCRAPER. 刮桑把

This instrument, which is used for scraping the grubs off the mulberry-trees, should be made of iron, with the edge upwards of an inch broad, and bent forwards ; it should be about three inches long, with a round hole at the near end, for the reception of the handle, which latter should be about two or three feet long.

32. THE SYRINGE. 噴筒

This may be made either of copper or bamboo, abou-seven tenths of an inch in diameter, and a foot long ; at the bottom it should be perforated with seven or eight holes, for the water to come out at ; besides this, take a round piece of wood, about half as long again as the tube ; at one end, put a short handle ; and at the other end, nail on two or three layers of leather, or bind it round with cloth, so that it may fit exactly to the tube ; insert this into the tube, and draw up water with it, in order to sprinkle therewith the snails and slugs.

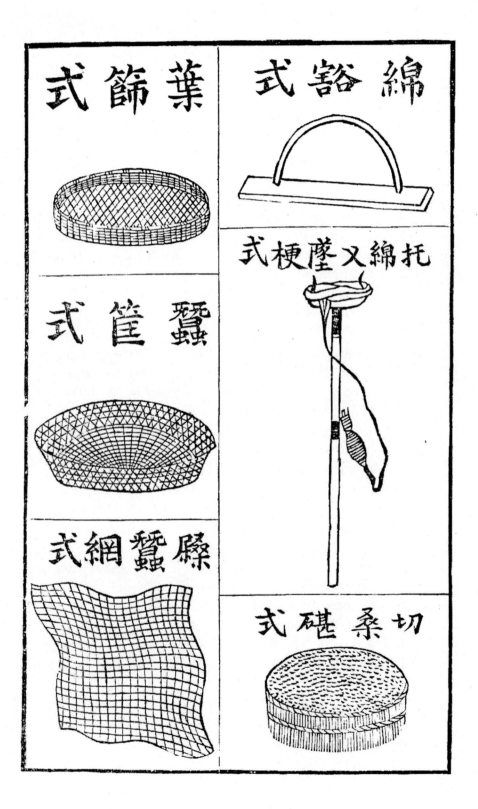

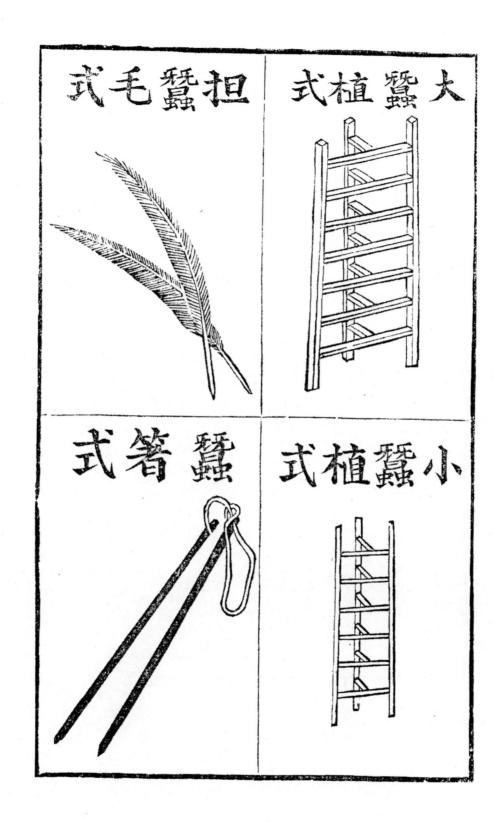

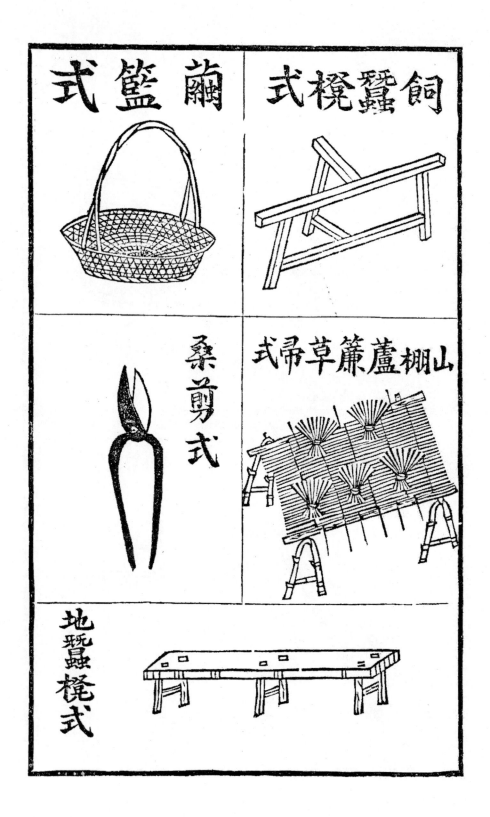

繭籃式

飼蠶櫈式

桑剪式

山棚蘆簾草帚式

地蠶櫈式

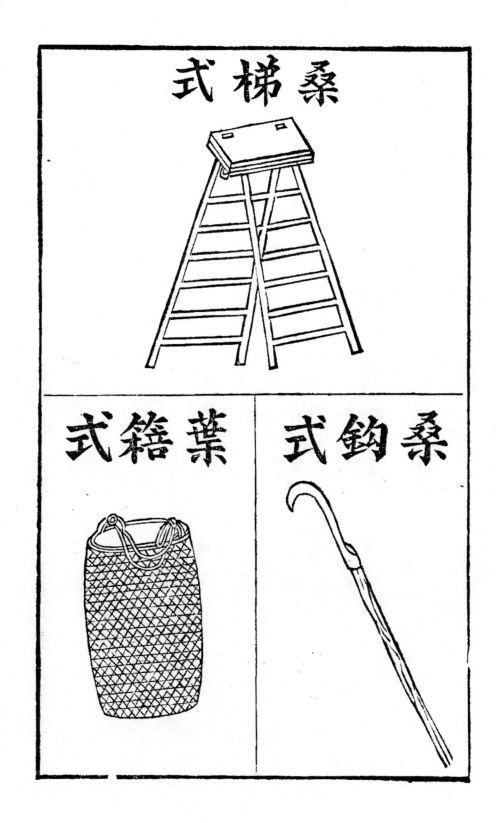

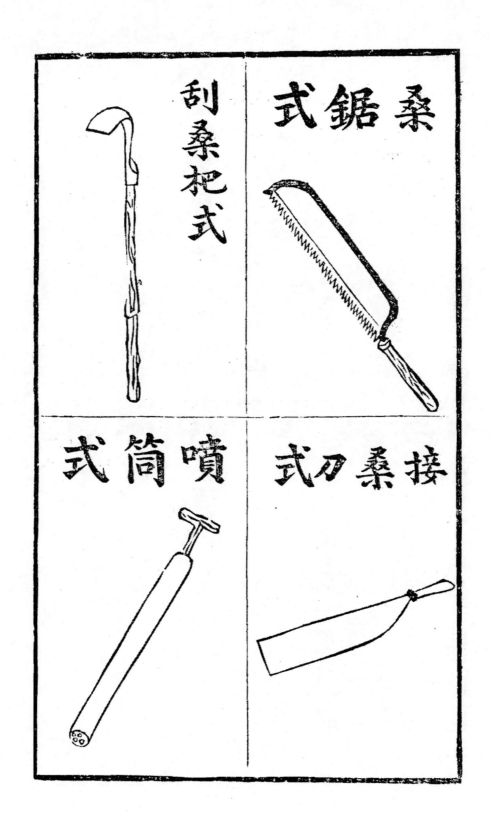

桑鋸式

刮桑把式

噴筒式

接桑刀式

中國內地一瞥：在絲茶產區的一次旅行期間所見

SOME FURTHER ACCOUNT OF HOO-CHOW.

Hoô-chow 湖州 is the capital of a prefecture of the same name. The form of the city, which was built A. D. 620, is irregular, being constructed to suit the windings of a river which surrounds it. The general shape is circular, with a considerable projection towards the east, and a smaller one towards the west, while on the north-east there is a corresponding indentation. The circumference of the walls was formerly 24 le, or 7 miles, but it has since been reduced in size. There is a pagoda on the north side of the city, called the 飛英塔 Fei-ying-tǎ, or "the tower of the flying hero," attached to a monastery of the same name. This monastery was built in the time of the 唐 Tâng dynasty, and has in it an image of a sleeping Buddha, and a very ancient tree, which are considered by the Chinese as remarkable. But temples and monasteries are no uncommon things with them, as there are about 300 religious houses in the two districts, included in the prefectural city of Hoô-chow. Some attention to the distresses of the living, as well as to the interests of the dead, is paid by the inhabitants of Hoô-chow; for there is a foundling-hospital near the west gate, and an asylum for old men near the centre of the city, besides other charitable institutions and public cemeteries. An altar or arena for sacrificing is erected on the south-west side of the city, dedicated to the spirits of the hills and rivers, and another on the north-west side, sacred to those of the land and grain. A terrace rises up near the middle of the city, at the back of the prefect's residence, called the 愛山臺 gnaé-shan-taê, or the "terrace of those who are fond of hill scenery;" and various public schools and examination-halls for literary candidates, are to be met with in this silk-producing capital.

The whole perfecture contains seven districts, or walled towns, of the third order, besides unwalled towns and villages in abundance. It is said to contain 3,000,000 mows of ar-

一一二

able land, or nearly 1,000 square miles. It is well watered, and beautifully diversified with hill and dale.

Of the hills of Hoô-chow, one of the most remarkable is 弁山 Peen-shan, or Cap-hill, so called from the resemblance which the top bears to a cap ; it is said to be upwards of thirty miles in circumference, and very high, insomuch that the snow does not melt on it during summer, while it is much infested by snakes and wild beasts. This mountain is remarkable for its high precipices, rising up several thousand feet in a perpendicular direction ; and for a cave called the yellow-dragon cave, because, they say, a yellow dragon was once observed there ; perhaps some fossil remains of the saurian tribe, which the Chinese have magnified into a dragon. Forests of upright stones, or stalactites are spoken of in this cavern, and one in particular, shaped like a flag, large at the top and small at the bottom, which shakes on the least force being applied to it. The depth of the cavern is unknown. Another remarkable hill is the 天目 t'heen-muh, or heaven's eyes, so called from a couple of lakes near the top, which look like two eyes. The Chinese say, that people who have ascended this hill have seen the clouds gather round the middle of the hill, and have heard the murmuring of the thunder far beneath their feet. From the summit of it four prefectures are visible, namely, 杭州 Hâng-chow, 寧國 Nìng-kwŏ, 徽州 Hwuy-chow, and 湖州 Hoô-chow, including an area of 2,000 le. On the top are to be found various medicinal herbs, which are very much celebrated in the Chinese books.

The principal sheet of water, near this prefecture, is the 太湖 T'haé-hoô, or great lake, from which 湖州 Hoô-chow derives its name. This lake receives the superfluous waters of the Yâng-tszè-këang, and is called great, on account of its capacity, rather than with reference to its extent. It was denominated 震澤 Chin-tsìh, in the time of the great 禹 Yù, and is referred to in the Shoo-king ; (see the translation of that work, page 98.) It receives the waters of 72 streams, which, not being able to reach the sea, disembogue themselves into the Great Lake.

A lake of some extent is spoken of, a little to the south of the city, called 碧浪 Pĭh-làng, or pearly wave lake, on account of the beautiful appearance of the waves when agitated by the wind; it receives the waters of the 天目 T'hëen-mŭh hill, and covers an area of 10,000 mow, or 1,666 acres.

A sheet of water occurs in the middle of the city of Hoô-chow, called the 月湖 Yŭĕ-hoô, or moon lake, from its resemblance to a half-moon.

There is a river, called the 四安溪 Szé-gnan-ke, along which our boat proceeded till we reached that town. The source of this river is in the hills about 廣德州 Kwang-tĭh-chow, but it is navigable only as far as 四安 Szé-gnan, proceeding upwards from Hoô-chow. This town is about 70 le, or 21 miles, from the prefectural city, and has an inspector placed over it. During the 隋 Suy dynasty, the town was surrounded by walls, with four gates, each having the word 安 gnan, or tranquillity, included in the composition of its name, hence the name of the town 四安 Szé-gnan, or four-fold tranquillity; the traces of these gates are still visible. In the 元 Yuên dynasty, a custom-house was established here, which has since been removed; the government wisely judging, that if toll were taken on the merchandize passing to and fro, between the tea and silk districts, such impost, added to the difficulties of the transit over the hills, would deter merchants from passing this way, and seriously affect trade.

The prefecture of Hoô-chow is said to contain 2,941,658 mows of arable land, or 490,276 acres, which at the rate of one mace, four candareens per mow, will produce 411,832 taels of silver for the land-tax; besides one tow and three quarters, or a peck of rice per mow; which will make 51,479 peculs of rice, for the taxes in kind. This amount, though large in the aggregate, is not so in the detail, as it averages little more than a dollar in money, and a pecul in weight of rice for every six mow, or English acre ; being the entire charge of government on this rich portion of the Chinese soil. The charges on hill-land and morass are proportionably lighter, being scarcely the 100th part of the above.

CONTINUATION OF THE JOURNAL.

April 2d. Early in the morning, we were on our way, and before daylight, had cleared the city walls. Our course was westerly, amongst ranges of hills, which, as soon as the sun was up, were gilded with his vernal rays. Thus illumined, the landscape displayed its varied beauties, set off by the sombre hue of the deep green foliage, reflected in the bosom of the noble stream, along which we passed. The windings of the river, presenting constantly a new prospect, the balmy breezes which were this morning favourable, and the warblings of the feathered songsters of the woods, all conspired to fill us with pleasing emotions, and to render this the most delightful part of the journey. To the south, was a lofty range of mountains, which we judged to be the 天目 T"hëen-mŭh hills, already alluded to. After sailing about eight miles, we came to a place, where two streams met, the larger one coming from the south-westward, where lies the town of 安吉 Gnan-keïh ; and the smaller one from the north-east, near the district of 長興 Châng-hing. We pursued the course of the latter, for about eight miles further, and then, instead of going direct for Châng-hing, we kept on in a westerly course, towards 四安 Szé-gnan. The entrance to the smaller stream, which we now began to navigate, was marked by a very high bridge of one arch, which appeared from a distance, as if suspended in the air, and as thin as if built of iron. The trees on either side concealed, with their exuberant foliage, the foundations of the bridge, and the absence of a parapet wall, gave it the attenuated and airy appearance alluded to ; but on a nearer approach, we found it substantially built of stone, and likely to endure for ages. The whole scene was such as a painter would have been glad to sketch, and I could not but regret my inability to secure a more durable impression of it, that I might gratify others by its representation. We had not proceeded above a mile along this new stream, when we met a boat crowded with well-dressed ladies, who were probably coming from 長興 Châng-hîng, to visit their friends in Hoô-chow. The banks of the river along which we now passed were high, and the water clear, evidencing the near approach to a hilly region. As we proceeded, the river increased in tortuosity, and gradually lessened in size. On its banks, were planted abundance of mulberry-trees, much larger than any I had previously seen. The stems were about a foot in diameter, and from the top of the main stem, which was generally four or five feet high, proceeded about eight or ten branches, the ends of which had a knob-bed appearance. From each of these knobs, a number of twigs shot forth, which were covered with new leaves. Passing along, we saw men driving stakes into the banks of the river, by means of an immense mallet, with a stone head, which it required the utmost strength of a man to raise above his head, when it fell with a heavy blow on the top of the stake ; proving at once, the strength and perseverance of the peasantry, in protecting their lands from inundation, and their soil from being washed away by the torrent. A little further on, we saw a company of men, employed in driving piles, as the foundation of a new bridge. For this purpose, they erected a stage of three tiers, with a certain number of workmen on each tier, each of whom held a string that was attached to the main rope, by means of which, the driving ram is raised to a certain height, and then allowed to fall suddenly on the head of the pile, in order to force it in. One of the number kept time by a lively song, in the chorus

of which, they all joined, and at a given signal, let go the
ropes together. In the absence of all machinery, this was
perhaps the best method they could have devised for effecting
their purpose.

About 4 P. M. we arrived at 四安 Szé-gnan, a small
town, situated about twenty miles from Hoô-chow. The
first object that struck our attention at this place was a temple,
in front of which were five ornamental gateways, erected
probably in honour of so many virtuous females, whose
relatives wished thus to prepetuate their fame. At the moment of our arrival, a play was in the course of being performed, which drew vast crowds of people from the town
and country adjoining, while it kept the attention of those
who were assembled pretty much rivetted on the performance, and prevented their noticing too curiously the newly-
arrived strangers. From the thousands of people assembled
in front of the stage, one might argue the populousness of the
adjoining district ; though it is probable, that the exhibition
of this buffoonery had attracted the villagers from a circuit
of many miles in circumference.

After passing the stage, we turned to the right, and going
under a bridge, we skirted the town, and, about half a mile
further on, came to the general lodging-place for strangers,
where a large number of boats were already at an anchor ;
one of our party went on shore to provide a place for our
reception, and soon returned bringing a number of coolees for
the baggage. On our arrival at the tavern, the host was very
polite, asking after the names and surnames of his honoured
guests, and inviting them to sit down and take tea. Of the ac-
comodations, however, I cannot speak flatteringly ; the reception-room had very much the appearance of a barn, with mud
floor, and no ceiling ; the dirt and cobwebs about it leading
to the supposition that it had not received any cleansing
since it was built. The front of this saloon was open to
the wind and rain, (except when a few bamboo screens were

中國內地一瞥：在絲茶產區的一次旅行期間所見

put up for temporary shelter,) and the little yard into which we looked was the receptacle of every species of filth and abomination. A table stood in the middle of the floor, with here and there a short narrow bench, on which the weary traveller might sit without reposing himself. Towards evening, an attempt was made to wipe the table, which would have required an hour's good scrubbing to render it free from dirt, but which was only the more ingrained with filth by the slight operation to which it was subjected. A number of dishes where then placed on the board, and rice enough and to spare was deposited in a tub at the end of the table, to which each guest might repair, and help himself at leisure. Though there was nothing tasty or delicate on the table, the host no doubt thought that he had afforded us an elegant repast, as was evidenced from his coming to the table, during our meals, and begging to be excused for putting so poor a dinner on the table ; which in a Chinaman's mouth means, see how richly I have provided for you. Before evening, I perceived my fellow-traveller taking out of his basket some slices of bacon and a salt fish, which he asked the cook to fry for him ; which done, the whole was deposited again in his provision-basket, to serve us for a meal on our future journey, when we might happen to lodge at places where neither fish nor meat was procurable. At first I was disposed to think that it would be much better to go without, than to resort to viands that had such a forbidding aspect ; but I afterwards found, these same salt provisions to be highly desirable, where nothing else was to be had. Before dark, we had rather a lively scene, occasioned by a number of rough and noisy coolees, who came in to look at our baggage, and to deliberate about the price to be paid for carrying it. The first requisite was to ascertain its exact weight, and to divide it into equal loads, so that every one might know what he had to carry, and that one might not have an ounce more than another. In this matter they are exceedingly particular,

weighing every trifling article ; as each one determines not
to carry more than his exact proportion.   So strict indeed are
they in this matter, that the next day, when I wanted one of
them to carry a coat for me, which was disagreeably warm in
the heat of the day, they all refused, because it would increase
their burthen by a pound or two, until something extra had
been promised them for so doing.   The weight assigned to
each coolee was about 150 pounds English, with which they
travelled about thirteen miles a day, for fourteen days in
succession, over hill and dale, in spite of mud or dust, or the
usual impediments of travel.   Much wrangling preceded
the final settlement of the bargain, and it was at length
arranged, that they should each receive a quarter of a dollar
a day, and start the next morning.

This matter being settled, the goods were all piled up in
one corner of the room, and some benches and boards being
brought out, our sleeping-places were contructed from these
materials, inclosing the baggage so that no person might
make free with it during the night.   Previously to our retiring
to rest, the boatman was settled with, who only received
about three dollars for the trip, from Shang-hae to this place,
with about one dollar and a half for the food of three of us,
for five days.   Thus, travelling in China is not very expen-
sive, at least to the natives, and those who travel in native
style.   The inn at which we were putting up is much frequented, and everyday accommodates a considerable number
of strangers ; which may be partly gathered from the fact of
more than a dozen persons being constantly employed to
attend to their wants, and partly from the hundreds and thousands met with the next day upon the road.

April 3rd.   After an early breakfast, the coolees came
blustering in, and bore off their heavy weights apparently in
great glee, and I was at first apprehensive lest they should
get out of sight before we were quite ready to follow them ;
but I soon found that there was little danger of their run-

中國內地一瞥：在絲茶產區的一次旅行期間所見

ning away from us. Indeed we overtook them before we got to the end of the street, and had to stop every five minutes, to enable them to keep up with us on the road. On quitting our hotel, the host and his clerk accompanied us to the door, and took leave with many protestations of the high consideration in which we were held, and of the gratification it would afford them, to have the honour of entertaining us again. Whilst passing along the street of the town, some remarks were made regarding me, not so much with reference to my strange appearance, as with regard to the curious circumstance of my wearing dark-coloured spectacles, which it seems are not usually met with in this part of the country. My guides, therefore, advised me to use others, which would be less likely to expose me to remark.

We had scarcely got outside the town, before we saw a hill before us, of a conical shape, standing in the midst of the plain, with no other rising ground for several miles around. On the south, at a considerable distance, were some of high hills, and on the north side, rose up a range of mountains of considerable elevation ; but this appeared to stand alone, as if it had been protruded by some subterraneous force from beneath. While the coolees proceeded slowly along, I had abundant opportunity for looking around me, and having been nearly a week confined in a small boat, I felt it the more agreeable to get abroad. I soon found that we were not the only travellers on the road, for the narrow pathway was crowded with bearers of burdens and wheelers of barrows, who where conveying goods backwards and forwards along this well-frequented line of road. It excited a little surprise, for the moment, to see how unceremoniously the fellows pushed along, without making the slightest attempt to afford one room to pass ; indeed one man made me get out of the pathway, and descend into the paddy-field, in order to make way for him. Having been accustomed to see the Chinamen turn out of the way for Europeans, and even jumping ditches to let them pass,

I was for the moment little prepared to be myself driven from the pathway in my turn; but when I recollected that I was then personifying a Chinese, I was rather gratified to think that I succeeded so well, as to be treated like one of themselves. My companion also chimed in by saying, that it was the custom in China for empty-handed people to make way for the carriers of burdens; also for these same coolees to make way for chair-bearers; and for chairmen, in their turn, to get out of the way for those who ride on horseback.

After skirting the foot of the hill just alluded to, we came to a stream of water, which I judged to be the same along which we had travelled from Hoo-chow, though here unnavigable, except for rafts. Here we found hundreds of people employed in collecting wood, as it was brought down from the interior, and making it up into rafts, for the purpose of being transported to the populous cities on the sea-coast for sale. Here also we met with an increased number of wheelbarrows, going and coming, the former conveying cloth and hides into the hill districts, and the latter bringing down rice and wood to the lowlands. At a moderate computation, not less than a thousand wheel-barrows passed or overtook us this day; some were driven along by one man only, and others were provided with two, one before and the other behind. Some were laden with goods, and others with passengers. It was not unusual to see two persons seated on the same wheel-barrow, one on each side, as in an Irish car; or one only, sitting astride his goods, as we should mount a horse. The Chinese wheel-barrows are somewhat peculiar, being provided with a large wheel, the axle of which is fixed near about the centre of gravity; so that the person employed to move such a machine has little or no weight upon his hands, and has nothing to do, but to guide and force onward the conveyance. In this way, a single individual will easily transport three hundred weight of goods,

N

while two will convey along double that quantity. It is possible that our own countrymen might derive a hint from this, in the better construction of wheel-barrows at home. One defect, however, is observable in the Chinese wheel-barrow, namely the narrowness of the wheel, by means of which the roads along which they travel are greatly cut up; and even the flag stones, laid down along part of the way, are cut into deep grooves by the narrow knife-like wheels.

In addition to the wheel-barrows, the road was literally covered with coolees, hurrying backwards and forwards with their burthens, continuing in one unbroken chain during the whole day; affording a specimen of the most busy scene I ever witnessed, not even exceeded by the crowding of the road that leads to a public market or fair; and this was but a usual specimen of what is exhibited here every-day. It was this uninterrupted throng of passengers that gave employment to the immense number of tea and cake shops all along the road; at every le, or a third of a mile, there were several of these *restaurateurs*, provided with benches and tables for the accommodation of passengers, who quaffed their simple beverage and passed on. At every ten le, also, there were rice-shops, where travellers could obtain a more substantial meal than the tea-shops afforded. During the first ten le's journey from Szé-gnan, the ground was tolerably fertile, being laid out in wheat, and great quantities of the mustard-plant, the seeds of which are used in the manufacture of oil; but as we advanced, the soil assumed a barren appearance, and being far elevated above the water-level, was incapable of irrigation; it was, however, planted with fir-trees, which flourished along the lower ranges of hills. The soil was of a light colour towards the surface, but red underneath; and in consequence of the wheelers of barrows having perpetually chosen new tracts for their vehicles, as the old roads became cut up and impassable, the whole country has been converted into one broad and uneven road,

approaching here and there to a focus, as it became necessary
to converge the lines, for travellers to avail themselves of a
bridge over a stream. In short, every man seems to do that
which is right in his own eyes, when pursuing his journey,
and hence the multiplication of pathways over these barren
tracts. After having travelled about nine or ten miles from
Szé-gnan, we came to a ledge of rocks, composed of coarse
red sandstone, in thin layers, and dipping towards the south-
west, at an angle of fifteen degrees ; about a mile further on,
we fell in with another ledge, similar to the former one ; and
observing the contour of the hills in the direction of the dip,
I calculated that the ledge rose up again at a distance of five
or six miles. On the road side we observed a plot of ground
covered with tea trees, but apparently in a languishing state.
We also passed several temples, which were generally in a
dirty and ruinous condition, as if regarded by no one. The
inhabitants of these districts were few and poor, seeming to
obtain a scanty subsistence by planting a little wheat, and
chopping wood for the lower and more populous districts.
After a journey of twelve miles, we came to a more level
and fertile region, where water was obtainable for the purpose of irrigation. But we observed, that in those fields
which were laid out in wheat, there was too much moisture ;
and the natives were in the habit of digging trenches a
foot broad, and equally deep, between every ridge of a foot
wide, upon which the wheat was sown. Thus giving up at
least one half of the soil, to render the other capable of producing the article required. During the latter half of the
year, when the same land is laid out in rice, every ridge
would of course be levelled, and the water brought in plenty
over the fields. Another mile further on, we came to a broad
stream, which was however very shallow, and unnavigable
except for small rafts. Across this river a wooden bridge
was thrown, about six feet wide, and 200 long ; the stream
flowed to the north-west. After passing the bridge, we came

to a paved road, and saw at a little distance a pagoda rearing its head, which pointed out the the situation of 廣德
州 Kwàng-tih-chow.

ACCOUNT OF KWANG-TIH-CHOW.

About half a mile on this side of Kwàng-tih city we
observed an elegant gateway, erected in honour of some
virtuous female, on the portal of which was written 金
心在中 Kin-sin-tsaé-chung, a golden, or perfect heart,
exactly in the centre; or hitting the due medium; the sentiment conveyed by which was much admired by my guide.
Towards evening, we arrived in the suburbs of the town,
and turned into a lodging-house. whose sign of moderate
accommodations and homely fare, hung out by the road side,
induced us to enter. In front of the lodging-house was a
small shop, where eatables were exposed for sale: passing
through this we crossed an open space. and came to a
rough kind of hall, or reception-room. with mud floor, and
tiled roof; on either side of this hall were bedrooms, but
so dark and damp that I was almost afraid to enter the one
which was allotted to us. There was no window, and all
the light it obtained was admitted through the door. which
opening into another apartment did not allow of the passage of many rays into this black and dismal abode. But as
there was no resource, we could only take our seats, and
wait for the evening meal. This day I found myself a little
unwell, through exposure to the sun, and sleeping in a current
of air.

April 4th. This morning we had a fall of rain, on which
account our party concluded not to move, and so nothing
was to be done, but just to sit still and wait for fair weather;
about ten o'clock, the rain stopped. and the sun shone out
brightly, which gave us a hope of making some way before
night; but, just as we were about to set forward, we found

that our coolees had already seated themselves at a table, to play at cards. And then, were an angel to exhort, or an emperor to command, it would have been of no use, as they considered the business of card-playing to be one of the most important, in all heaven and earth ; under these circumstances, the wish of their employers to proceed was, of course, treated as unworthy of the slightest attention. Among the rest of the coolees was one pre-eminent for impudence, who had the audacity to ask one of our party, whether the boxes he was transporting contained opium or not ? to which he replied, you may open every bundle, if you please, and should there be opium concealed in the boxes, we shall be accounted as offenders, and you may take us before the magistrate ; but should there be no traces of the drug, you will then be an offender, and we shall take you before the mandarins. Upon hearing this, he desisted from further enquiries. On looking round about the walls of our lodging-house, I found a proclamation from the magistrate of 廣 德州 Kwàng-tĭh-chow, stating, that for some time past a set of villainous rascals had, under pretence of searching for opium, obstructed honest travellers in their way, compelling them to open their packages, that they might steal their money ; on which account, the chief magistrate severely prohibited this kind of villainy, and also interdicted the keepers of lodging-houses from harbouring such a set of scoundrels. This proclamation had been issued a few months previously, in consequence of an attempt to rob some travellers, under false pretences, between this town and 四 安 Szé-gnan ; so that our friend the coolee, would have found himself in an evil case, had he persevered in requiring the packages to be opened, and found them to contain nothing but silver, the result of the tea sales recently made by my fellow-travellers in Shang-hae.

Whilst waiting for our men to set out, I had an opportunity of observing a poor sick girl, lying in a sort of portable bed-place, to be conveyed on the shoulders of two men, by means of a pole fixed longitudinally ; this pole was fitted about two or three feet above the bed-place, with a cloth flung over it, falling down on each side, to protect the person inside from the sun and rain.　The wretched traveller referred to, was being borne in this manner from 湖州 Hoô-chow, to 徽州 Hwuy-chow, a distance of 200 miles ;　on her arrival at each separate tavern, the bed-place was put down, with its sick inmate, in some open hall, and left there, till the coolees were ready to start the next morning : no change of clothes after a hot day or a cold night ; no attentions or services of any kind rendered to the feeble ; even necessary food was not thought of, till the cries of the hungry girl aroused the whole household, when her hard-hearted bearers condescended to furnish her with a morsel ; it was such an outcry that drew my attention this morning, and caused me to make the enquiries, which resulted in the information above detailed.　To add to all her troubles, it turned out that the poor girl was deaf and dumb.

Having nothing else to do, I occupied myself in observing the way, in which the master of the shop manufactured his vermicelli.　He first made a paste of flour and water, which having been well pounded in a stone mortar, was put on a thick table, across which, was placed a pole, with one end fitting underneath a strong bamboo, on the opposite side of the table, and the other projecting a foot on this side, so that the workman could sit on it, without touching the table itself ; this pole being made to cross the dough, was pressed forcibly down upon it by the weight of the man's body applied to the near end.　In this way, by constantly shifting the pole backwards and forwards, and by perpetually jumping up and down as he sat upon it, he effectually kneeded the dough, and brought it by repeated foldings and pressings into exceedingly thin layers.　Then rolling these up together, he, by the application of a sharp knife, cut off thin stripes, which formed the vermicelli. In the evening, we had this same vermicelli for supper; it was simply boiled and served up, as hot as may be, being seasoned with a bit of bacon, which we had brought with us. When night came on, every individual coolee obtained from the lodging-house keeper, one of the dirty thick quilts, which are kept in store for such purpose and wrapping himself up in it, soon fell fast asleep; with the exception of those who loved gaming better than sleep, and who preferred to stay up the whole night playing at cards.

April 5th. This morning we started about seven o' clock, having previously furnish d ourselves with spiked leather shoes, to enable us to get along over the muddy and slippery ways. These are uncomfortable things to walk in, but it is better to wear such on a rainy day, than to travel in cloth-soled shoes, which immediately become wet, and take a week to get dry. After passing the suburbs, we came to the gate of the city, in front of which was a bridge, with the words 新河橋 sin-hô-keaóu, or "new-river-bridge," written over it; from this I gathered, that a new canal or water-course had been dug, from the navigable part of the river, where the two streams that flow past the city, on the east and west sides of it, in a north-westerly direction, meet about a mile or two lower down; by means of this cut boats may be brought up to the city itself, and the inhabitants enabled to carry their produce to a good market, or get what they need from abroad. When we entered the city gates, we immediately turned to the left, and walked along the walls; my companions took this course, with the view of screening me from the observation, to which I should have been exposed by passing through the crowded streets; a precaution which, though scarcely necessary, afforded me a better opportunity of taking a general survey of the city, than I should have enjoyed by passing through its main street. I observed, that the walls were about fifteen feet high, but out of repair in several places, as if they had been built several hundred years ago ; while in some places, there were marks of recent repairs. The form of the city resembled a parallelogram, with the longer part lying east and west ; about three 里 le in one direction, and one 里 le in the other. There seemed to be but one main street through the city, intersected here and there by short cross streets, which however did not extend to the walls on either hand, not even in the vicinity of the north or south gates. A large part of the area within the walls was occupied by rice-fields, insomuch that nine tenths of the ground, may be considered as devoted to the sustenance of the population, who occupy the remaining tenth with their houses. I cannot account for this, otherwise than from the circumstance of the city having declined much in importance, since the period at which it was first built ; and because the soil within the walls is more rich, and less burthened with imposts, than the ground outside. There are, however, no vacant spots in the suburbs, but the most is made of every inch of ground everywhere, except where the sterility or steepness of the ground, render it incapable of improvement.

In the early days of Yaou and Shun, until the Han dynasty, this city went under the name of 楊州 Yáng-chow ; and, after having received various appellations, it came, in the 宋 Súng dynasty, to be designated by the name which it now bears. The first monarch of the 明 Ming dynasty, directed his generals to fix their head-quarters here, when the walls were built, about three miles in circumference, fifteen feet high, and eight wide. There were then six gates, towards the north, south, east, and west, together with the north-east and south-east ; some of these, however, are now turned into water-gates. In the fourth year of 正德 Chíng-tíh, (A. D. 1,510) the walls were repaired by the then existing magistrate, and the mud defences received a facing of brick ; in the time of 嘉靖 Këa-tsing, (A. D. 1,530) the magistrate of the district added battlements ; from which time to the present, the walls have been frequently out of repair, and as often re-edified ; the last repair recorded was effected in the time of 康熙 Kang-he. (A. D. 1,670.)

The most remarkable hill in this district is the 橫山 Hwăng-shan, or "cross hill ;" it lies to the west of the district city, and assumes a transverse appearance, from whichever way viewed, hence the name. Another hill has the designation of " parrot beak," from its fancied resemblance to the hooked bill of that bird. To another is assigned the appellation of " stone fairy," and " stone Buddha," from an upright stone at its foot, resembling a tall figure.

The stream that nearly surrounds the city, flowing from the south-west, in two branches, one on each side of the city, and uniting together about a mile lower down, is the 玉溪 Yŭh-k'he, or " pearly stream."

The military force at present stationed in the town of 廣德 Kwàng-tih, is a 遊擊 Yêw-keïh, major, a 守備 shòw pei, captain, a 千總 lieutenant, and two ensigns, with thirty-eight horse, and eighty-five foot soldiers, and two hundred and ninety one men for mounting guard ; these numbers are, however, to be found rather on paper, than in reality.

The arable land in this district, amounts to 171,642 acres, On this is levied a land-tax of 50,896 taels, with an impost in kind of 13,744 peculs of rice, and 1,550 of pulse, besides 205 taels on waste land, fisheries, &c. amounting in the whole to less than half a tael per acre.

In the centre of the city, is a pagoda, seven stories high, in a dilapidated condition ; a pavilion, however, of three stories, on the south side of the city, dedicated to the spirit presiding over letters, had been recently repaired ; from which one may argue, that the inhabitants are more concerned to propitiate the genius of literature, that they may attain advancement in the present, than to flatter Buddha, in order to acquire happiness in the future life.

After quitting the city, my fellow-traveller facetiously remarked, that we should soon see an individual who could point out the road to others, but could not walk therein. I was unable at first to comprehend his meaning; but about ten le from the city, we came to a place where two ways met, and a friendly sign-stone stared us in the face, with this inscription on it, " the road to 徽州 Hwuy-chow turns off here," which explained the enigma of my friend. The more direct of these two roads, pointed in a southerly direction, towards 嚴州 Yên-chow; while the other led off to the south-westward, in the direction in which we had to travel. After walking.about five le further, we came to the other branch of the stream, which flows past 廣德 Kwàng-tih, and partially surrounds it; this stream flowed in a northerly direction, and was beautifully clear, but not navigable. After wandering along its banks, for about a mile, we came to a wooden bridge, near which was a tea-shop, where we stopped to take a cup of tea; my companion remarked. that on his former journey, he had not observed this accommodation: to which the woman, who kept it, replied, that their little hut had been erected, for the convenience of travellers, who might happen to arrive at the banks of the river, soon after a freshet, when the bridge was generally washed away. The travellers in that case, would have no place to remain in, whilst the storm lasted or the bridge was repairing, hence the necessity of this accommodation. During our stay at this tea-shop, half a dozen travellers came, by, who had a very suspicious appearance; and looked as if they would be glad to make a disturbance, for the purpose of profiting by the result, on the principle of there being good fishing in muddy waters; but after a hasty cup of tea, they passed on, and we saw no more of them.

After parting with these suspicious-looking fellows, we saw few persons on the road, and fewer wheel-barrows ; it is probable, that the large number of travellers seen on the road between Sze-gnan and Kwang-tih, is owing to the road between those two places being the medium of communication between the two rivers, the one terminating at the former, and the other commencing at the latter place ; which neck of land being crossed. the goods are subsequently carried forward by water. It seems that the question has been agitated at court, whether it would not be better to establish a custom-house at this point, but the compassionate ruler of China wisely judging, that for every little advantage which he might derive from the tolls thereby collected, many grievous burthens would be laid on the people by the collecting officers, and the trade be thereby driven into other channels, determined on leaving the people to pass to and fro at this point unmolested.

Having crossed the river in question, and walked about a mile, we entered a most romantic velley. on each side of which the hills were covered with the blue bell and convolvulus, while the crystal stream murmured through the dell, and the feathered songsters warbled in the grove, altogether contributing to cheer the heart, and lighten the fatigue of the way. I here observed some layers of rocks. consisting of a red-coloured mica slate, intermixed with other shades, some of a light and others of a darker hue, according as the laminæ lay near to, or far beneath the surface. The dip was towards the north-west, at an angle of 20 degrees from the horizon. The dip was the same on the hills on both sides of the valley : not up one declivity and down the other, but always towards the north-west, wherever the strata were found ; hence it might be inferred, that the disturbing force. which threw these strata into the oblique form, was entirely independent of the protruding of these small hills. and in fact involved them in the rupture. There must have been some uprising of the ground, occasioned by volcanic action far to the south-east, which has upheaved the whole mass of previously-formed strata, and let it fall in broken portions (which form the present hills) in a north-westerly direction. But at such a period of terrible convulsion, one may be led to ask, what organic life could have existed, or have endured the shock ?

Having passed through the windings of this valley, by a good paved road, we came to a place where two ways met ; one turning to the west, and the other pursuing the usual south-west course, in the direction in which we had all along been travelling. About a mile further, we came to a Buddhist temple, in a sequestered spot, called the 石嶺奄 Shǐh ling yén, or monastery of the rocky mountain ; here we found three or four priests residing, who busied themselves in boiling rice and preparing tea, for the travellers who passed by, not of course without good and sufficient payment for the same. The temple was in good repair, and tastefully adorned, while some of the side apartments appeared clean and decent ; so that a botanist or naturalist, whose business was to search for curiosities in the mountains, might spend a few days or weeks at such a temple, without inconvenience : if he could manage to conceal his origin and object from the priests who entertained him. People say, that frequent robberies used to be committed in this valley, the perpetrators of which were sheltered by the priests, who shared in the booty ; but that latterly the officiating friars have been changed, and such irregularities have ceased. Throughout this region three kinds of flowers were most frequently observed ; one of a red colour, shaped like an inverted bell, growing on an arboraceous stem, several inches high, with few leaves ; these the women were very fond of gathering and sticking them in their hair, while the men delighted in garnishing their newly-ploughed rice-fields with the same beautiful production. The second kind was of a lilac colour, growing on trees, about ten feet high, which sometimes covered the whole side of a hill, and

gave it a splendid appearance. The third was white, and
although plain, when mixed with the other flowers, produced a very pleasing effect. A light blue-coloured bell-
shaped flower was gathered by the natives in great quantities,
to be boiled down as vegetables. Many stems of bamboos
were planted over the hills, but scattered wide apart, which
when acted on by the wind, waved their graceful tops, like
ostrich feathers on the crown of the mount ; a few miles further on, we came to a temple, in good repair, dedicated to 司
山大帝 Sze-shan-tá-té, the great god who guards the
hill ; in the middle of this temple, I observed a board hung
up, enumerating the names of those who were in the habit
of contributing candles and incense, for the service of the
temple ; it was further stated, that on the day of the winter
solstice, the contributors should all attend and burn incense ;
and in case of a single individual absenting himself, he
was to pay a whole year's incense as a fine. Thus strict do
these villagers appear in attending to their idolatrous services.
I also observed in a tea-shop where we stopped, a 門牌
mûn-paê, or door-tablet, such as those mentioned by Morrison, and other writers on China, as hung up in every house,
for the inspection of the local officers, and said to contain the
names, sex, and profession of every inmate ; for the failure
in recording which, according to the laws of China, every
master of a family is subject to the infliction of 100 blows.
There was a blank schedule on this tablet, to be filled in
by the master of the house, describing the inmates, whether
wearing a beard or not, whether married or single, the
name of his wife, concubine, children, brothers, sisters,
nephews, nieces, cousins, and hired labourers ; such indeed
was the law, but as is the case in China with most other
regulations, it was honoured more in the breach than in
the observance ; for there was only one thing written on
the tablet, and that was the master's name. I had an
opportunity afterwards of seeing another door-tablet, in

a different part of the country, which had nothing on it, but the master's name and surname: and on asking him, whether he did not expose himself to punishment for neglecting to insert the other inmates of his family, he said, that the only thing required was the payment of forty-eight cash, about two-pence a year, to the man who delivered out these tablets from the government office, and no account was ever taken of what was written on them. Thus the boasted care, which the Chinese are said to take of their population-returns, turns out to be an exaggeration. The census grounded on such tablets must be very unsatisfactory, and if the government returns are merely taken from these, the number of inhabitants must greatly exceed what the local officers give in.

THE VILLAGE OF YANG-T'HAN-POO.

In the evening we came to a small village, called 土橋 T'hoò-keaóu. or 陽灘舖 Yàng-t'han-poo, about forty-five le from 廣德 Kwàng-tih, where we passed the night. The accommodations resembled those of our previous lodging-place, the rooms having no place for the admission of light, except through the door ; but an advantage was possessed by our present residence over the last, viz. a boarded floor. The room was so small, that our three bed-places, and four cooly-loads filled the apartment, while our hands could touch the ceiling over our heads. It was as well, however, that the room was dark, otherwise the dirt, cobwebs, and filth, would have been revealed too plainly. On the wall of the shop, I observed a paper, containing an exhortation to people to bury their dead speedily out of sight, and not to listen to the stories of the 風水 Fung shwùy, wind and water teachers. who pretended to find out lucky sites and propitious days for sepulture, and by this means kept the dead out of their graves for months or years, until this discovery should be made. Our coolies, who had been gaming a day and a night at Kwàng-tĭh-chow, no sooner arrived at this place, and got their feet washed, and their dinner finished, than they set to work in a back apartment to gamble again; and from the noise they made, and the high glee which seemed to prevail, they evidently went about it with a greater zest than ever: thumping the table and rattling the cash, during more than half the night, when after a short sleep they had to set out with their burthens. This time, however, the man most fond of sport lost all his money; and the rest were not inclined afterwards to renew the game. At this place my fellow-travellers observed some very suspicious-looking men, whose prying curiosity, bold assurance, and absence of all ostensible means of support, excited some alarm in the breasts of my friends. Accordingly they tried to keep me as much as possible out of the way, and requested me to remain in our dark room, till meal-time arrived, after which I went out to walk in a back garden. The hill at the foot of which this village was built, was very steep and well-wooded, so that it rose like a dark green screen at the back of the house, and threw a sombre hue over all the surrounding objects. I found the cool breeze very refreshing, after a whole day's exposure to the sun, and having regaled myself with the evening air, I went in and retired to rest.

THE VILLAGE OF PIH-TEEN.

April 6th. Notwithstanding my wish to remain quiet on the day of rest, I could not induce my companions to do so, and harrassed as they were by the presence of the fore-named suspicious-looking personages, they were anxious to set forward as soon as possible. During my walk, however, I failed not to lift up my heart continually, to the God of nature and of grace, who had spread such a beauteous scene around me, and who had added to all his earthly bounties, the richer gift of his dear Son, of whose resurrection the Christian Sabbath was a commemoration. After walking about fifteen le, we came to a place called 柏墊 Pih-tëen, or 栢店 Pih-tëen, where we met with a considerable stream, flowing towards the north, and navigable for rafts; over which was thrown a bridge, of seven buttresses, built of stone; the top of one of them was arched, and the rest covered with flat rafters and boards; it was about 180 feet long, and 20 broad, but in several places out of repair; so that passengers generally avoided it, and passed over a temporary bridge, about twenty yards higher up the stream. The bottom of the river was covered with light-coloured sand; which, on inspection, turned out to be composed of broken pieces of quartz, felspar, and mica, mixed with hornblende, which all appeared to have been washed down, from the granitic or gneiss mountains in the south, from between two ridges of which the river seemed to have wound its way. The sand, I was informed, had increased in quantity of late years, so that the bed of the river is sensibly raised, and the stream at every considerable fall of rain overflows its banks. This was evident, from the circumstance of the footway being removed from the edge of the stream, to a part higher up the bank, while in places where the river was inclosed by high rocks, travellers were unable to pass, until the freshets had subsided. If the sand goes on increasing at this rate, the road by the side of the river will be altogether impassable, and must be removed to another track. The bed of the river is wide, but the body of water that flows on ordinary occasions is not large, and it is only during the heavy rains, that the river fills up all its banks. Pih-tëen, is a small village, containing three or four hundred inhabitants, with several eating-houses and butcher's shops; always an indication of a gathering among the Chinese. A mile or two further on, we came to a small place, called San-meaou, which contained only a few houses;

after passing which, we fell in with the same river, along the banks of which we travelled for several miles. Here we saw many shelves of rocks, dipping towards the north-east, at the various angles of ten, twenty, and some even fifty degrees, from the horizon ; at length, we came to a temple, recently repaired, and dedicated to 伏魔東平王 the subduer of demons, and the pacificator of the east. The names of those who had contributed towards the repairs of the building were emblazoned on a tablet, from which it appeared, that two clans had distinguished themselves in this work of superstition. The road here turns suddenly to the west, leading away from the river ; and after twenty le of travelling over some low hills, brings one to a broad valley, along the bottom of which runs another stream, in a northerly direction, spanned by a bridge, of five arches ; this bridge seems to be seldom used, except when the river is swollen by rains, and travellers generally pick their way from rock to rock, across the stream, by which a small distance is saved. This bridge, however, appears to have been better built than the former one, and is now in a tolerable state of repair. The river here consists of two streams, running side by side, which are probably united in one, when freshets come down ; across this second stream, is a wooden bridge, which is not calculated to withstand the torrent, and must require frequent renewal. After passing this double stream, we came to a place called 陽溪 Yâng-k'he, where we passed the night. Here, however, as well as at T'hoò-keaóu, we had to guard against a set of meddlesome fellows, who, under pretence of searching for contraband goods, were desirous of inspecting our baggage, and involving us in difficulty ; providentially we escaped their hands.

THE TOWN OF HO-LOO-K'HE.

April 7th. On starting this morning, a number of these idle people were assembled in the street, in front of our lodging-house ; as we passed out, we heard them remarking on my appearance, as having something singular about it. We passed on, however, and saw no more of them. For the last three days, our road has been amongst ranges of small hills, not about three or four hundred feet high, with narrow vallies between them, which just admitted of a strip of cultivation on each side of the road, not more than 1000 feet wide ; these long narrow fields were occupied with wheat, pulse, and mustard-seed, all of which were in a state of advancement, ready to be cleared in the month of May, and give place to rice, which is the staple commodity, and the staff of life among the Chinese. The hills were not planted, except with bamboo and fir, designed for house-building and fire-wood. The character of the rocks had mostly been of the primary strata, but in thin layers, and of a light yellowish colour, passing into a darker hue, and deposited in thicker strata, as the slates lay lower down, or were more mixed with hornblende. From this place, however, the vallies became more open, and the cultivation more extensive.. One beautiful tract of country, through which we passed this day, was covered with fruitful fields, the population being proportionably more dense ; while before us lay a broad open region, with cloud-capped mountains, appearing in the distance higher than any we had hitherto approached. The roads, too, gave intimation of their being more frequented, by being kept in better repair, and being almost uniformly paved with large flag-stones, of a black colour, and worn quite smooth by the many feet that perpetually passed over them. After a journey of 45 le, we came to a broad river, spanned by a well-built bridge, skirted by a populous town, and thronged by small boats and rafts, which altogether presented a very lively scene. This place is called 河路溪 Hô-loó-k'he, or 洞渡鎮 Hô-t'hoó-chin. The current of the river is towards the north. The name of the stream is 東河 Tung-hô, and it is the same with that which passes Ning-kwŏ-hëén, and afterwards Ning-kwŏ-foo ; flowing on

until it empties itself into the Yâng-tszè-këang, at 太平府
T'haé-pìng foò.   The bridge over it is well-built, and in
good repair, with a level road, more convenient for passengers
than the mountain-like bridges, high in the middle, and low
at each end, which the Chinese are so fond of building.   The
bridge consists of eight arches, is upwards of 300 feet in
length, 20 in width, and frequently crowded with passengers.
The town lies on each side of the river, and is a place of considerable traffic, carried on between the hill people to the
south-east, and the inhabitants of the low country in the
neighbourhood of the Yâng-tszè-këang, into which river this
stream empties itself.   While crossing the bridge, I was
noticed by some people, perhaps on account of the long and
steady steps I took, in order to measure the length of the
structure, or because I held my umbrella rather low over my
face, as if to conceal my countenance.   Some had the curiosity to come and look under my umbrella, and others
turned their eyes towards my hair, at the back of my head,
but no remarks were made, nor hindrance met with ; my
fellow-travellers, however, were in great consternation, lest
a discovery should take place, which might involve us all in
difficulty.   They were particularly apprehensive at this
place, also, because being a place of some traffic, it was the
resort of strangers from all parts, who having come in contact with foreigners on the sea-coast, might the more readily
recognize one even in the native garb.   Something which they
heard in the street, or saw at the inn, increased the alarm
of my guides, so that they began to consider the propriety of
separating the company ; one of them accompanying me, and
travelling by chair before, whilst the other would follow with
the baggage, which contained silver, to the amount of several
thousand taels.   This plan would have been carried into
effect immediately, but for the difficulty of procuring chairs,
which led them to postpone it until our arrival at the next
stage.   The mind of one of my guides was in a considerable

state of agitation, and I could hear him sighing and crying, in the most earnest manner, for some time after the others had retired to rest. His chief consolation seemed to be the purity of his motives, having nothing in view but the diffusion of knowledge, without aiming at personal benefit. The inn at which we put up was one of the roughest imaginable, though the business done at it was sufficient to have warranted a little more being laid out in accommodations. After passing through the front shop, which was occupied with the traffic of the inn-keeper, we came to a shed, the roof of which was in one slope, open both at the top and the bottom, so that the slightest rain would have rendered it untenantable, except in the middle ; with a mud floor, and every thing as damp and dirty as possible. One side of this shed was partitioned off for a sleeping-room, but so badly done, that it answered every other purpose, but that of a private apartment, and was calculated to exclude every thing but the wind and rain. The company at this place of *entertainment* was of the most noisy kind, and in their quarrels I heard them make use of the epithet 鬼子 kwei-tszè, devil's son ; but whether with reference to a supposed foreigner, or in reproach towards one another, I could not tell. To add to my own apprehensions, and those of my companions, I was heard several times crying out in the Malayan language during my sleep, which of itself was enough to excite the strongest suspicions.

THE CITY OF NING-KWŎ HEEN.

April 8th. The next morning, we were all glad to get away from this place, and set out in the direction of 寧國縣 Ning-kwŏ-hëèn, which was only two miles distant. On the way we saw an altar or area of earth, about eight feet high, and forty or fifty feet square. These places are designed for the purpose of offering sacrifice, at the spring and autumn festivals, to the spirits presiding over the land and grain, but not as with the Jews for the sake of presenting burnt-offerings. A little further on, we saw a number of persons, in front of a temple, offering incense ; at the head of them were three mandarins, the sight of whom so near at hand alarmed my guides very much, lest their attendants, who are eagle-eyed, should discover something unusual about our little company, and endeavour to get up an accusation against us. Hurrying past them, we observed on the boards carried before the magistrates the following words 寧國縣 正堂 Ning-kwŏ hëën chíng tâng, the chief civil officer of the district of Ning-kwŏ. Leaving them, and moving on a quarter of a mile further, we came to the city of Nìng-kwŏ hëën. This district city is said, in the statistics published by the Chinese, to be situated ninety le south-east of the prefectural city of the same name ; forty-five le west from that of Kwàng-tĭh-chow, which we had just left, and 110 east of 績溪 Tseĭh k'he, whither we were travelling. This city was founded in the time of the 三國 San-kwŏ, three kingdoms, A. D. 220 ; and rebuilt in the Súng dynasty, about the tenth century of the Christian era. Having fallen into decay, it was thoroughly repaired in the time of 正德 Chíng-tĭh, of the 明 Mìng dynasty, (A. D. 1,506) ; and judging from the appearance of the bricks and mortar, of which the walls are composed, the city defences must have undergone a thorough repair within the last few years. The walls are said by the Chinese to be 5,190 feet, or about one mile in circumference ; by counting my steps, as I walked round the walls, I judged the city to be about three le in circumference, which agrees very nearly with the Chinese account. The walls are 15 feet high, provided with embrasures, and having well-finished half-moon bastions, at each of the gates. Thus the city is small, but compact and neat, affording an idea of a Chinese town, exactly corresponding with what they represent them to be in their drawings. This district of Nìng-kwŏ is distinguished for its teas, particularly that description called 松蘿 Sûng-lô. It also produces hemp, varnish, lime, linseed-oil, fir, ginger; and chesnuts : while a great quantity of paper is manufactured here. Between this district and Tseïh-k'he is a large range of hills ; the most celebrated of these is the 籠叢 Lùng-tsúng mountain, the narrow passes of which are said to have been formerly much infested with robbers.

On the west side of the city is a pavilion, three stories high, called 文祠亭 Wăn-sze-tîng ; and further on, we observed a terrace, on which sacrifices are offered ; it was four-square, about six feet high, and thirty broad. We also saw a sort of redoubt, which might have been used as a fortified camp in ancient times, but is now completely deserted.

About half an hour after leaving Nìng-kwŏ hēên, we entered again among the hills, the winding vallies between which were here narrower than any we had previously seen ; so that the hills on either side, appeared to approach each other foot to foot, leaving only a small pathway between them. The road was, however, well-paved with flag-stones, about three feet in width. In the evening, we arrived at a village, called 橋子舖 Keaóu-tszè-poò, or 蟠龍舖 Pwan-lûng-poò.

TRAVELLING IN CHAIRS.

April 9th. Finding my feet very sore with travelling, it was agreed, that we should hire chairs, and that one of the guides should go with me, while the other remained with the stuff. An agreement was made with the bearers, for 3,600 cash, to carry each chair 230 le ; besides which, they were to have money for provisions and wine. This indefinite arrangement soon proved very costly, for the fellows ate three hearty meals a day of rice, besides one of vermicelli soup, and about ten tea beverages, accompanied with cakes ; so that when it came to be reckoned up, each man consumed 300 cash a day in expenses ; a sum equal to half of what had been promised them for their labour.   When the chair-bearers, who travelled faster than the coolies with the baggage, passed the latter on the road, there was a great deal of complimentary language lavished on both sides ; the one party protesting, that they were verily guilty in thus passing their brethren ; and the other party exclaiming, that they could not think of detaining their honourable companions ; at last, they settled it by the chair-bearers, saying, you come quietly along, and we will go a little slower, to wait for you.   After travelling a couple of miles, we came to an ascent ; and ten miles further on, we arrived at a hill, about 1,000 feet high.   Here we were obliged to walk, as the bearers could not carry the chairs, with us in them, up so steep an acclivity.   On the top of the hill was a tea-shop and a small temple.   On the way up the hill, I observed some people burning lime ; and on examining the stone which they used for that purpose, I found, that it was a dark-coloured marble, with white glistering veins.   The people dig out this stone from the sides of the hill, and employ the fir, that grows on the summit, as fire-wood. When we obtained a view of the other side, we observed a conical mountain, which seemed to be of volcanic origin. On a nearer approach, we perceived, that the top of the hill, was divided into two or three peaks, and eventually we saw something like the extinct crater of a volcano.   It was probably at this point, that some disturbance of the earth's surface formerly took place, which threw the surrounding rocks out of their position ; some falling to the north-east, and others to the south-west ; thus producing the present inclined appearance of the strata.

At the foot of the hill was a stream, spanned by a wooden bridge ; on the opposite banks of which was the town of 胡樂司 Hoô-lŏ-sze.   The river flowing past this place,

海上絲綢之路稀見文獻叢刊

is the western branch of the 東河 Tung-hô, which we crossed at 河渡鎮 Hô-toó-chin, a little below which the two streams meet. The town of Hoô-lŏ-sze, is large and thriving; the trade consists in the purchase and transport of the grain and fire-wood brought from the mountains, which is conveyed on bamboo rafts to Ning-kwŏ foo, and thence to the great Kĕang. We travelled along the banks of this stream, in a south-westerly direction, for about seven miles, until we came to 觀音橋 Kwan-yin-keaóu, or 叢山關 Tsung-shan-kwan, where we halted for the night, having gone about twenty miles since morning.

THE CITY OF TSEIH-K'HE.

April 10th. We continued journeying along a fertile and well-watered valley, producing abundance of wheat, and pulse, which were grown in the ground, without deep trenches between the rows of grain, as seemed to be necessary in the more damp regions. After a journey of about twenty miles, we came to the district city of 績溪 Tseïh-k'he, the walls of which were low, and very much out of repair; indeed in many places, they were entirely destroyed. The bearers insisted on our alighting to walk through the city, which we did, without appearing to attract the attention of any of its numerous inhabitants. At the west gate, nothing would satisfy our coolies, but they must sit down in the very gateway of the city, to eat vermicelli soup; and thus I was obliged to sit in the most public place possible, with hundreds of people coming and going, to the gaze of all of whom I was exposed, for about an hour. No one, however, saw any thing in us that attracted attention; and so, after drinking a cup of tea, we quietly passed on. Outside the gate of this city, we passed under a number of memorial arches, which had been erected over the road, for the purpose of commemorating various chaste and

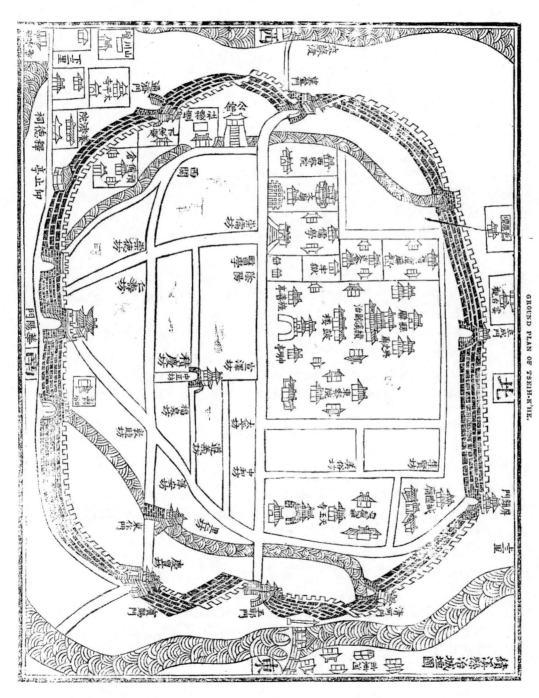

GROUND PLAN OF TSEIH-K'HE.

virtuous females, who had graced the community of Tseïh-k'he in former times. These memorial tablets were particularly large and handsome, shewing the sense entertained by its inhabitants of female worth. There is here a river flowing to the south-west, which afterwards passes Hwuy-chow, and then traversing the northern part of Chĕ-këang province, empties itself into the bay of Hang-chow. A-long this stream, the greatest part of the green teas are conveyed, which are sent to Ningpo and Shanghae. The river at this place, is spanned by a bridge of seven arches, about 250 feet long, and 20 wide, very strongly built, and with a level road over the top of it.

The town of Tseïh-k'he was first settled in the 梁 Lëang dynasty (A. D. 502), under the name of 良安 Lëang-gnan, but was afterwards put out of the list of corporate towns; until the time of 太宗 T'haé-tsung, of the 宋 Súng dynasty, (A. D. 770) when it was established as a district city, under the name of 績溪 Tseïh-k'he, or interwoven stream; this name was assigned it from the curious wind-ings of the river, which flows past the place, the two branches of which appear as if interwoven with each other. The walls of the city were built in the last year of 嘉靖 Këa-tsing, of the Ming dynasty, A. D. 1,566, by the magistrate of the place.

In the 30th year of Kang-he, (A. D. 1,692) a benevolent individual, at his private expense, formed a new road, at the 新嶺 Sin-ling, a mountain lying between Tseïh-k'he and Ning-kwŏ hëen, to save people the trouble of crossing over the top of the mountain.

The walls of Tseïh-k'he are 8,410 feet, or nearly two miles, in circumference; it is provided with eight gates; the residence of the magistrate is in the northern quarter; it has a college and examination hall, with public granaries, and an hospital for old men.

From Kwang-tih-chow, up to this place, the strata of the

rocks, consisting of clay-slate and lime-stone, were observed to dip towards the south. Here again we met with red sand-stone, dipping in the same direction. We saw in the district of Tseïh-k'he, some mills driven by water, and used for the purpose of pounding and cleansing rice, or grinding wheat ; the wheels were, however, very roughly finished, and the whole of the machinery was of wood.

VILLAGE OF HEUNG-LOO-CHIN.

About three miles on the south side of Tseïh-k'he, we came to a village called 雄路鎮 Heung-loo-chin, having passed through which, we were beset by a number of beggars, who were clamorous for cash, and thrust their hands into the sedans, being determined not to be denied. I had no cash about me, my companion being the cash-keeper ; this I told them ; but they would not believe that a person, who could afford to ride in a sedan, could possibly be destitute of cash ; or that any one in his senses would trust his fellow-traveller with all his money ; so that they kept on pestering me for some time, till my companion came up to the rescue. After this I thought it better to provide myself with a few copper coins, to avoid such annoyances in future. At this place, also, a number of suspicious-looking men came about us, who seemed determined to pry into our affairs, with the view of finding something about us, which they might complain of to the magistrate, and thereby promote their own selfish ends ; we, however, avoided them, and at 臨溪 Lin-k'he we halted for the night. The road along which we had travelled this day was well-made and broad, paved with flag-stones in the centre, and smaller pebbles on either side ; so that carriages might easily have been driven along the way. The flag-stones of which the road was constructed were of lias, some of them more than ten feet long, and two wide. The soil appeared fertile and the people happy. The distance travelled to-day was about 70 le, or 21 miles.

THE CITY OF HWUY-CHOW.

April 11th. After a journey of 40 le, we arrived at 徽州 Hwuy-chow, on entering which we observed four idle vagabonds, lying down on the road side, who called on us to stop; we, however, passed on without heeding them.

The road to the prefectural city of Hwuy-chow, lies through the district city of 歙 Heih, which latter is joined on to the former, as it were an excrescence, on the eastern side. Both cities are walled; the wall of the prefectural city forming the defence of the district city on one of its sides; the other three being surrounded by a wall inferior in height and strength to the wall of the larger city. The stranger, on entering the gateway of the smaller city, does not immediately perceive the houses of the district city, which are hidden by a few small hills within the inclosure, so that it appears as if the district city wall were merely an outwork of the defences of Hwuy-chow itself. We entered by the 新安 Sin-gnan gate, on the north-east side of Heih-hëen, where there are few if any houses within the walls; the inhabited part of the district city lying to the left as we passed along, where the district magistrate resides, and where all the public offices are situated. The principal entrance, however, is by the 紫陽 Tsze-yâng gate, in the south-eastern quarter.

The district city of 歙 Heih is spoken of so far back as the time of 秦二世 Tsin ûrh shé, the successor of him who burned the books, B. C. 246, and was so called from a marsh of that name, which lies to the south of the city. In the 唐 Tâng dynasty, silver and lead were extracted from the 鄣 Chang hill within this district. The mines were, however, exhausted, after they had worked but a few years. The city was originally without defences, but in the Ming dynasty the Japanese attacked the place, which induced the district magistrate to erect the city walls, which in the 39th year of 嘉靖 Këa-tsing were completed. The walls are about 10,000 feet, or two miles in length, and 30 feet in height : being ten feet wide at the top, and 20 at the bottom. The cost of the erection was 100,000 taels of silver. A Chinese writer on this subject, says, " the most agreeable thing for the people is to pass their lives without annoyance. This was the case at Heïh, for 190 years after the settlement of the district ; during which period they never heard of wars or confusions : until those cruel Japanese suddenly disturbed the eastern districts, when the poor people, seeking to escape them, crowded into the fenced cities. These not being sufficient to contain the multitudes, who trode one upon another, the necessity of building more walled cities became apparent. The rulers, therefore, solicited those in higher stations, and urged the peasantry and villagers, until even women and nurses came forward with their contributions, amounting to 800 taels : some sold part of their lands, in order to remunerate the workmen : some composed songs for labourers to sing and forget their toils ; while others afforded the more substantial aid of materials ; in this way the walls were completed, and the city was secure."

From the district city of Heïh, to the prefectural city of Hwuy, the passage is by the 德勝 Tih-shing gate, situated about the middle of the line of wall which, running north and sorth, separates the two cities. This gateway is large, and provided with a half-moon bastion, on one side of which there is a gate through which the road passes, and then. turning sharp off at an angle, enters the principal gateway of the chief city. Here are to be seen a number of commemorative arches, intended to keep alive the recollection of the various virtuous females, who have adorned the city of Hwuy-chow ; these arches are in such numbers, and so lavishly adorned, as to lead a stranger to imagine that all the feminine virtue in the empire has been congregated in

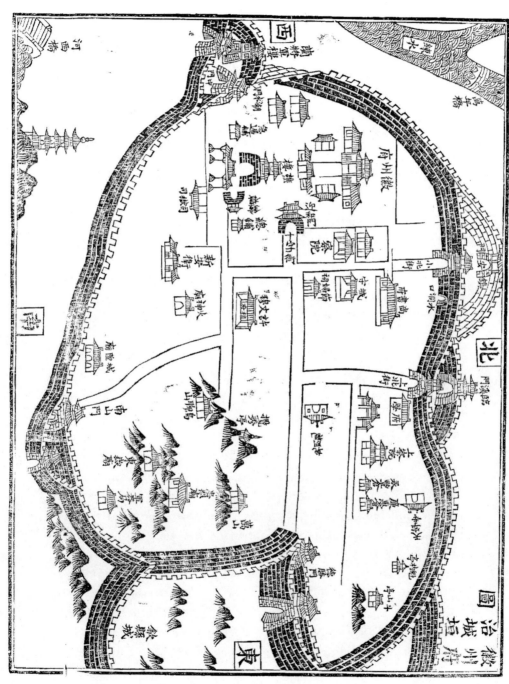

中國內地一瞥：在絲茶產區的一次旅行期間所見

GROUND PLAN OF HWUY-CHOW.

一四九

Hwuy-chow.   Just as we entered the gateway, we met a government officer, seated in his sedan, with a large retinue following him : our chair-bearers immediately stopped, and we alighted to let the great man pass.   He was a dark-visaged man, and looked scrutinizingly at me ; but I turned off into a shop, and avoided his further inspection.   The main street of Hwuy-chow was long. and thronged with busy people, amongst whom none took the trouble to look at us, and so we passed on unobserved.   Our course lay along the main street of the city, which is called the 十字街 Shih-tszé-keae : passing on the right the public college and granaries, and on the left a number of temples situated on an elevated spot within the walls.   Arriving at the streets running north and south through the city, and which by their crossing thus give the name to the principal way along which we travelled, we went under an ornamental gateway, called 迎和門 Ying-hô-mûn, and thence across a broad square, well paved and clean, which was in front of the prefect's mansion, and so out at the west gate of the city.   Here our bearers insisted upon sitting down to enjoy some vermicelli soup, and we were therefore obliged to take shelter in a tea-shop which stood close by.   Here my companion was much disturbed by the appearance of several myrmidons from the public office, who stood for some time in front of tea-shop where we were, pointing hither and thither, and making signs as if they were in search of some one ; but it is very probable that his fears were groundless, and that the men in question were looking after something that more nearly concerned themselves than us.   Leaving the tea-shop, and resuming our journey, we passed over the great Hwuy-chow river, which was spanned by a bridge of many arches. about 750 feet long, and twenty-five wide. One of the arches was however broken ; and the communication thus interrupted was kept up by beams and planks laid across.   Having passed over the bridge, we observed preparations for the acting of a play ; a stage was erected by the side of the river, and a great number of benches spread out under an awning, on which were already seated some well-dressed females, waiting for the play to commence.

A little way from this we passed near another bridge of seven arches, very well formed and in good order, along which a road passed, leading to the westward, towards the city of 休寧 Hew-ning. To give the reader some idea of the bridges at Hwuy-chow, we subjoin a sketch of one called the 紫陽橋 Tsze-yâng-keaóu, situated on the south side of the city of Heih just described. The sketch is by a native artist, and of course the perspective and proportions are very defective ; still it will serve to exhibit the character of Chinese bridges in this region.

The city of Hwuy-chow, is mentioned in the Shoo-king, as existing during the reign of 禹 Yù, B. C. 2200: under the name of 陽州 Yâng-chow: (see English Translation of the Shoo-king, page 97.) During the period described by Confucius, in his History of his Own Times (B. C. 500), it formed part of the 吳 Woò country, which extended from the hills of Hwuy-chow to the sea-coast near Shanghae. After the Woò country was destroyed, it formed part of the region of 越 Yuĕ: then of the kingdom of 楚 Tsoó. In the 25th year of 秦始皇 Tsin-chè-hwâng, the whole region was called 鄣 Chang. The emperor 光武 Kwang-woò, of the 漢 Hán dynasty, (A. D. 17) called it 丹陽 Tan-yâng: during the reign of 獻 Héen, (A. D. 203) it was denominated 新都 Sin-too; the 晉 Tsín dynasty, (A. D. 264) altered it to 新安 Sin-gnan. During the reign of the first monarch of the 隋 Sûy dynasty, (A. D. 598) it was altered to 歙州 Heih-chow. During the reign of 徽宗 Hwuy-tsung, of the 宋 Súng dynasty, it was called 衛州 Hwuy-chow, on account of the beauty of the situation, and perhaps out of compliment to the reigning monarch ; which name, with slight occasional changes, it has retained to the present day.

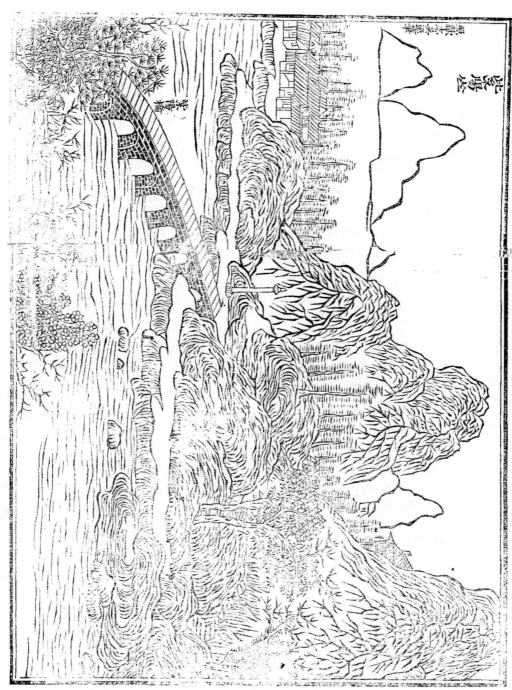

VIEW OP A BRIDGE AT HWUY-CHOW.

The prefecture of Hwuy-chow is 390 le from east to west, and 250 from north to south ; it is 650 le distant from Nanking, and 4,000 from Peking. The city walls are 11,340 feet, or a little more than two miles in circumference ; they are from seventeen to twenty feet in height, and from eight to ten in thickness ; it is oblong in form, being longer from north to south, than from east to west. The city is provided with five gates, each of which has a half-moon bastion to cover it ; and barracks for troops to guard it. Seven towers are to be met with in various parts of the walls, for the purpose of espying the approach of an enemy. On three sides of the city, there is a moat, twenty-four feet wide, and twelve deep ; but on the remaining side, the hills are supposed to be a sufficient guard.

THE TOWN OF TUN-K'HE.

On leaving the city of Hwuy-chow, we took a southerly course ; having travelled about ten le, we perceived that the road was paved with large flag-stones, of a light colour ; the road itself was about six feet wide. Thirty le from the city, we observed a small hill, about three hundred feet high, with a round top, consisting entirely of stratified red sand-stone ; there were a number of hills around, of the same character. Ten le further, we perceived that the stones with which the roads were paved, those with which the foundation of the houses were constructed, and those of which the bases of flag-staffs in front of the temples were made, were all red sand-stone ; from which I concluded, that such rocks abounded in this region. On examination, the sand-stone was found not to be of the coarse kind, for the people seemed to be in the habit of using these stones for sharpening their knives and axes ; so that the buttresses of the temples and houses were very much worn away in many parts, by the process. Having proceeded ten le further, the chair-bearers wished to halt for the night, at a small village ; but as we were within a short distance of a large mart for business, where my fellow-traveller wished to see a friend, they were constrained to go on ; whilst we walked a part of the way to relieve them of their load : in this way we arrived at 屯溪 Tun-k'he.

This Tun-k'he lies in Latitude 29. 48. North, Longitude 2. 4. East of Peking, and though an unwalled town, is one of the largest places of commerce in the green tea district. It is situated on the 縣港河 Heen-keang-hô, which falls into the Hwuy-chow river. It is about three miles long, and contains at least 100,000 inhabitants, amongst whom are the most extensive tea-dealers, who purchase the teas that are grown in the surrounding country, and after preparing and sorting them, despatch them by means of a water communication that passes through the town, by way of Hwuy-chow to Shang-hae ; or if they think they can find a better market, they have only to transport them over a range of hills to the westward, when they descend the stream that passes by Woo-yuen, into the Po-yang lake, and thence southward to Canton. In the town, there are not only large house of business in the green tea line, but also every kind of handicraft is practiced, that is in any way connected with the packing and transporting of the teas ; together with a host of shop-keepers, who live by disposing of eatables and wearing-apparel to the traders and mechanics thus engaged. Seven or eight hundred chops of tea are annually sent from Tun-k'he, in the directions above specified. My fellow-traveller, being well acquainted with the managers of one of these tea-establishments, stopped at his house for the night. We were, on alighting from our chairs, greeted with a hearty welcome by our kind host, who entertained us in a hospitable manner, and treated us with every mark of kindness and respect. We were first regaled with basins of hot vermicelli soup ; and as the even-

中國內地一瞥：在絲茶產區的一次旅行期間所見

ing set in, a large feast was prepared for us in the central hall. The lights upon the table, however, were very dim, and as I wore a pair of dark-coloured spectacles, to prevent any remarks being made upon my eyes, I was unable to see distinctly what was in the dishes before me. With a great deal of difficulty I was enabled to take up with the chopsticks, a few pieces of meat from the dishes, in the centre of the table, which I not unfrequently let fall before they reached my plate, or could be conveyed to my mouth. Our kind host saw the dilemma I was in, and persisted in assisting me to secure the most dainty bits, and lodge them in my plate; he must have seen, however, that I behaved myself most awkwardly, and acted as no Chinaman would have done under the circumstances; indeed nothing but his native politeness could have led him to overlook the slips, or prevented him from attributing them to the right cause, viz. a want of familiarity with the instrument employed. His son, a young man between twenty and thirty, must certainly have suspected something unusual in their guest, for I could perceive him watching my every motion, and eyeing me from top to toe. I was very glad, therefore, when the feast was ended, and we removed from the ill-lighted table, to sit in a still more gloomy part of the room. Here the host engaged me in conversation, and asked me particularly respecting a new Chinese firm, which had been recently established in Shanghae. Happening to know something respecting the said house of business, I was enabled to give him some information; while I was at the same time surprised at the accurate knowledge which he possessed of things as they existed in Shanghae. Finding from the tones of my speech that I was acquainted with the Fokien dialect, he asked me more particularly respecting matters in that province, and the manners and customs of the Fokien people. Thus we passed the evening, until overpowered with the fatigue of a long journey during the day, I asked to be shown to my

R

一五五

room, and took my leave of our kind host, expecting to depart early the next morning.   A sleeping apartment was allotted us in the rear of the great hall, which, though neither to be admired for its cleanliness, nor beauty, was a prefect palace, compared with many places, where we had already lodged ; here tired with the business of the day, I soon fell asleep.

PROSECUTION OF THE JOURNEY.

On the 12th of April, we set out early from Tun-k'he, and after travelling about five le, came to a curious assemblage of rocks, about 100 feet high standing in the midst of the plain. The principal rocks were two, standing opposite each other, with a temple built between them, which they appeared to overshadow and protect.   In this part we saw frequent specimens of the tea-shrub, on each side of the road ; but planted on raised pathways between the rice-fields, or in the corners of enclosures, as though they did not form the chief article of cultivation, but were merely attended to as a secondary object.   The plants were bushy, about three feet high, with new leaves coming out, while the old leaves were still on the tree ; the new leaves only appeared to be gathered by the cultivators.   One plant is estimated to produce about a pound of tea-leaves during the season ; but seven pounds of the green leaves are calculated to make only one pound of the dried and prepared tea.   The common people merely use the little stalks and refuse leaves, while the best part of the produce is sold to the tea-dealers.

After travelling about ten le in this direction, we came to a ruined bridge, over the 縣港河 Heuén-këàng-hô, across which the road formerly lay ; but this being now broken down, we were obliged to go on, about a le further, until we came to a ferry, at which we paid six cash for each chair, and one for each individual.   Three le further on, we crossed another river, called the 南港河 Nàn-këàng-hô ; here we observed people making bamboo rafts, by first peeling off the outer green rind of the reed ; after which they varnished it of a black colour, in order, as they said, to make the raft float more lightly on the top of the wave : the ends of the bamboos, which formed the head of the raft, were bent upwards by means of heat, to enable those who used them to get more easily over the rapids, with which these rivers abound. We passed this day several tall elms, and others trees, in full growth and vigor. One spot was especially to be admired, surrounded with these high trees, with their thick foliage, full of the feathered songsters of the grove, who appeared happy in being exempted from the fowler's gun. Here we stopped to take tea, and were enabled to enjoy the scenery, while our bearers rested themselves.

About twenty le further on, we came to 南山古廟 Nân-shan-koò-meaóu, an ancient temple under the southern hill. At this place, according to the saying of the geomancers, was once discovered the foot of a dragon ; on which account it was esteemed a most fortunate place for sepulture, insuring that any, who had their parents buried there, would attain to no less than imperial dignity. It is said, that the owner of the ground, surnamed 汪 Wàng, was desirous of securing the site for a tomb, when the people interfered, lest the consequence would be a revolution and change of dynasty : they therefore subscribed a large sum of money, purchased the property, and built the temple ; which, however, out of compliment to the former owner, they dedicated to 汪公大帝 Wàng kung tá té. It is futher reported, that the emperor, who reigned at the time, also contributed a sum of money towards the building of the temple ; lest the succession to the throne, in his own family, should be disturbed by a person belonging to any other house obtaining this fortunate site for a grave. All this in consequence of what they term a dragon's foot having been discovered in the soil ; which after all was perhaps nothing more than the remains of some ichthyosaurus or plesiosaurus, which among us would have been of far greater interest to the geologist than the geomancer.

We passed this day through a considerable town, called 龍巖 Lûng-yên, or 五城鎮 Woò-chîng-chin. At this place, we met with the river formerly mentioned called Nân-këäng-hô. navigable for rafts or small boats, and flowing towards 屯溪 Tun-k'he, from which it is distant by the road about 40 le ; at Tun-k'he it joins the 縣港河 Hëén-këäng-hô, when they both flow on to Hwuy-chow, and from thence to Hang-chow bay. Here the people from 婺源 Woó-yuên, who have to convey teas and other produce towards Ningpo and Shanghae, take advantage of the water-carriage, and transport their goods by means of this stream ; after having crossed the chain of hills which here separates the district of Woó-yuên from those of 休寧 Hew-ning, and 歙 Heïh. All the rivers on the south side of this chain of hills flow to the southward and westward. into the Po-yang lake, by which means the valuable produce of Woó-yuên is transported to Canton.

After travelling ten le further, we came to a small hamlet, called 新嶺局 Sin-ling-keŭh ; here the rain and wind prevailed so much, that the chair-bearers would not venture to ascend the hill which lay before us, so that we were obliged to put up at a miserable hovel which presented itself, in the name of an inn, at the foot of the hill. The accommodation was of the most wretched description ; we procured shelter from the rain, it is true ; but that was nearly all. The hut in which we had to lodge, admitted the wind at every corner ; and a recess was offered us as a bed-place, which must have been tenanted by beggars and thieves for many a day previously. For provisions the people could furnish us with nothing, but coarse red rice, and a few pickled beans to tempt it down. They did not forget to charge, however, as much as if we had been favoured with the best accommodation and supplies. This hill appeared to be of the clay-slate formation, mixed with conglomerate; the dip was toward the north-east.

The hill itself, which is called 新嶺 Sin-ling, is said by the Chinese to be 6,000 feet high. I found it, however, by counting the steps we ascended, to be no more than 1,500 feet, from the hamlet at the foot to the pass over which we crossed. The peaks of the neighbouring mountain were much higher. It adjoins on the west the 芙蓉 Foô-yûng, or marsh-mallow hill, and constitutes, with the 對鏡 Túy-king, 手鬪 Shòw-tów, and 得勝 Tih-shíng hills, the five lofty mountains for which this region is celebrated. There are various caves and rocky dells amongst these hills, which are adorned by temples and pavilions, where the traveller or devotee may rest; and in the recesses of which priests are found, fostering and perpetuating the system of Buddha. In one of these pavilions there is a 石筍 Shih-sun, or stalagmite, twenty feet high. A Chinese poet has celebrated these five mountain peaks, in his song, as follows:

" The five-pointed mountain rears its lofty head,
Where the marsh-mallow lifts its blossoms to the sky;
At every step we ascend higher and higher,
And as we mount upwards dare not look back.
Winding and turning we seem as if scaling the Heavens,
And fancy we shall never reach the summit.
It is not necessary to enquire whither we are going,
But we press on until we reach the azure clouds."

JOURNEY OVER THE HILLS.

April 13. The rain having ceased, my companion determined to proceed, and I was obliged to accompany him. I directed my thoughts, however, to Him, who will have mercy and not sacrifice, and whilst seated in the sedan was enabled to refresh my mind by the perusal of the Scriptures. We passed in succession over five different mountains as described above. The road was well-paved the whole way; flat stones having been laid down, six feet wide, and formed into regular steps, up and down the hills. Sometimes the road was paved with slabs of coarse marble, and sometimes with large round pebbles, brought from the brooks below. We observed also a white kind of stone, which appeared to be pure felspar, resembling that of which the Chinese porcelain is made, interspersed with a hard red stone like porphyry. All of these appeared to be quarried out of the neighbouring hills. The natives informed us, that the paved road was constructed by a man, whose surname was 汪 Wáng, belonging to the district of 婺源 Woó-yuên; some part of it is ascribed to an old vintner, who, on account of the restoration of an only son to health, exhausted his property in the construction of this road. The whole is the result of voluntary effort, and charitable contribution, without any government order or imperial benefaction. The mass of the rock of which the hills are composed seems to be gneiss, mixed occasionally with the felspar and porphyry, above alluded to. On one side of the hills, the dip of the strata is towards the north-east, and on the other towards the south-west; hence the disturbing force which upheaved the mass must have been somewhere about the central ridge. The angle of the dip is from thirty to fifty degrees, and sometimes the strata are quite vertical.

The scenery, whilst winding amongst these hills, I found to be picturesque in the extreme. Here and there a rocky dell, in the bosom of which lay a Buddhist temple; now and then, a monumental pillar or gateway, intended to perpetuate some supposed benevolent act, or virtuous female; while the works of nature, more sublime by far than the works of art, with which they were intended to be adorned, rose in awful grandeur, and overtowered them all. Whilst passing over these hills, we met some tea-merchants from Woó-yuên, going to purchase teas. They had long white bags, slung to the poles across their shoulders, which on enquiry, I found to contain silver. Each of them seemed to be conveying the worth of a thousand dollars, unconcealed and undefended, over these retired heights, far from the busy haunts of men, without apparently the slightest apprehension of being attacked by those who might covet their wealth. Indeed our companions were doing the same thing, and though they were sometimes alarmed, when lodging at inns, near crowded cities, where sharpers might have sought a quarrel with them, and by bringing them before the mandarins, have squeezed them to the extent of their property; they never dreaded mountain bandits, nor open plunderers. This speaks much for the secure condition of the wild and unfrequented parts of the interior; but not much for the justice and protection afforded by the magistracy, in the cities of China.

After passing two villages called 塔坑鎮 Tä-k'hang-chin, and 茗坦村 Ming-tan-ch'hún, we came to the town of 江灣村 Këang-wan-ch'hún, where we saw a river flowing to the southward, called 婺河 Woó-hô, the same which afterwards passes by 婺源 Woó-yuên and from which that city derives its name. After this it empties itself into the Po-yang lake, and forms a medium of export to the inhabitants of this district, towards the south and west. Leaving the town of 江灣 Këang-wan, and travelling about five le, we came to a very well-constructed bridge, called 宏齊橋 Hûng-tsê-keaóu, which was built over the Woó-hô. It consisted of strong buttresses, from one to the other of which beams were laid across, having planks nailed on them. We annex an illustration of it by a Chinese artist, which is not unlike the original. The bridge is twenty-four feet long, and the space between the buttresses, from thirty to forty feet. The width of the bridge is fifteen feet. On the centre of the bridge is a pavilion, to screen it from the weather. Underneath the pavilion, are two small shrines, in which offerings are made to the spirits under whose charge the bridge is supposed to be. Near these shrines is a board, containing the regulations under which the bridge is placed; according to one of these, beggars are forbidden to cook their rice, or to pass the night, under shelter of the pavilion; according to another, heavily-laden carriages are prohibited from crossing the bridge; according to a third, cattle are required to wade through the stream, and not to cross the bridge at all. There is also a board hung up at the bridge, recording the names of those who contributed to its erection; according to this, it appears, that the magistrate at Woó-yuên had subscribed fifty taels of silver; whilst some others, had given one or two hundred taels. In this way, most of the bridges and canals in China, with the roads and other conveniences for travelling, are constructed, and maintained by the efforts of private benevolence.

THE VILLAGE OF WANG-K'HOW-CH'HUN.

Having crossed over this bridge, and travelled about ten le, we came to 汪口村 Wáng-k'hòw-ch'hún; here we found a junction of two rivulets, one the 婺河 Woó-hô, which we had already seen, and the other flowing from the 龍尾 Lûng-wei hill, in the north-west. The two rivulets united here, form a considerable stream, which is navigable for large boats. Having crossed this river, we put up for the night at the town on the opposite bank. The inn at which we were accommodated, however, was excessively filthy; and as there was no private parlour, we had to take our meals with the family. This instead of being a privilege, was a complete annoyance, as all the inmates, as well as lodgers, who were not of the highest class of society, considered themselves privileged to elbow and scrutinize the

中國內地一瞥：在絲茶產區的一次旅行期間所見

guests, no matter who they were, or from whence they came. Thus we were subjected to all sorts of inspection and remark; while the interchange of compliments at a Chinese dinner-table, such as have been described on a preceding page, were under these circumstances anything but agreeable. The chair-bearers for instance, who dined with us, thought themselves entitled to take every liberty, as if they were on the most friendly footing; and all this was to be endured, lest by a little manifestation of disgust, they should discover, that they had some among them who were not familiar with Chinese habits. At night, we were shewn into a large upper room, where all sorts of people were reclining on the floor, in promiscuous confusion, amongst whom we should have been compelled to lie down, had we not discovered a small chamber, particularly inclosed in one corner, where there was the semblance of a bedstead; upon this we stretched ourselves, and should have enjoyed a little repose, had we not, every now and then, been aroused by the noises which issued from the large room, where the numerous occupants of the floor were either fighting or playing, during the whole night. Once or twice I started up, but my companion begged me to be still; and thus we passed the troubled night, till the break of day informed us, that it was time to rise.

April 14. My fellow-traveller discovered that our own chair-bearers had been drinking, gaming and quarrelling the whole night, with some of the lodgers at the inn; and on reproving them for it, he and they came to a disagreement; whereupon the bearers shouldered their chairs and went away, leaving us to do the best we could for the rest of the journey. Being thus left by our own coolies, my fellow-traveller engaged places for us in the passage-boat, which was that morning moving down the river. Here we had to sit in very close contiguity with all sorts of people, face to face, and eye to eye, so that if any discovery was to be made of the foreign extraction of any on board, that was the time to make

S

it. The passengers expressed to each other, as is usual on such occasions, their opinions relative to the origin, character, and intentions of each individual stranger. Their surmise respecting myself was, that I was some literary graduate, who, having succeeded at the district examination, was now proceeding to the provincial city to try for higher honours. They seemed, however, much more taken up with smoking, than with the observation of men and manners; for the pipe, which was a sort of water-pipe, somewhat approaching to a hookah, went continually round amongst them, and was pulled at successively by every one, without cessation. During our voyage this morning, we passed over ten or more rapids, where the water ran with the fiercest violence, among the rocks and over the shallows. The boat, when arrived at these places, darted away of its own accord with considerable velocity; and all that the people on board could do, was merely to guide it, so as to avoid the dangers that threatened on every side. Having been accustomed to the place, and the work, they managed tolerably well, and brought the boat safely through, where a stranger would expect a certain wreck. The voyage down the river was thus speedy in the extreme; the attempt to ascend, however, must have been proportionably difficult; and what took us only one day in the descent, would have required at least ten days to accomplish in the opposite direction. To the north, on a hill at some distance, we observed some stone pillars, or peaks of a great height. These appear to have been situated on the 高湖 Kaou-hoô, 'or High Lake hill, which separates Woó-yuên from 休寧 Hew-ning; the hill is thus denominated, on account of a lake near the top, covering several acres of ground, which during all seasons of the year never becomes dry. The pillars we noticed are called 摩夫頂 Mo-foo-ting, and 斧峰 Foo-fung; the latter is so denominated on account of its resemblance to a hatchet; on one side of the former there is an orifice, from which gas or smoke is emitted, which

中國內地一瞥：在絲茶產區的一次旅行期間所見

the Chinese call 通天竅 T'hung-t'hëen-k'heaou, the open-ing that communicates with heaven. We annex a rough sketch of the scene taken by a Chinese artist.

The rocky strata on the river-side dipped towards the south, the banks of the stream were well-wooded; this. and its perpetual winding, presented us with an ever-varying but pleasant prospect, which relieved the tedium of the voyage very much. After travelling 40 le, we arrived at the dwelling of my fellow-traveller. He had been nearly two years away, and I was curious to see, under such circumstances, what sort of reception a Chinese father of a family, would meet with on his return home; on arriving at the village, one or two persons recognized him, but without stopping to converse, he passed on to his own dwelling. Entering this, he found his younger brother, who had been left in temporary charge of his abode, and to whom was entrusted the out-door work connected with his little farm, sitting in the front room, enga-ged in shelling some beans. This man, on recognizing his bro-ther, merely gave him a nod, after which he rose up, cleared a-way the beans, and proceeded to sweep the floor, which much needed it. The wife then came in, and without any salutation proceeded to wipe the table, and spread the tea-cups. The daughter, a young woman of eighteen, was equally indifferent; and both she and her mother seemed only anxious to know what fine things he had brought with him. His baggage not having arrived, they were obliged to wait for the grati-fication of their curiosity.

April 14—18th. I remained in this family, enjoying their hospitality, until the arrival of my other fellow-traveller, with whom I had to prosecute my journey a little further. Having thus had an opportunity of seeing the interior of a Chinese household, as one of themselves, I shall be the more particular in describing the domestic arrangements. The house was small: the front and central room, in which the guests were received, and where the family meals were eaten, was a sort of shed, open in front, and surrounded on the other three sides by the remaining rooms of the dwelling, one of which was a pig's-stye, and the other my sleeping apartment. Common earth served for the floor, about the evenness of which the inmates were not very particular; for every successive foot, on entering, in rainy weather, brought an additional quantity of earth with it, which the bringers were not careful to deposit in the places most needed; hence the passage from the entrance to the back apartment was higher, in consequence of the increased deposits of mud, than the more unfrequented parts of the room. As to the maintenance of cleanliness, such a floor afforded peculiar advantages; all liquids soaking at once into the earth, and smaller particles being easily trodden into it; while the bones, which fell occasionally from the table, were gladly carried away by the half-famished dogs. The stench arising from such a floor, however, combined with the pig's-stye on one side, and an uncleaned drain in front, was rather disagreeble to those unaccustomed to it; but being on a keeping with the rest of the establishment, it was not worth while remarking thereon. The room which was allotted for my reception was sufficiently secure to keep the weather out, and as it afforded the advantage of retirement, its other inconveniences were the more easily tolerated. The apartment appropriated to the females was not much better than the front room for the reception of visitors; for that too was open on one side, for the admission of air and light, while earth in its native state constituted the floor. Another apartment appropriated to lumber made up the dwelling. And this was the private residence of one of those tea-dealers, who are in the habit of visiting both Canton and Shanghae, to transact business with foreigners, though in a secondary capacity.

However poor the dwelling of these people, the provisions

of their table was by no means deficient. My hostess seemed to feel a pride in bringing forward something new and nice at every meal ; and when her husband was necessarily absent on business, she would press me to eat, and seemed dissatisfied if I did not devour the greater part of what was put on the table. Though forbidden by Chinese etiquette to sit down at the same table with a stranger, she would stand on one side, and frequently come from her inner apartment, to insist on my eating more ; as though she was afraid lest her husband should scold her, if he found his guest in indifferent keeping. Her unmarried daughter, who frequently went in and out of the front apartment, was always well-dressed, and had remarkably small feet, the shoes to fit on which were not above four inches long. Her principal employment seemed to be to feed the pigs, which she very industriously attended to, about every half hour ; affirming that it was not good to give pigs their food all at once, but that it was better to supply them with smaller portions and at more frequent intervals. Thus she might be seen all day long, hobbling through the front apartment, with the slush-bucket, wherewith to supply her pets, who evidently seemed to flourish under her care.

In one part of the house was a range of coppers, for firing and preparing the tea, which during the season, occupies the attention of this and almost every other household in the district, day and night, until the leaf is brought to a marketable condition. Then comes the work of picking, or selecting ; by which means, from the same mass of prepared leaves, the various kinds of tea are procured. from the commonest Hyson, to the finest Imperial. The tea plants grew around the dwelling, on every spot of ground that could be spared from rice-cultivation, not in regular plantations, but under the hedges, and along the pathways which separate the rice-fields, as though the tea-cultivation was only a secondary, and the five kinds of grain the principal, object of attention.

THE DISTRICT OF WOO-YUEN

The city of 婺源 Woó-yuên, which was only ten le, distant from the residence of my host, was founded in the 28th year of 玄宗 Heuen-tsung, of the 唐 Tâng dynasty (A. D. 741); when, from the circumstance of its lying on the river 婺 Woó, it received its present name. The city walls were built in the Súng dynasty, they are said to be 5,310 feet, or a little more than a mile in length; the river Woó flows round it on the north, east, and west, thus forming a moat on three sides of the city; the remaining side is defended by a moat, twenty feet broad, and eight deep. These defences had, however, fallen into decay, when in the 45th year of the reign of 嘉靖 Kёa-tsing, (A. D. 1,567,) on account of the incursions and depredations of some banditti from the Chĕ-kёang province, the then presiding magistrate had the walls and ditches repaired, and enlarged to the extent of more than 9,000 feet. The city has now five principal gates, defended by half-moon bastions, and three smaller ones, for the convenience of the people. The residence of the magistrate is near the centre of the city, on the north side of the main street leading from the east to the west gates; there are two arched gateways, with galleries over them, built across the main street, the one on the right and the other on the left hand of the mandarin's house, to grace the entrance of the abode of magistracy, or to inspire the people with some awe of their rulers. Near the west gate is the college and examination hall, adjoining the temple of 文帝 Wăn-té, the god of literature. In the southeast corner of the city, is an hospital for the reception of old and infirm persons, and on the north-east the barracks of the military.

The city of Woó-yuên is 210 le to the south-west of the prefectural city of Hang-chow. The territory embraced in this district is 220 le from east to west, and 150 from north

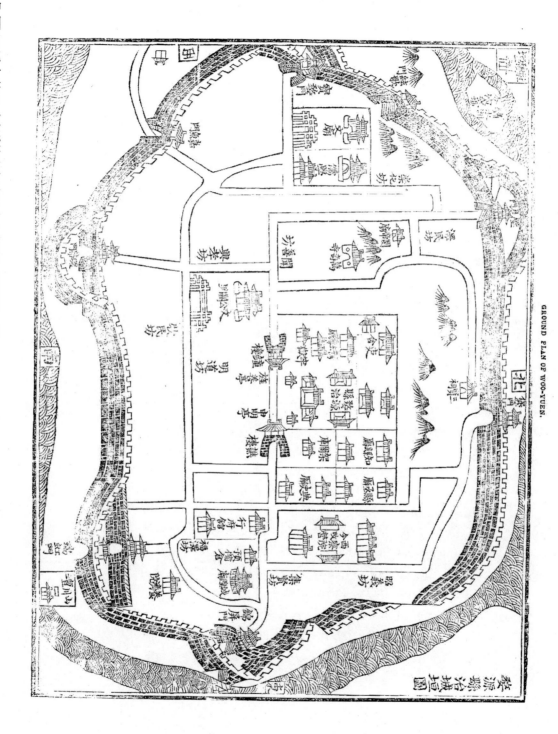

GROUND PLAN OF WOO-YUEN.

to south. It is 190 le from the city of 開化 K'hae-hwá, on the east, and 155 from that of 浮梁 Fôw-leâng, on the west. It is 105 le distant from the city of 德興 Tíh-hing, on the south, and 180 le from that of 休寧 Hew-ning, on the north.

In order to give the reader an idea of the resources and expenditure of the various districts, alluded to in this narrative ; we extract from the statistics of 徽州 Hwuy-chow, a detailed account of the capitation tax, the tax on fields and land, and the sums expended on various accounts, shewing what balance is left to to be carried to the Imperial Treasury.

CAPITATION TAX.

Originally estimated number of masters of families, in the district of Woó-yuên.	30,718
On striking the census, it was found, that there had been a subsequent increase of	2 193
Total	32,911
Deduct persons privileged and exempted from service ; such as, the descendants of Choo-foo-tsze, and the gentry, or the graduates of purchased rank, viz. Tsín-sze, Keu-jin, Kung-săng and Kĕen-săng, amounting to	673
Balance of persons really fit for service	32,238
Originally estimated number of persons belonging to Lŏ-ping and Tíh-hing districts, in Kĕang-se, who have purchased land on the borders of Woó-yuên district, and reside in farmsteads to manage their taxes	87
Total number of males in Woó-yuén district, and residents of purchased farmsteads	32,325

Taking each man at taels,	.10458455912	
gives for 32,238 men, taels		3371.5970169105 6
Taking each man at taels	.103	
gives for 87 men, taels		8 961
Total amount at which 32,325 men are estimated, taels		3380.55801691056

TAX ON FIELDS AND LANDS PAID IN MONEY.

	King.	mow.	fun.	le.	haou.
Originally estimated amount of rice-land	4,291	50	1	6	9
Dry land, 735 king, 97 mow, 7 fun, 4 le, 8 haou, allowing each mow of dry land an average of 6 fun, 1 le, 5 haou of rice-fields	452	62	6	1	5
Hills, 1,215 king, 22 mow, 3 fun, 3 le, 6 haou, allowing an average of 2 fun, 2 le, 2 haou, of rice-land per mow	269	77	9	5	8
Embankments, 16 king, 47 mow, 2 fun, 5 le, 8 haou, allowing an average of one mow of rice-land, per mow	16	47	2	5	8
Total rice-land, and averages of ditto, allowed on dry land hills, and embankments	5,030	38	0	0	02

N. B. A Chinese mow is the sixth part of an English acre, and 100 mow make a king.

Estimating each mow at taels

.674913134436 Total taels 33,950.6953455573

Original estimate of vassalage fees, payable on the rice-land, of the farmsteads, purchased within the border of Woó-yuên, by the inhabitants of Lŏ-ping and Tih-hing districts, in Kéang-se, which are not subject to grain and village tax, taels .168398737 per mow of rice-land. There being altogether 75 king, 54 mow, 2 fun, 5 le, 2 haou, of such rice-land, it will pay taels   127.14552

Brought forward   34,077.8408655573

Each mow of dry land pays taels .005 ; there being total land, 4 king, 37 mow, 6 fun, 3 le, 2 haou, it will pay   taels   2.18916

Each mow of hill-ground pays taels .005 ; there being total hill-ground, 8 king, 89 mow, 4 fun, 5 le, 6 haou, it will pay   taels   4.44728

Each mow of embankment pays taels .01; there being total embankments 18 mow, 4 le, 2 haou, 2 sze, it will pay   taels   .180422

Total amount obtained from rice-land and vassalage fees   taels   34,084.6567275573

Deduct cultivated lands belonging to the descendants of Choo-foo-tsze, the literati, the Lëen-hwuy store, and such like official purposes, amounting to 20 king, 40 mow, 1 fun, 1 le, exempting each mow at the rate of taels .02614765627, making a total deduction of   taels   53.344095329897

Balance estimated at   taels   34,031.3126322227403

TAX ON LAND PAID IN KIND.

Estimating each mow at .01309284786 shĭh or peculs of rice, gives for 503,038 mow, a total of rice   shĭh   6586.2

Estimating each mow at .00072559131 shĭh or peculs of yellow peas, gives for 503,038 mow, a total of peas   shĭh   365.

                       6951.2

A shĭh, or pecul is 133⅓ lbs. avoirdupois.

SUMS SENT UP TO THE PROVINCIAL CAPITAL FOR SUNDRY CHARITABLE PURPOSES.

Original estimate for Woó-yuên district,   taels   30.

T

Proceeds of rent of the Lëën-hwuy fields,   88.6675
Less estimated expenditure for clothes,
   fuel, and coffins to the destitute and
   poor, which is put to the general account,   30.0000
             Balance   taels   58.6675

(Note. See expenditure for sundries, not placed to general account.)

EXPENSES ON FORWARDING TAX TO THE PROVINCIAL CAPITAL.

Regular sum for Woó-yuên district, taels 31,504.95607869321
For porterage money for the above, taels 291.261049936675
For materials for yearly manufacture of
   silk piece-goods, bedding, cushions, taels 261.9838
For gifts to carrying porters, loss on
   exchange, and expenses,   taels   75.6769992
             Total taels   628.921849136675

Here follows an enumeration of additions to, and deductions from this sum, made in different reigns, and upon various accounts.

SUM SENT UP TO THE PROVINCIAL CAPITAL, FOR THE PURCHASE OF VARIOUS ARTICLES.

Originally-estimated sum for Woó-yuên
   district,   taels 166.513813357127
Bedding and cushions   15.897
Porterage and loss by exchange   .5712
             Total taels   182.982013357127

Here follows an enumeration of different articles, the combined value of which makes the above sum : viz. vermilion, cinnabar, black plums, indigo, Tung oil, tutenague, hempen cloth, tea, yellow wax, and white wax. These different articles are sent one year in kind, and another year in money; in the years 'when the latter is sent, the district magistrate takes the value 'of the qualities originally fixed, the porterage and the making up of loss in exchange, in money, and 'sends 'it 'in, whatsoever the amount may be; and in the years, wherein the articles are sent' in kind, the originally-fixed values are entered into the estimate-papers, and the purchases of the articles are then made, according to the market-value current through the whole province.

EXPENSES ON THE TRANSPORT OF RICE.

Original estimate for Woó-yuên district, of Këang-nân Setsang rice, shǐh 899.	Attendants in charge, sifting, drying, and carriage, taels 35.96
Waste 89.9	Attendants in charge,
Do. Këang-nan' Shwuy-ting rice shǐh 5597.3	sifting, 'drying, and carriage, taels 183.5211
Total rice shǐh 6586.2	Total taels 174.4811

EXPENSE ON THE TRANSPORT OF PEAS.

The transport from Woó-yuên district was originally in Këang-nan *Kung-yung-koo* hemp, but it is now changed to 365 shǐh of yellow peas; and the gifts to attendants in charge, with transport and carriage expenses, amount to 29 taels 2 mace.

TRANSPORT EXPENSES OF MONEY SENT UP TO TREASURY.

Share of Woó-yuên district taels 157.2.

EXPENSES OF OFFICERS AND ATTENDANTS.

Total expenses of officers of the Woó-yuên district, taels 1432.376.

中國內地一瞥：在絲茶產區的一次旅行期間所見

In the above are included the salary of the sub-
assistant prefect of Hwuy-chow-foò   Taels 60.

Card-paper	20.	
Two door-keepers	12.	
Eight policemen	48.	
Twelve runners in the van of processions	72.	
Two lantern-bearers	12.	
Seven chair, umbrella and fan-bearers	42.	266.
Salary of district magistrate	45.	
Card-paper	20.	
Two door-keepers	12.	
Sixteen van-runners	96.	
Eight horse-police, including fodder	134.4	
Fifty militia	300.	
Four lantern-bearers	24.	
Eight gaol inspectors and lictors	48.	
Repair of granaries and gaols	20.	
Seven chair, umbrella, and fan-bearers	42.	
Four treasury-keepers	24.	
Four Tow-keihs	24.	789.4
Salary of assistant magistrate of district	40.	
One door-keeper	6.	
Four van-runners	24.	
One horse-keeper	6.	76.
Salary of secretary of the district magistrate	31.52	
One door-keeper	6.	
Four van-runners	24.	
One horse-keeper	6.	67.52
Salary of instructor and sub-instructor of district	31.52	
Three *tae-ting* bearers	36.	
Three door-keepers	21.6	
Fodder for horses	6.	
Incense and candles	7.776	102.896
		1301.816

一七九

Carried forward Taels		1301.816
Salary of police inspector, Tae-pĭh-sze	31.52	
Two van-runners	12.	
Salary of police-inspector of Hang-tsun-sze	31.52	
Two van-runners	12.	
Salary of police-inspector of Ta-yung-sze	31.52	
Two van-runners	12.	130.56
		1432.376

MONEY SENT TO GOVERNOR TO EXPEND.

Woó-yuên district, original estimate, for
pay and labour   taels   89.978938732

MONEY SENT TO LITERARY CHANCELLOR TO EXPEND.

Woó-yuên district, original estimate, for
presents, &c.   taels   15.10492

Expenses of attendants who bear this sum   .7

taels   15.80492

MONEY SENT TO COMMISSIONER OF FINANCE TO EXPEND.

Woó-yuên district, original estimate   taels   53.391

Expenses of attendants who bear this sum   1.135

taels   54,526

In this is included, for examination-shed at Nan-hing,
taels 49.8793 ; assistance in defraying pay and food of persons required in the examinations of Shang-yuen, and Këang-
ning, taels 1.8467 ; expenses of bearers of the money, taels
1.1 ; towards expenses of visit of treasurer to imperial levee,
1.367 ; offer of what is thought necessary to the military
Keu-jin of Tae-ping foo, tael 1.9117 ; expenses of bearers of
the money, tael .035.

MONEY SENT TO THE PREFECTURE TO BE EXPENDED.

Woó-yuên district share originally laid
down   taels   983.7541648

Here are enumerated sundry little expenses, which combined make up this sum.

Woó-yuên district; originally fixed sum, taels 2188.36839
In this sum are included, saluting, and bullock to meet
the spring, taels 15. Support of 20 *Sew-tsae*, taels 124;
banners, tablet, wine, and expenses of one *Kung-săng*, every
two years, taels 33.5, payable per year; paper and gifts towards quarterly examinations of *Sew-tsae* by the literary
district officers, taels 30; providing of rewards necessary for
the general examination of new candidates and picked
scholars, by the literary chancellor, and sending newly entered *Sew-tsae* to the literary officers' office, gilt flowers, and
red cloth, taels 30. per year; purchase and sending of wine
and eatables to the civil and military *Keu-jin* of the metro-
politan examination, taels 40.664 per year; expenses and
feasting at the triennial examinations for *Keu-jin*, by the district literary officers, taels 43.575; almanac at the close of the
year, taels 12; money for the vernal and autumnal sacrifices at
the Confucian temple, and the fanes of the descendants of the
sage, of Choo-wei-chae and Choo-foo-tsze, of famous minis-
ters and village worthies, at the altars of the hills and streams,
of the land and grain, and of the city; the sacrifices to the
ground, the banners at the Shwang-këang term, taels, 139.9;
village banquets, two per annum, taels 8; treasury-keeper
of fane of Choo-foo-tsze, board and wages, taels 3.6; two
door-keepers of court of learned men in ditto, taels 7.2; five
chair and umbrella-bearers, taels 36. twelve archers of Ta-
pǐh-sze, taels 43.2; twelve archers of Hung-tsun-sze, taels
43.2; twelve archers of Ta-yung-sze, taels 43.2; sixty-three
foot soldiers, taels 453.6; ditto additional for intercalary
months, taels 15.12; newly-fixed annual allowances for pay
and provision of men and horses engaged in the postage depart-

ment, including intercalary month additions, taels 280.14 ; (this is a sum erased elsewhere, and appropriated to be given to attendants and horses); repair of the college and the literary officers' quarters, taels 30 ; repair of city walls, taels 30 ; ferrymen at all the ferries, wages and food, taels 61.5 ; tablets, banners, and triumphal gateways, in honour of successful *Keu-jin*, taels 79.33333 per annum; same for *Tsin-sze*, taels 62; same for military *Keu-jin*, taels 13.33333 per annum ; picked graduates, taels 40 per annum ; rice for storage to give to the poor, taels 329.4 ; do. intercalary months, taels 5.4 ; hospital for charity, clothes, fire-wood, and coffins, for the destitute and old, taels 145.

MONEY SENT TO PROVINCIAL CAPITAL FOR EXPENDITURE, FOR SUNDRIES NOT PUT TO GENERAL ACCOUNT.

Woó-yuên district prescribed amount payable

taels 171.658544

In this are included the proceeds of rent of the Lëên-hwuy fields, taels 88.6675, less taels 30. already entered to general account, for providing clothing, fuel, and coffins, to the poor and destitute, the balance taels 58.6675, being left in the district for charitable purposes ; also Tsëang-pan, taels 112.991044, which is sent to the treasurer as duties.

Some things are worthy of remark, in the above estimate. First. The whole income in money arising from the Woóyuên district appears to be 34,031 taels of silver, together with 6,586 peculs of rice, and 365 peculs of peas, paid in kind. Out of the income in money, there are taken certain sums for salaries of officials and other charges, while only 31,504 taels are forwarded to the provincial capital from this rich district. Secondly. the whole amount paid in salaries to the officers of the district appears to be but 1,432 taels: we say *appears*, for the fact is really not so. It is not to be supposed that the magistrates of such an extensive and rich district as Woó-yuên should be content with 60 and 45 taels annually ; neither are they.   The way in which they make their money is by charging for inferior officers and assistants, without paying them ; by concealing from the government the amount of cultivated fields ; by exacting from the cultivators more than the amount sent in ; and by levying toll on articles, and in a way, not specified in the tariff.   To instance only one thing : it is well-known that Woó-yuên produces large quantities of the best green teas.   And yet in the statistical account of the district, published and intended for the eye of government, there is not one word said about *tea*.   Judging from this record, a stranger would not imagine that a single leaf of tea was exported from Woó-yuên.   The English merchants in Shanghae best know how many chops of tea they obtain from this district every year ; and the writer has been informed on the spot, that upwards of 20,000 taels are annually exacted from the tea-merchants as they export this article from the district, by regular levies of so much per pecul.   If however this were to be complained of to the Chinese Government, as an improper levying of transit duties, they would reply that according to the information before them, there was no such thing as tea grown in Woó-yuên. Besides all this, the magistrates all over China make *immense sums* by receiving bribes, to influence them in judicial proceedings.

Thirdly. The ostensible salary of the magistrates being so low, the emperos is apt to imagine, that his government is carried on on the most economical plan ; and when he becomes angry with a magistrate, and mulcts him in a whole year's pay, he fancies that he has nearly deprived the poor wretch of subsistence ; whereas it is only a thousandth part of his real income.   Fourthly, it is ridiculous to observe, how particularly the small items for articles used in sacrifice, for incence and presents to literary graduates are specified, as if to lead the government to imagine, that a large proportion of the income of the state was expended in these charitable and pious purposes ; whereas the proportion of sums thus expended is extremely insignificant, compared with what is obtained by means of bribery and corruption.

CONTINUATION OF JOURNAL.

Whilst residing in the house of one of my guides, near Woó-yuện, I heard one evening a great lamentation, and on inquiring the cause, found, that an old woman, related to the family, had lost by death her intended son-in-law. As the marriage between the young people had not been concluded, nor was intended to be for several years, I wondered that so much grief should be manifested, regarding a person who was not at the time related to the family. To this the reply was made, that the young man just deceased had been taken into the family when quite an infant, and kept and fed there all his life long, with the expectation of being married to a daughter of the parties, of the same age with himself. Having nursed, educated, and cared for him, during the last twenty years, the old people had begun to look upon him as their son, and felt for him accordingly. I asked, how it came to pass, that the boy was thus obtained in his infancy, having always understood that daughters only, being lightly valued by their parents, were passed over during infancy nto other households, but never knew that sons were thus disposed of. My informant then said, that there was an exchange in this case ; the one family having two sons, and the other two daughters born, within a few years of each other ; and thus to suit the convenience of both, this family parted with a daughter, to become the future bride of one of the sons of that family ; while the other son of that family was transferred, to become the future bridegroom of the remaining daughter of this. This arrangement is certainly

U

preferable to the one common in the south of China, of making away with superfluous daughters, when they increase, in their wretched parent's estimation, too rapidly; but still, under this system of exchange, little account is taken of the future predilections of the young people, who must marry the persons designated for them in infancy, whether they like them or not. Such being the circumstances of the case, I asked again, why the parties, living under one roof, and now grown up to a marriageable period, were not forthwith united; and was informed, that the expenses necessary to arrange the marriage ceremonies were still wanting, and the family did not know when they should be in circumstances to enable them to complete the nuptials. Thus young people in China, are not only affianced in infancy, to parties of whom they can know nothing; but are kept when marriageable, and the prize, if it be one, almost within their grasp, year after year, in a state of single blessedness, because the funds necessary to celebrate the wedding, according to the foolish vanity of the parents, are not forthcoming. In the mean time, the intended bridegroom dies, and the affianced bride has to wait, perhaps, until some one else should choose to ask her in marriage. The grief of the old lady referred to above, was most likely on account of the serious loss they had incurred, in expending so much money to so little purpose.

April 19th. My former guide having arrived and arranged his business in Woó-yuên, we set out for the district of 浮梁 Fôw-lëâng, where the moral reformers formerly spoken of resided. We started on foot, having only one or two coolies to transport our luggage. During the first few miles of our journey, we wound our way among the low hills, to the northward and westward of the city. The soil was here of a light colour, and the rocks consisted of recent formations of sand and stone. Wherever a low or level place could be found, the Chinese had taken advantage of it for rice-cultivation, which seems to them of first importance; while here and there only a strip of ground was devoted to the tea-plant. About ten le from the city, we came to a considerable hill, called 吳坑山 Woŏ-k'hang-shan, at the foot of which was a small village, where we stopped to take tea. The scenery about this was very romantic, and the ascent though steep, was in some degree pleasant, as affording us an extensive view of the surrounding country. Before we had reached the top, we were glad to rest, and a small house of refreshment afforded us the desired opportunity. The higher ground of the hill was covered with crops of barley, and a plantation of small shrubs, very regularly disposed, which I took to be tea. At the top of the hill, we had a view of the country, on the opposite side, exhibiting a lovely interchange of hill and dale, in a high state of cultivation. The pleasure of our journey was, however, soon interrupted by a shower of rain, which necessitated a resort to umbrellas and clogs : the one tiring the hands, and the other crippling the feet. Descending again to the plains, we found the tea-plant more plentiful, and the frequency of villages, together with the paved roads, and well-built sheds over them, indicated the wealth of the region, and the attention of its inhabitants to the wants of the traveller. After a toilsome journey of about forty le, we came, wet and tired, to a village, where we sought lodgings for the night.

A poor inn, by the side of the way, soon appeared, which promised us the accommodation we desired ; we accordingly turned in thither, and sitting down, called for some tea. The room into which we entered, being the principal one of the house, was about ten feet square. The host had to be roused from his sleep, which appeared to annoy him not a little, in order to attend to his guests. His wife, however, was more attentive, and kindling a fire, soon procured us warm water. A party, which had but recently preceded us, had left the benches and table in a most filthy condition ; covered with the refuse of rice and vegetables, mixed with grease and dirt, which the landlady vainly attempted to brush away. The tea she gave us, which in a country a-bounding with the plant, was inexcusably bad and sparse, was put into one of the basins, previously used for the rice and vegetables of the former guests ; this made it so nau-seous, that the Chinaman's stomach could scarcely bear it. This might have been remedied by not partaking of so dis-gusting a beverage; but we were soon to be annoyed in another way, from which we could not so easily escape. The little room we occupied was, after a while, crowded by other guests; first a dealer in fowls, with his stock in trade, filling up the whole of one side of the chamber; the noise and stench arising from these was almost intolerable. Then entered a couple of travelling tinkers, with their bel-lows, furnaces, tools, pots, and pans, all requiring space in the confined apartment. After that, came two or three fel-lows, far less respectable than either of the former ; being idle vagrants, who were moving about from place to place, to see what could be picked up to their advantage. The garrulity and strife of these various parties, were sufficiently annoying, to wet and jaded travellers ; but the prospect of being fallen upon and robbed, under some vain pretext, so easily got up by these gentry, made us emphatically desire their room, rather than their company. There was, however, no resource, but to bear it and be still. The dinner was common to all, consisting of rice, with soup, made of pulse-jelly, (a preparation so heavy, that it sinks in the water,) and portions of the putrid mustard-vegetable to tempt it down. The approach of night under these circumstances was wel-come, and when the landlady thought proper to announce that the beds were ready, we were glad to retire. Here, however, our annoyances had only to begin. The upper room assigned to myself, my guide, and cooly, was six feet square, and only as many high ; forming a kind of box, in which we had to make ourselves comfortable for the night. It had, however, a door, having closed which, and spread our mats on the floor, we lay down, thinking we should at any rate be alone till the morning. Vain expectation! for we had no sooner put out the light, and covered ourselves over with our quilts, than we were attacked at once, by untold millions, who beset us in every part of the body, and by their sharp bites and never-ceasing onsets, soon convinced us that rest for the night was impossible. The tinkers and poulterers, in the adjoining apartment, seemed to be used to such kind of things, as they slept soundly and comfortably through it all.

April 20th. Leaving our uncomfortable abode, we started on our journey, and soon found, in the freshness of the air, and the beauty of natural scenery, some compensation for the inconvenience suffered the previous evening, by too near a contact with the busy haunts of men. One of the hills ascended this day was called 天堂山 T'hëen-tâng-shan, the hill of paradise ; and in many respects it seemed not to belie its name. The prospect presented was grand and extensive, and the fertility of the soil afforded the conveniences of life at an easy rate to those who inhabited those secluded regions. A neighbouring hill, called 船槽嶺 Chuên-tsaôu-ling, or dry dock hill, derives it name from five grooves in the top of the hill, bearing some fancied resemblance to dry docks. Behind the hill is a stone-screen, or rocky precipice, flanked on either side by hills, called 日山 Jíh-shan, and 月山 Yuĕ-shan, sun and moon hills. The older inhabitants say, that the vallies which lie between these were formerly occupied by water, over which people had to be ferried in boats ; the water is now, however, dried up, and the space formerly covered by it is laid out in cultivated ground. Underneath the precipice is a cave, which the natives say, connects itself with the Po-yang lake, in Këang-se. Lime-stone is, however, dug from the cave, which doubtless yields much more profit to the people. than their fabulous inventions about under-ground communications. After crossing several of these hills, we arrived in the evening at 項村司 Hëang-tsún-sze, where we put up for the night at an inn, a little better than the one occupied on the preceding evening.

April 21st. We started on our journey over another range of hills, called 風爐嶺 Fung-loo-ling, the top of which is crowned by various peaks, interspersed with small pools, of which the natives avail themselves to irrigate their rice-fields. There is also a hill in this direction, called 三靈山 San-ling-shan, the mount of the three spiritual ones, so named, because in the 晋 Tsín dynasty, three adherents of the Taou sect, pursued their study of alchymy here. One of the hills, which we passed over during this day's march, was remarkable for being exceedingly bare on one side, and well-wooded on the other ; owing, as I understood, to the one side of the hill, having been let to a contractor for wood, who, regardless of the interests of those who should occupy it when his lease was expired, cleared away every stick and shrub, which the hill produced. The other side we observed, as we descended, was not only well-wooded, but covered with a large plantation of tea shrubs, over the whole declivity. At the foot of the hill, was a considerable village, where we stopped at an inn, for the sake of refreshment ; but could procure nothing, except some cold rice, which was so unpalatable, that I could not eat it. My guide also fancied, that he saw some one in the room eyeing me with rather too curious a gaze, whereupon we abruptly left, and proceeded on our journey. The path we pursued, led us through a most romantic valley, along the bottom of which dashed a foaming torrent, the whiteness of whose spray contrasted beautifully with the black rocks over which it hurried, in its headlong way towards the south-west, where it joins the river Woo, and proceeds in concert with its waters

to the Po-yang lake. We now ascended the 滘嶺 Keaou-
ling, and from thence proceeded to the 潹源山 Júy-yuên-
shan, so called from its giving a name to the romantic
torrent just described. This hill is said, by the Chinese, to
be upwards of 3,000 feet high, and forms the boundary
between the districts of 婺源 Woó-yuên and 浮梁 Fôw-
lëâng. In the Súng dynasty, it is said, that this hill was
frequented by golden pheasants, hence it is also called, the
Golden Pheasant hill. It was with much difficulty, that
we toiled to the top of this mountain, but when once there,
the labour was sufficiently compensated, by the glorious
prospect which presented itself of the 浮梁 Fôw-lëâng
district of 江西 Këang-se province; as its extensive
rice-fields, interspersed with tea-plantations, stretched themselves as far as the eye could reach, glowing with the reflection of the western sun. The descent was easy and pleasant, but the further journey, of more than twenty le, along
uneven roads and bye-ways, after the darkness had set in,
was but labour and sorrow; until arriving at the hospitable residence of my guide's friends, I was completely overcome by fatigue, and glad to avail myself of the earliest
opportunity to rest myself. The politeness and cordiality
of these friends, on meeting after a long separation, presented a striking contrast, with the coldness and indifference manifested by the family of my former guide, on wel-
coming home their lord and master. The real affection was
doubtless greater in the latter case than in the former, but
it is not usual with the Chinese to exhibit their domestic feel-
ings; while in the intercourse of friends, polite attentions are
fully expected, and must be abundantly displayed. Tired
as I was, the evening was not allowed to pass away, without
a long conversation and discussion with various learned
men of the reforming school, previously alluded to; and the
opportunity was not lost of unfolding to them a general view
of religious truth, including the being and perfections of the

中國內地一瞥：在絲茶產區的一次旅行期間所見

Deity, the creation, fall, and redemption of the world, and ending with a free declaration of the internal peace and happy prospects of those who knew and embraced these glorious truths. An impression was produced in favour of the speaker, conclusive at least of his sincerity in the maintenance of his own views, however much they might demur to the adoption of them. Up to that time, no one but the guide supposed, that there was anything peculiar in the speaker's origin. At length overcome with travelling and talking, I begged to retire, and was shewn into a tolerable room and bed, far better than any which I had occupied for some time.

April 22d. Awoke this morning with a grievous pain in one of my feet, which if caused by a fit of the gout, was brought on most certainly by any thing but ease and good living. It was never the less sharp on this account, and had to be borne with patience, until it had run its course, alleviated occasionally by the few remedies which I had fortunately brought with me.

April 23—28. These days were spent in the house of my guide's friend : who though informed, after the first day of the character of his guest, was not the less kind and attentive ; indeed, after the first surprise was over, he appeared rather pleased than otherwise to have a foreigner in his house, putting a variety of questions to me regarding my country, its distance from China, extent of dominion, the amount of population, character of the inhabitants, religion, literature, manners, customs, &c. Frequent discussions were held on religious subjects with him, and the rest of the school of reformers, who are congregated hereabouts. The prevailing character of their minds appeared to be an earnest desire to carry out the system of Confucius, as they thought, in its genuineness, free from that atheistic gloss which the Commentators of the Súng dynasty had put upon it ; and an especial aim to cultivate the virtues of benevolence and righteousness as laid down by him. Some of their ob-

一九一

servations and sentiments regarding self-examination, victory over evil desires, constant vigilance, searching after their own errors, and ingenuous confession of them when ascertained, were tolerably good, and would not have disgraced a Christian moralist. But while they had some sense of sin, they had of course no idea of an atonement, and were utterly in the dark as to the manner in which their sins could be pardoned, or the Divine Being reconciled. Their prevailing errors appeared to be, too great a veneration for the sages, whom they actually idolized, and in many instances put upon a level with the Author of wisdom ; as well as too high an estimation of their deceased parents and ancestors, to whom they paid divine honours, and from whom they expected protection and every blessing. It was found very difficult to give them any idea of the difference between the veneration and respect due to parents, and the worship which was demanded by the Supreme Author of our being. The Chinese term for worship being one which applies to all sorts of obeisance and compliment, it sounds strange in their ears to be told that they must not 拜 paé, that is, behave civilly towards their parents and brethren. But as these subjects are familiar to those well-acquainted with Chinese matters, and are not very interesting to others, we shall pass over the discussions then held ; and content ourselves with observing generally, that the matter took very fast hold of one of the parties, who could not rest in his mind, until he had discovered where the truth lay. He was heard praying, in the dead of night, very earnestly, to the Giver of light, that he might be directed in his search after truth, and it is pleasing to add, that, as the result proved, he did not pray in vain.

Having some leisure during my stay at this place, I availed myself of the opportunity thus afforded, and drew up a brief summary of the Christian religion, for the information of the aged instructor of this college, who was too unwell to

中國內地一瞥：在絲茶產區的一次旅行期間所見

pay me a visit. This treatise, amounting to 30 or more pages, was afterwards printed and many thousands of it circulated through all parts of the country.

Whilst I was living at the house of my guide's friend, a circumstance occurred which greatly alarmed those who had undertaken to see me safely conveyed through the country. After sitting at table some time, engaged in discussion, I rose, and retired to the bed-room; where, in a few minutes afterward, I observed my guide coming in, with my cue in his hand. It had dropped off, whilst I was sitting in the chair, and had of course been left behind. My guide was very much agitated as he brought in the detached cue, and I could not help sympathizing with him. He said, that he had just escaped a fearful danger, for had the cue become loose, and fallen off during our previous march, or at any one of the numerous inns and tea-shops at which we put up, we could not have prevented our secret from being discovered; which would have been much more detrimental to him than it would to me; inasmuch as he would thus have been convicted of bringing a foreigner into the country: and the result would have been his imprisonment and ruin. He felt thankful, however, that the accident had occured in a friend's house, and proceeded as speedily as possible to repair the damage. This he did, by unwinding the locks of hair, and tying them separately with thread on to the locks of my own hair, behind the crown. His fear, lest another accident of the kind should happen, made him tie the knots so much the faster, thus greatly inconveniencing the wearer of the cue, by the tightness with which it was attached. This, however, was cheerfully borne, and greater care was of course taken in future, lest the like mishap should occur in a more public place, where the evil might be irreparable.

On another occasion, whilst sitting alone in the front room, a stranger entered, who without ceremony sat down and began to converse. I soon perceived that he was a for-,

tune-teller, who pretended to ascertain the future condition
of individuals by the examination of their physiognomy. I
could see, after a while, that he was surveying mine ; and as
mine, under the circumstances, would not bear too close an inspection, I got up and retired into the inner apartment. Soon
after, my host entering was accosted by the fortune-teller, who,
referring to me, said that 容貌非凡 yûng maóu fei fân, the
countenance was not of the common order. This startled
my host, who got rid of him as soon as posible, and from that
time took care that the outer gate of the premises was carefully barred. Thus I was immured for some days, between the
four walls of my host's premises, and in the loneliness thus
experienced began to think of the deprivation of society which
some missionaries experience for years ; who, in order to re-
side in China without molestation, are obliged to seclude
themselves from all observation, and keep as much within
doors as possible. I was not entirely abridged of liberty,
however, as I availed myself of a back door which remained
open, to take frequent walks into the woods and fields, where
I enjoyed the fresh air, and the surrounding scenery.

The house where I resided was situated in a widely-ex-
tended plain, surrounded by lofty mountains ; one of these
was the famous 高嶺 Kaou-ling, abounding in the purest
felspar, whence the clay is obtained of which most of the
porcelain used in China is made. The white quarries
were visible from the plain just outside my host's dwelling.
An account of the porcelain manufactory, where this same
Kaou-ling is spoken of, may be found in Morrison's English
and Chinese Dictionary, under the head " Porcelain," and
in Davis's Chinese, Vol. II. chap. 17. With reference to those
accounts, however, I may be allowed to make one observation,
with the view of correcting any mistake about the spot, from
which the best porcelain clay is obtained. Both Morrison
and Davis say, that the principal part of the clay is obtained from the district of 浮梁 Fôw-lëâng, in the prefec-

ture of 饒州 Yaou-chow, in Këang-se; but that the best kind is found in the district of 祁門 Kè-mûn, in 徽州 Hwuy-chow, in Këang-nan; from which the reader might infer that two distinct regions produced this substance, situated in different provinces: whereas 祁門 Kè-mûn is the district of Hwuy-chow which borders closely upon 浮梁 Fôw-lëâng, separated only by a chain of hills, on the southern side of which hills the valuable clay in question is found; so that although the hill in which the best clay is met with is nominally in another district and province, it is really but a few miles from the spot, where the larger mass of it occurs, constituting in fact but one region.

COURSE HOMEWARD.

Having finished what business I had to attend to in Këang-se, I began to think of returning; and much discussion took place, as to the best route to be taken. One course proposed was southerly and then easterly; viz. across a chain of hills to 開化 K'hae-hwá, thence along the 衢河 Keu-hô, to 衢州 Keu-chow; afterwards following the course of this river to 嚴州 Yên-chow, and 亢州 Haug-chow; and from thence to Shang-hae. The chief obstacle, however, that deterred my companion from taking this route was the difficulty of passing the troublesome custom-house at Hang-chow. The officers stationed there are said to be most annoying, examining every part of a traveller's baggage, and looking narrowly after every thing strange and unusual; so that there was great danger of their discovering our secret, and subjecting us to much inconvenience. for the sake of getting what they could out of us. The other course was to proceed northward, until we came to the Yang-tsze-këang, down which we might proceed leisurely, until we arrived at Nan-king and Soo-chow, from which place we might soon get to Shang-hae. There were custom-houses, it appears, on this route, also, but the officers stationed there were by no means so annoying, nor so much dreaded by travellers as those at Hang-chow, whose ill-fame had spread all over this part of the empire. It was therefore decided that we should take the course last described.

April 29th. Having thanked our kind host, who accompanied us part of the way, we set off this afternoon for 鵝蛋鎮 Gnò-tan-chin, or Goose-egg village ; where the brother of my guide resided. We put up for the night at his shop, in which the combined business of apothecary, grocer, pork-butcher, dyer, and pulse-jelly-maker was carried on. Such a heterogeneous mixture of trades might be supposed to have yielded some profit ; but, whether owing to improvident outlay or bad management, the business, once flourishing, was now in a declining state ; and the chief customers appeared to be the rats, who visiting the shop by night, instead of by day, greatly annoyed me as I lay on one of the counters. The keeper of it did not appear to notice his guest very particularly ; for when on a later occasion he was met by the writer in Shanghae, and asked if he had ever seen the individual addressing him before, declared again and again that he had never had that pleasure ; much to the amusement of some standing by who knew the circumstances of the case.

April 30th. Having engaged a couple of sedans, and a cooly to carry a little luggage, we started this morning in a northerly direction, on our way back. After proceeding a few miles we crossed the river that leads to 景德鎮 King-tĭh-chin, the great pottery of China, where two or three hundred furnaces, are constantly burning, and several hundred thousand workmen are employed. Had it consisted with my guide's idea of what was necessary for the safety of his fellow-traveller, I should have rejoiced to avail myself of this opportunity to visit one of the most important manufactories of the empire ; but the least display of curiosity on my part was sufficient to awaken his suspicions and fears ; on which account I thought it better to pass on. After crossing the stream in question, we began to ascend a portion of the famous 高嶺 Kaou-ling hill, up the greatest part of which the coolies bore us without complaining, until we thought it better to relieve them of their burthen by walking. Unfortunately the road we took did not bring us near the quarries. The ground was however strewed all over with fragments of felspar and quartz, and people were frequently observed carrying loads of stone to the neighbourhood of the streams, where they could either pound it, or transport it to the place of trade. Many of the pathways along which we passed appeared exceedingly perilous, passing along the edges of cliffs, and turning suddenly at the heads of deep gullies, where one slip of the foot might have precipitated us, chairs and all, into the abyss that yawned beneath. The coolies, however, were very sure-footed, and though we were sometimes held over deep gulfs, with one bearer on one side and the other on its opposite, having nothing but the long poles of the sedan to keep us from falling into the yawning cavity, yet by the good Providence of God we were carried over in safety.

Descending the heights, we crossed two branches of a broad stream called the 渭水 Wei-shwùy, which was here flowing in a south-westerly direction. There appeared to be considerable traffic on these rivers ; the boats with earths and minerals floating merrily down the tide ; while those with provisions and necessaries for the workmen had to be drawn up with extreme toil, and at a very slow rate. On crossing this river, we took advantage of a gratuitous ferry-boat; a notice on the river side informed us, that the benevolent in that region had subscribed together for the purpose of assisting travellers across the stream, and that as the boat was purchased and the boatman's wages paid out of this fund, there was no necessity for passengers to pay anything. According to the nature of things, one might have expected that the ferry-man, not being overlooked by his employers, would be indifferent to his duty, and rather hold his office in the light of a sinecure ; but no such thing ; there was the old gentlemen at his post, from morning till night, ever ready to ply his oar ; and after ferrying over a boat-load of passengers, he kindly wished them a pleasant journey, and put back to ferry the next batch, who were waiting to cross the stream. This is benevolence, not in theory only, but in practice.

REGION OF PORCELAIN CLAY.

Finding an inn at the village on the north side of the stream, we turned in and put up for the night. Here we soon had convincing proof that we were in a busy and productive country. On every side we perceived water-mills at work, and were kept awake by the pounding of the wooden hammers, worked by the wheels which the ever-flowing waters turned. Here, as we read in the account of 景德鎮 King-tih-chin, partly translated by Dr. Morrison, "The people who procure the 白不子 Pih-tun-tszè, avail themselves of 溪流 K'hè-lêw mountain streams, where they erect 水碓 water pestles, to 舂之 pound it. After pounding the stone, they 澄洗淘淨製如磚式 目白不 wash and scour it quite clean, and moulding it into the form of bricks, call it 白不 white tun. The 黄不 yellow tun clods are 大而堅 large and hard. The white tun, however, is 稍鬆細 rather loose and fine. At present the very best tun is that produced in 壽溪塢 Shòw-k'he-woo, and all dealers, when they come to market, call their own commodities 我壽溪不 my Shòw-k'he-tun."

May 1st. We proceeded on our journey this morning, and soon came to the hill of 吳嶺 Woò-ling, from which the 壽溪 Shòw-k'he mentioned above probably takes its rise. We were here met by a couple of Chinese sportsmen, with matchlocks on their shoulders, preceded by a brace of dogs, and going forth to see what game they could find. They were hearty healthy-looking men, and appeared to enjoy the prospect of a day's sport, as did also their companions. Proceeding onwards, we crossed the 小北港 Seaòu-pĭh-këàng, a stream flowing in a south-westerly direction, which joins the 渭水 Wei-shwùy, where the city of 浮梁 Fôw-lëàng is situated, and from whence their united waters flow on past 景德鎮 King-tĭh-chin, into the Po-yang lake. After this we crossed another range of hills, called the 搖嶺 Yaôu-ling; and passed through a village named 大惟舖 Tá-wei-poò, situated on the borders of Këang-se, from whence proceeding northward, we soon arrived at 橫頭村 Hwăng-t'hôw-tsún, in the province of Këang-nan. Here we put up for the night, at a respectable kind of inn; where the landlord was exceedingly obliging and civil, answering our questions with readiness, and giving us something like clean and wholesome fare. He described the town in which he dwelt, as one of importance, owing to its being the great thoroughfare between the two provinces of Këang-se and Këang-nan; and since it had neither pass nor custom-house, travellers much preferred it, in order to escape the annoyances of the mandarins. He informed us, that many of the teas, produced in Këang-se, were conveyed across the hills through this town, in order to be sent down the Yang-tsze-këang, to the foreign traders at Shanghae, and that the transport of teas in this direction was becoming more and more common.

RE-ENTER KEANG-NAN PROVINCE.

May 2d. Leaving 橫頭村 Hwăng-t'hôw-tsún, we began to ascend the 石門嶺 Shĭh-mûn-ling, and were soon convinced of the truth of our host's assertion, that numerous chops of teas were conveyed in this direction; for we overtook and met at every turn, merchants going and coming, to purchase and convey the article in question. At first, I was not aware of the mode in which the teas were primarily collected together, and conveyed to those who prepared the leaf; but passing by one of their tea-drinking shops, where a number of peddlers and carriers were resting themselves, I observed a row of white cloth bags by the road side, full of something, which I took to be a species of culinary vegetable, partially dried and intended for winter use; on enquiry, however, I found, that the contents of these bags were none other than the newly-picked leaves, which, after being sun-dried, were bought up by the tea-dealers, from the cottagers and small farmers around, in order that they might be conveyed to some manufactory, and be properly fired and separated for the market. After this process is gone through, the teas are packed in baskets, tubs, or boxes for sale.

Having crossed the 石門嶺 Shǐh-mûn-ling, we came to a small village called 石門街 Shǐh-mûn-keae. After resting awhile, another hill had to be encountered, called the 桃墅嶺 T'haôu-shoó-ling. The road which wound amongst these hills was exceedingly romantic, presenting an ever-varying scene of peaks and ravines, rocks and dales in succession. At length, we found the streams taking a northerly direction, and we began to descend into the level plains of Këang-nân, bordering upon the Yâng-tszè-këang. These streams collecting together, soon swelled into a river, which bore the name of the 前河 Tséên-hô. In the direction of this water, we pursued our journey, when we found the country gradually opening, presenting on all sides cultivated fields and smiling villages. One thing struck us as new in this region, with respect to the tea-cultivation, viz. the entire occupancy of most of the small hills by the tea-shrub, which was here planted in beautiful rows; and, as it happened to be the spring season, when the cultivators, men, women, and children, were scattered over the plantations gathering leaves, the whole presented a very lively scene.

ARRIVAL AT YAOU-CHING.

Towards evening we arrived at the town of 堯城鎮 Yaôu-ching-chin, situated on the opposite side of the river to the city of 建德 Këen-tih. This district city is included within the prefecture of 池州 Chê-chow, and was built in 45th year of 嘉靖 Këa-tsing, of the Ming dynasty, (A. D. 1,547), when the walls were raised 18 feet high, with a breadth of ten feet, and a circumference of five le. About the year 1,628, however, when the Ming dynasty was in its decline, two famous robbers disturbed the neighbourhood, and the presiding magistrate induced the people to add four feet and a half to the height of the wall.

The town of 堯城 Yaôu-ching is a very busy populous place, which might be inferred from its connecting the hill country with the region watered by the great Këang. The goods displayed in the shops, however, appeared to be chiefly those of native manufacture. It could hardly be expected, indeed, that those of foreign origin should present themselves prominently; for, independent of the partiality which all nations have for articles of home production, the quantity of foreign goods, though large, is by no means so great as to arrest attention at every town of the interior. As usual my guide became very anxious on entering this town, and insisted on my sitting in the sedan, by which means I was borne rapidly along the streets; not so rapidly, however, as to prevent my making a few observations. We found a tolerably comfortable lodging in the centre. The people who kept the inn made some remarks about the fairness of my complection, which my companion parried by asking, if they expected all the people in the world to be alike? The evening was occupied in seeking for, and making an agreement with a boatman, who for a small consideration was to take us to 東流

Tung-lêw, the first town on the Yâng-tszè-këang ; or, if we could agree about terms, further on.

JOURNEY TO TUNG-LEW.

May 3rd. We set off this morning to walk to the place where the boat was anchored, a few miles lower down the river. The people, I thought, looked rather intently at us, as we passed along the street, and over the bridge, outside the town ; but as it was no doubt farthest from their thoughts to meet a foreigner there, they did not seem to suspect the peculiarity of my origin. After pursuing our way for about a mile along the banks of the river, we came to a ferry just at a time when a party of beggars were crossing. One of these was carrying a young woman on his back, who had been probably deprived of her feet in infancy, in order to render her more the object of pity ; others were bearing their children, or pots and pans, with a few articles of dress ; and altogether they formed a group of the most noisy, impudent creatures I ever saw. They spoke excellent Mandarin, appeared to be acquainted with every step of the road, and could, from the appearance of each individual, make a pretty shrewd guess, regarding the origin and profession of all whom they met. They were thus making their remarks on the bye-standers. when my companion intimated to me, that it would be better to keep out of their way. As soon, therefore, as the boat came to land, we hurried on, and left them to hobble and jabber as best pleased them.

Arrived at the boat-anchorage, we found that the boat we had engaged was a large roomy vessel, broader in the beam than the generality of canal boats, and calculated to stand a stiff breeze, and a heavy swell, such as is very frequently to be met with on the Yâng-tszè-këang. Having nothing to detain us. we set sail, and dropped down the broad stream that leads to Tung-lêw. On the way we passed a number of boats, deeply laden with grass or reeds, which at first I supposed were intended as fodder for cattle, but afterwards I discovered that they were designed for mending, and, with a due mixture of mud, consolidating the banks of the great river in the neighbourhood. We had not proceeded far down the river before we were hailed by a person on the bank, who wanted a passage to Tung-lêw; the boatmen were disposed to afford him the accommodation he required, expecting no doubt to increase thereby the amount to be realized by the trip; but my companion, knowing the peculiarities of our situation, and judging that the fewer strangers we came into contact with the better, resisted the application. His remonstrances, however, proved unavailing, and the stranger was taken on board. Finding him a well-behaved man, my guide soon got into conversation with him, and the stranger, seing himself noticed, scrupled not to tell his history. He said, that only a few days previous, he had purchased a boat from the fruit of his earnings, and had freighted it with a little cargo, when he set sail, accompained by two relatives, on a voyage down the Yâng-tszè-këang, to see what could be made by the speculation. A storm, however, suddenly arose; the waves beat into his little vessel; it was capsized, his goods all went to the bottom. his companions perished, and his own life was spared only after he had been some time in the water. The story was told with much feeling, and I was pleased to see, that the boatmen, who had expected to gain something by his coming on board, now proposed a subscription in behalf of the shipwrecked stranger, heading it themselves by a hundred cash each; my own companion and myself threw in our mite, and the stranger went on shore at Tung-lêw glad of heart, and exceedingly grateful for the relief afforded. I mention this to shew, that fellow-feeling is sometimes displayed towards sufferers, in the heart of China, and that the cry of distress is not always heard in vain. Our boatmen assured us, that such instances of disaster on the waters of the Yâng-tsze-këang, were by no means unfrequent; and that when the wind was a little strong, the waves got up so high as to endanger the small craft that navigated the stream.

The city of 東流 Tung-lêw, at which we arrived in the evening, was formerly an unwalled town; but in the first year of 萬歷 Wán-leïh, of the Ming dynasty, (A. D. 1,573) the magistrate of the district asked leave to construct a wall three le and a half in circumference. Fifty years afterwards, this wall was raised three feet higher, and fenced by an earthern rampart and a deep ditch outside. During the troubles which prevailed about the close of the Ming dynasty, the defences were much defaced; but in the 6th year of 順治 Shún-ché, (A. D. 1,650) they were repaired, and five gateways erected, with watch-towers over them; thus the town was rendered stronger than before.

CITY OF GNAN-K'HING.

May 4th. Having agreed with our boatmen to convey us farther on our journey, we started this morning from Tung-lêw, and soon found ourselves on the broad stream of the great Këang, which passes on with majestic flow to the north-north-east. This giant river of China, is here upwards of a mile wide, with waves occasioning the rocking of our vessel like a little sea. The traffic on it appeared to be very large, and numerous junks were passing up and down the stream. The former, at that time making equal progress with the latter, as the wind was blowing strong from the northward, which enabled them to do more than stem the current. We passed a long island in midstream, with a rocky islet called 哪叱磯 No-cho-ke, and arrived towards evening at 安慶府 Gnan-k'hing-foò, the captial of 安徽 Gan-hwuy province.

This city was erected in the 10th year of 嘉定 Këa-tíng, of the Súng dynasty, (A. D. 1,025) in consequence of the irruptions of the 金 Kin Tartars. It had then five gates,

and the walls were upwards of nine le in circumference.
In the Yuen dynasty, the general in command of the city
raised the walls to the height of twenty-six feet, and dug a
triple ditch outside, into which he led the waters of the Yâng-
tszè-kéang. In the Ming dynasty, the ditches were deep-
ened to ten feet, the inside of the walls also were faced with
glazed tiles. Others repaired the occasional breaches which
time had made, and added steps wherewith to ascend the
walls, with a horse-road all round, on the top within the
parapet: during the present dynasty, efforts also have been
frequently made to repair the injuries occasioned by heavy
floods, and thus the city has continued to the present day.

VOYAGE DOWN THE YANG-TSZE-KEANG.

May 5th. We got under weigh, and sailed down the
洋子江 Yâng-tszè-kéang; at first the wind was moderate, but towards evening, it increased to a gale, which being
at the same time adverse, obliged us, as night approached,
to put into a small creek, where we lay all the next day,
unable to stir. The river, during this storm, exhibited
all the appearance of a little sea, so that few vessels could
venture out. Those that had the wind in their favour, appeared to scud fast, almost under bare poles; while our boatmen shrugged their shoulders, and lay down till the gale
moderated. Whilst lying in this creek, I heard a great up-
roar between two of the boatmen on board another boat;
and on listening to ascertain the cause, found that it origi-
nated in one of them, calling the other a 鬼子 kwei tszè,
devil's son; which so exasperated the young man, that he
seemed almost beside himself with rage. Thus it appears,
the term which the Chinese so unceremoniously bestow on
foreigners, is, when employed by one of themselves towards
his fellow, considered most opprobrious and vexatious in
the extreme. The creek where we had taken shelter, was a
little to the north-eastward of 池州 Chê-chow, which we

had passed without entering. This city was founded in the
唐 Tâng dynasty, about the 8th century, and after having
been taken and destroyed by robbers, was repaired. In the
Yuen dynasty, the city was demolished, and the district left
defenceless, but it revived again in the Ming dynasty, when
the walls were raised twenty-three feet high, and proportionably thick, 14 28) feet in circumference, with seven gates, for
the convenience of the inhabitants.

May 7th. This morning we again proceeded on our
course. The river appeared to widen as we proceeded, but
it became proportionably more shallow; so that in many
places, we could see the ripples, occasioned by the water
rushing over a shallow bottom. We passed on our way
several immense rafts of timber, floating slowly down the
stream. Some of these were at least a mile long, and of
great width, as well as height, and of course drawing
much water. In order to get them moved along, it appeared
that the force of the current was not sufficiently powerful;
and therefore the owners of the raft adopted the method
of sending out boats ahead, carrying an anchor, which they
dropped at some distance forward of their position; and then
by means of a windlas, which was worked by a number of
hands, warped the immense mass along. In this way, their
progress was slow, but sure. The process, however, necessitated the employment of a large number of persons, who
lived in regular houses, built in rows, forming a street along
the raft; in this street, all sorts of trades and handicrafts
were carried on, as in a town on shore. There were barbers, tailors, shoe-makers, butchers, bakers, pulse-preparers,
rice-venders, and vintners. All floating together in one
moveable town, going on to the place of their destination.
These large rafts are broken up, as soon as they arrive at
Nan-king or Chin-këang foŏ, where the grand canal crosses
the great Këang, and then, the timber which they contain

is conveyed in smaller rafts, to the north or south, where it may be most needed.

May 8th. This day we passed 銅陵 Tûng-ling, a district city, situated on the right bank of the Yang-tsze-këang, in the prefecture of 池州 Chê-chow. This city was built in the third year of 萬歷 Wán-leĭh, of the Ming dynasty, (A. D. 1,576); the walls are 7,000 feet in circumference, and 21 feet high. Without stopping at this city, we passed on, and anchored for the night at some distance lower down.

ARRIVAL AT WOO-HOO.

May 9th. We arrived about mid-day at the district of 無湖 Woô-hoô, situated in the prefecture of 太平 T'haé-ping; the walls of this city also were built in the time of Wán-leĭh, are five le in circumference, and thirty feet high. At this city, there is a custom-house, and all boats are obliged to come to, in passing up and down the river, in order to be examined. My guide felt anxious, on approaching this place, and asked me if I had anything about me that would lead to suspicion, should we be subjected to a personal examination. He remembered, he said, seeing a little book in my hand, in which I was always writing in pencil, and wished to see it. On taking it into his hand, he found, that it was my note-book, which contained a description of our whole journey, of the places at which we stopped, and of the events which had happened by the way. This he said, was the very thing to lead to a detection of our whole plan, and if discovered, would involve all connected with us; he therefore considered it his duty to destroy it. I had previously taken the precaution to transcribe it when lodging at one of the houses, where we made several days' stay; this copy was still in my girdle where I thought it best to let it remain. The precaution of my guide was, however, unnecessary, as the custom-house officer, on our arrival at Woo-hoô, merely came to the head of the boat, and finding we had no goods for sale passed on.

We observed opposite this city, on the other side of the Yâng-tszè-këang, a great number of imperial grain-junks anchored, and waiting either for wind and tide, or the arrival of other vessels, which were expected to join them on their voyage northward. These had probably come down the 裕溪 Joo-ke, from 廬州 Leu-chow, and the parts adjacent, and would in a few days start in a north-easterly direction, towards the mouth of the grand canal, at Chin-këang-foò.

Some time after leaving 無湖 Woò-hoô, we arrived at the 東梁 Tung-lëâng hill, where we entered a tributary stream, which empties itself into the Yâng-tszè-këang from the eastward, called the 水陽河 Shwùy-yâng-hô. Several pagodas adorned the place, and fixed the position to the navigator of the Great River; a water-gate, thrown quite across the stream, brought to all vessels that might be passing to and fro, for examination and the payment of impost. From the former we experienced no annoyance, and the gatherers of the latter were satisfied with a few cash, after the payment of which we passed on.

The change for us was now very great, from a broad and sometimes turbulent stream, to a narrow canal, not a hundred yards wide; and from the high mountains and broad rivers, which almost bewildered by their vastness, to the close banks and low cottages which here met the view.

This water is the outlet from Nìng-kwŏ-foò, and it is the same which we had previously crossed at 河渡鎮 Hô-toó-chin, on the upward journey. In order, however, not to be led again amongst the hills we had left, we were obliged, after sailing about ten miles along this river, to pass into another stream, which led us in a north-westerly direction, apparently in an almost opposite course to that which we had just taken. After proceeding a few miles, we got into another river, which flowed to the south-east, and passing the town of

薛鎮 Seih-chin, we arrived about dusk at the district city of 高淳 Kaou-chun, in the prefecture of 江寧 Këang-ning, and within 100 le of the city of Nân-king. Kaou-chun is only partially defended by a mud wall, and for the protection of the other parts reliance is placed on a natural bank on one side, and the river Chun on the other.

May 10th. This morning we were in some doubt about the propriety of starting, as a strong wind was blowing right a-gainst us, and we had to cross a broad lake, where the waves are easily excited in a storm, and owing to the shallowness of the lake break short, thereby exposing vessels which at-tempt to cross it to great danger of being knocked in pieces. The name of the lake was 固城湖 Koó-chíng-hoô; it is broader than it is represented in the maps; after some deli-beration, our boatmen resolved to attempt the passage, and poling the whole of the way, by dint of great and unwearied exertion, succeeded in crossing it in safety, early in the after-noon. Having reached the town of 定埠鎮 Tíng-fow-chin, the boatmen informed us that they could take us no further, as a neck of land, several miles in extent, here breaks the water communication, and separates the western from the eastern waters. There seems also to be a difference of level, not only between the waters on either side, but also be-tween them and the small canal which traverses the neck of land, that divides the two water communications from each other. We were therefore obliged to land, and enter the busy town above-named, in order to seek a passage across the isthmus. The transport of goods from the river to the canal-boats occupies great numbers of coolies, and the rush of pas-sengers to secure places is uninterrupted. The canal-boats for the conveyance of goods and passengers are long barges, ca-pable of carrying great quantities of merchandize, with a sort of hold near the stern, where the passengers are stowed away. Into this compartment, eight feet square, about a dozen passengers were thrust together, notwithstanding my guide

had expressly stipulated that we should be left alone. One
of the passengers was addressed by the boatmen as a 少爺
Shaòu-yây, young squire, and treated with great deference; on
enquiring into his name and rank, it appeared that he was the
son of the district magistrate of Kaou-chun. As these young
gentlemen are particularly celebrated for possessing all the
rapacity and none of the literary attainments of their sires,
they are more to be shunned than courted: particularly by persons who possess any secret, the finding out of which might
endanger their own safety, and add to the profits of their dis-
coverers. We were, however, now so close together, that there
was no possibility of our avoiding each other : my guide therefore put a good face upon it, and began to enquire into the pedi-
gree and prospects of the young mandarin, by which he
kept alive his attention, and prevented him from taking too
much notice of me. A slight return of the pain in my foot,
which had come on with more acuteness that day, kept me
sufficiently occupied, and finding that I was unwell, he
did not disturb me any further. It was quite dark before we
reached the 東巴 Tung-pa, where we were to get accommodations for the night, and a boat to carry us on the next
day. To the former we were directed by the barge-master,
and soon found ourselves tolerably well housed, and a supper
spread out before us sufficiently satisfying. Our host was
now requested to look out for a boatman, with whom we
might make some arrangements for our onward course. A
man was soon brought, who demanded an exorbitant price
for conveying us to Soo-chow. The landlord professed to
be our friend, and declaring that he considered our cause his
own, sought to bring down the demands of the boatmen;
this he did in some degree, but after all made an arrangement for what appeared to be much more than was just or requisite. The high price demanded went, according to him, to
satisfy the exactions of the mandarins, who required a portion of the profits of every voyage made by each boat ; this
was the more willingly given by the boat-people, in order to

prevent annoying enquiries and examinations before the officers. Some of it, however, I was afterwards informed, went into the pocket of our landlord, who so zealously defended our cause, and laboured with such earnestness to get our arrangements made. We obtained a ticket, at this place, which exempted us from further exactions and interference, until we reached the end of our journey.

May 11th. This morning we embarked in a large and comfortable boat, with half a dozen men to propel us forward, and though the wind was contrary, we still advanced with tolerable speed. The river called 滑河 Seu-hô, along which we went, was narrow, but sufficiently deep to be navigable for such a boat as the one on which we were embarked. The banks were lined with mulberry-trees in great numbers, apparently larger and more flourishing than any we had previously seen ; perhaps they only seemed so, however, owing to the more advanced season of the year. The inhabitants were busy picking the leaves for the young silkworms, which they did by means of ladders or steps, with props on the other side, so as to enable the gatherers to mount without injuring the trees. We soon passed the towns of 廣通 Kwàng-t'hung, 鄧埠 Tăng-fow, and 社渚 Shay-choo ; all very thriving places, filled with contented inhabitants. By travelling most of the night, we arrived next morning opposite the city of 漂陽 P'heaou-yâng, in the prefecture of 江寧 Këang-ning. As far back as the 南唐 Nân-tâng dynasty, (A. D. 924) an earthen wall, four le in extent, had been thrown up around this city, outside of which was a ditch fifty feet wide ; this wall was enlarged in the 宋 Súng dynasty ; in the 元 Yuên dynasty the town was admitted into the list of sub-prefectural cities. In the Mîng dynasty a wall was built on the foundations of the original earthen bank, upwards of 9.000 feet in length ; the ditch was likewise dug much deeper ; battlements and semi-bastions were afterwards added, and the city became, in the Chinese estimation, fortified.

May 12th. This morning we pursued our voyage, and passing by the towns of 鐘溪 Chung-k'he, and 湖埭 Hoô-taé, entered about midday the grand canal, the waters of which were covered with vessels passing up and down, contrasting in its busy scene with the stillness of the streams along which we had previously passed. The imperial grain-junks were pursuing their journey northward, each propelled by their score of men, but as they were of unwieldy bulk, and moreover, belonged to the emperor, the navigators on board seemed unable or unwilling to advance at more than a snail's speed. The boats and vessels belonging to the people, being pushed on by the spirit of private adventure, went at a faster rate. The bustle increasing, we found that we were approaching a city, and 無錫 Woô-seïh soon rose to view. This place appears in a prosperous condition, both on account of its trade and manufactures. Situated on the grand canal, mid-way between Soo-chow and Chang-chow, it has always a great influx of strangers, which of course makes business thrive; besides this, it is very much celebrated for its potteries and its iron-foundries. For about two miles before our arrival at the city, we passed one continuous line of glazed pots and pans, arranged in piles, in the various pottery-stores, along the banks of the river. An island of considerable length, surrounded on every side by the waters of the grand canal, was covered with pots from one end to the other; and there seemed sufficient of these articles to supply the whole empire. The iron-foundries here, are also very much celebrated, and the numerous specimens of vases, tripods, and pagodas, some of them twenty feet high, cast both in iron and bronze, shew that Woô-seïh has not belied its name. The water carriage is here very convenient for the transport of heavy goods, having the grand canal winding completely round the city, and being in the immediate vicinity of the 太湖 T'haé-hoô, or great lake. The walls, which are in a good state of repair, were built in the Súng dynasty ; they are upwards of eleven le in circumference, and about twenty feet high. The origin of its name 無錫 Woô-seïh, or " no tin," is variously accounted for. There is a small hill in its neighbourhood, called 錫山 Seïh-shan, or " tin hill," from the name of which one might gather, that tin has formerly been procurable here, until the exhaustion of the mine led the neighbouring inhabitants to cry out " no tin ;" which might have given rise to the name of the city. The natives of the place have, however, a strange story, that the tin mines were once so productive in the neighbourhood, as to cause a great influx of strangers to the place, who contending for the possession of the mines, created such disturbances, that the emperor forbad their being worked altogether, and, in order to discourage people from coming thither for such purposes, commanded the city to be called Woô-seïh, " no tin."

We proceeded on our voyage the same afternoon, and towards night, arrived at a pass, within a few miles of Soochow, where, finding the gates which were constructed across the canal closed, we were obliged to come to for the night.

May 13th. Early this morning, our boat, in conjunction with a number of others, was waiting outside the canal-gate, until the custom-house officer should see fit to awake from his slumbers, and examine the fleet. My guide was of course in great trepidation lest any discovery should be made, and we endeavoured to have every thing as snugly arranged as possible, so as not to excite suspicion. About seven o'clock the approach of the official became apparent, by an unusual stir among the boats, and presently a low underling from the custom-house came on board. He asked what merchandize we had, and being informed we had nothing but a box of clothes, he required to see it ; on its being placed before him, he opened the lid, and rummaged it to the bottom; finding nothing particular, he took a glance around the cabin, to see if he could spy any contraband goods on board, and not heeding the principal contraband article that sat in a Chinese garb before him, he passed out through the stern of the cabin and we saw him no more. Immediately the gates gave way and we passed through, after paying a small sum as a porterage-fee, and we proceeded unmolested on our voyage. The name of the pass is 許墅關 Heù-shoó-kwan. Approaching Soo-chow from the north-west, we found both sides of the canal lined for several miles with houses, the wharves in front of which presented a most busy scene; after passing through this populous suburb, we arrived at the city, the walls of which did not appear so high, nor in such good repair, as those of Woô-seïh, which we had left the day previous. Still they were much more extensive, including a vast area, more than sufficient, if covered with houses, to accommodate a million of inhabitants. The space within the walls is, however, by no means filled up with human dwellings, and except in the direction of the principal streets, and cross-ways leading from them, a large portion of the ground is laid out in fields and gardens. A description of this city cannot be crowded into a journal like the present, and well deserves a separate notice. My guide having conducted me faithfully thus far, and put me in a fair way of reaching Shanghae, left me at this place, whilst I proceeded alone in the same boat to the end of my journey. As I slowly passed along, under the walls of the city, I was struck with the vast quantity of timber left to soak in the canal, or hauled up on the shore, in the different wood-stores outside the city. Then the number of grain-junks laid up in ordinary drew my attention; these moored along the side of the canal, in an unbroken succession for miles, shewed how large the fleet of such vessels must have been, in the aggregate, when these were only the overplus of the still larger number which had already sailed for Peking. Some of them were, however, completely dismantled, and others in a most ruinous condition, with all the upper works torn away, apparently for the sake of using the word for fuel; while not a few were sunk, and had only the deck above water.

Having passed along the north side of the city, we arrived at the gate, which lies on the east side, but near the north-east corner of the city. Here we found a canal which led eastward, towards 崑山 Kwăn-shan, along which we proceeded, and soon lost sight of Soo-chow. This canal is broad and deep, and from its pursuing such a direct course, appears to have been the work of art. Along this the imperial grain-junks proceed, in their course from Shanghae, and the adjacent towns, in preference to following the course of the Woô-sûng-këang, which after leaving the neighbourhood of Kwăn-shan, is spread out into the shallow lakes of the 泖湖 Maòu-hoô, 澱山湖 Tëen-shan-hoô, 金鴻湖 Kin-hûng-hoô, and 沙湖 Sha-hoô. As the day declined, we arrived at 崑山 Kwăn-shan, and anchored for the night under its wall. This city includes two towns in one. The walls are said to be 12 le in extent, and 28 feet high. Near the north end of the city is a hill, crowned with pagodas, from the galleries of which may be seen, in a northerly direction, the hill of 常熟 Châng-shŭh, which seemed from its appearance to be at least 1,500 feet high, and in a southerly direction the whole of the city and its adjacent lakes, together with the hills about Tsing-poo, appear in the distance. As this city, however, lies within reach of the European residents of Shanghae, it will be less necessary minutely to describe it.

May 14th. We again got under weigh, and without meeting with anything worthy of particular remark, we arrived about nine o'clock at what is called the Soo-chow bridge, near Shanghae, from which I got two of the boatmen to carry my baggage, and arrived in an hour after before my own door; where having got the bearers to deposit my baggage, I discharged them, and quietly walked in; those who had accompanied me not knowing who I was, and those at home not dreaming of the direction in which I had travelled, or the way in which I reached home, except in so far as I chose to inform them.